Dear Reader,

Emily Austin is universally adored. We receive many love letters for Emily from booksellers across the country, calling her a "mainstay of queer contemporary fiction" and saying that she made them "laugh just as often as she broke my heart." Emily's most recent novel, *We Could Be Rats*, was an Indie Next Pick and was hailed by *USA Today* as a "touching portrait of the messy, transcendent nature of sisterhood."

Is This a Cry for Help? is Emily Austin's best work yet. Darcy is a signature Austin character, hearkening back to Gilda in her breakout debut, *Everyone in This Room Will Someday Be Dead*. Having enthusiastically followed Emily's rise at Atria—before jumping at the opportunity to work with her—I'm happy to say *Is This a Cry for Help?* represents a deepening, an expansion, and a triumphant culmination of so many of the themes she has been building on over the years.

At once a moving portrait of life post–coming of age in the queer community and a love letter to the importance of libraries, *Is This a Cry for Help?* will appeal to readers of Alison Espach, Catherine Newman, and Rufi Thorpe. I hope you'll join me in helping continue to grow the legions of readers in the Emily Austin adoration society.

Warmly,

Sean deLone
Editor
Sean.deLone@simonandschuster.com

ALSO BY EMILY AUSTIN

FICTION
We Could Be Rats
Interesting Facts about Space
Everyone in This Room Will Someday Be Dead

POETRY
Gay Girl Prayers

IS THIS A CRY FOR HELP?

EMILY AUSTIN

ATRIA BOOKS
NEW YORK   AMSTERDAM/ANTWERP   LONDON
TORONTO   SYDNEY/MELBOURNE   NEW DELHI

> Do not quote for publication until verified with finished book at the publication date. This advance uncorrected reader's proof is the property of Simon & Schuster. It is being loaned for promotional purposes and review by the recipient and may not be used for any other purpose or transferred to any third party. Simon & Schuster reserves the right to cancel the loan and recall possession of the proof at any time. Any duplication, sale or distribution to the public is a violation of law.

ATRIA BOOKS

An Imprint of Simon & Schuster, LLC
1230 Avenue of the Americas
New York, NY 10020

For more than 100 years, Simon & Schuster has championed authors and the stories they create. By respecting the copyright of an author's intellectual property, you enable Simon & Schuster and the author to continue publishing exceptional books for years to come. We thank you for supporting the author's copyright by purchasing an authorized edition of this book.

No amount of this book may be reproduced or stored in any format, nor may it be uploaded to any website, database, language-learning model, or other repository, retrieval, or artificial intelligence system without express permission. All rights reserved. Inquiries may be directed to Simon & Schuster, 1230 Avenue of the Americas, New York, NY 10020 or permissions@simonandschuster.com.

This book is a work of fiction. Any references to historical events, real people, or real places are used fictitiously. Other names, characters, places, and events are products of the author's imagination, and any resemblance to actual events or places or persons, living or dead, is entirely coincidental.

Copyright © 2026 by Emily Austin

All rights reserved, including the right to reproduce this book or portions thereof in any form whatsoever. For information, address Atria Books Subsidiary Rights Department, 1230 Avenue of the Americas, New York, NY 10020.

First Atria Books hardcover edition January 2026

ATRIA BOOKS and colophon are trademarks of Simon & Schuster, LLC

Simon & Schuster strongly believes in freedom of expression and stands against censorship in all its forms. For more information, visit BooksBelong.com.

For information about special discounts for bulk purchases, please contact Simon & Schuster Special Sales at 1-866-506-1949 or business@simonandschuster.com.

The Simon & Schuster Speakers Bureau can bring authors to your live event. For more information or to book an event, contact the Simon & Schuster Speakers Bureau at 1-866-248-3049 or visit our website at www.simonspeakers.com.

Interior design by Erika R. Genova
Manufactured in the United States of America
1 3 5 7 9 10 8 6 4 2
Library of Congress Cataloging-in-Publication Data is available.
ISBN 978-1-6682-0023-0
ISBN 978-1-6682-0025-4 (ebook)

*Dedicated to my grandma Gloria Faith Austin,
who volunteered many years for the
Friends of the Library in St. Thomas*

IS THIS A CRY FOR HELP?

CHAPTER
ONE

A patron is watching porn out loud. My job at the library requires I walk behind him to verify what kind of porn it is, and if it involves anything illegal, I get to call 911. If it doesn't, I'm not supposed to do anything.

I walk behind him discreetly. While pretending to adjust a book display about earthworms, I see the film stars three women who appear to be of consenting age. It's titled *Vintage Lesbian Cuckhold*, which I find curious. A cuckhold is the husband of an adulterous wife; however, this film has no men cast, and it appears to have been taped on film stock from the 1970s. Same-sex marriage wasn't legalized anywhere at that time, so these women couldn't possibly be married. Therefore, it's impossible for this to be a true "cuckhold" film.

I also doubt, based on the performances, that any of the women are actually lesbians. I'm somewhat of a stickler for categorization. It bothers me when material is mislabeled. I care that things are marked and classified properly.

Several people are milling around the computers. A middle-aged woman. An elderly couple. A small pack of goth teens. Rather than speak directly to the man watching porn, I announce to the room, "Please remember to use headphones, or to mute your devices so you don't disrupt others. If you need headphones, come see me. I'm happy to lend you a pair."

The man mutes his porn, and I return to the reference desk, satisfied to have fulfilled the demands of my role. I eye the bouquet of yellow tulips my coworkers left by the computer. There's a note affixed to the vase. It says, WE MISSED YOU, DARCY.

My coworker, Patty, is manning the circulation desk nearby. She waves at me.

I smile at her. Today is my first day back at work. I was gone for two months because I had a mental breakdown.

A child left a picture book titled *A Slug of a Different Color* on the floor. I flip through it and see it's about a slug who was born on a horse farm. He tries to live like the horses. He samples their salt lick, grazes in their pastures, and attempts to whinny and neigh. He dreams about galloping through their trails—feeling branches comb through his coarse mane. Of course, he can't grow hair, run, or withstand salt or sunshine. He's a slug. He has no legs, but a moist, soft body that would dehydrate if salt came anywhere near his sensitive skin. It could kill him. He's also nocturnal, and thrives in humid, cool, dark spaces. Unless there's a magical element to this story, the slug will never become a horse, and he'll probably die if he keeps trying—

"Are you aware a pervert is watching adult films over there?"

I look up from the book. The medication I'm taking affects my eyesight, so I have to squint at the hazy woman.

"Are you aware a pervert is watching adult films over there?" she asks again, louder.

"Oh," I say. "Yes. I am."

She crosses her arms. "Why hasn't he been stopped?"

"Because you're allowed to watch adult films at the library."

"Excuse me?"

"You're allowed to watch adult films at the library," I say again.

This isn't my first rodeo when it comes to porn consumption here. I know the protocol. In my orientation, I distinctly remember being taught what to do in cases like this. After listening to monotonous employee onboarding about how to operate e-readers and request vacation leave, my ears perked up when the subject of porn was breached. Furthermore, I doubt we've ever gone more than one month without someone watching porn here. This is a *public* library.

"I'd like to speak to someone in charge," she says.

I rub my eyes. "That'd be me at the moment, but if you'd prefer someone more senior, I can get you a form."

UNABLE TO ATTEND DUETO MEDICAL ISSUE. SRORY.

I wrote this email two months ago. Prior to taking sick leave, I was in the middle of an interview process for a branch manager position. I sent this poorly written email to decline the invitation for a second interview. I have no recollection of writing it.

I dreaded returning to work today partly because I couldn't remember if I'd actually declined the interview. I'd convinced myself that I just didn't show up. My short-term memory is weak due to my recent mental health crisis. My therapist told me emotional overwhelm can make it hard to process and store new information.

I woke up several times last night worrying about this. I kept picturing emails with red flags, titled FOLLOW UP ON MISSED INTERVIEW, and stern voicemails asking, "*Where are you?*"

Job applications generally follow a repeatable formula. I have strong pattern recognition, and I'm good at following procedures, so I have the skills to navigate a job interview process successfully. The wrench my mental breakdown threw into my application rattled me—not just because I wanted the job, but also because it disrupted a process that I should have been able to complete. I am dysregulated when I try to follow steps, do what I'm supposed to do, learn the rules, and still manage to mess things up.

I'm relieved to see I sent this email. I wish I remembered I did. I might have slept better. Though it's bizarre I can't remember writing it.

I usually have a good memory. I rarely have to look up library policies or procedures. I know the steps to request an interlibrary loan, submit a supply order, or issue a new library card. I can even remember what I wore on my first day of second grade, cloud formations I saw one Christmas morning, and how the grout peeled around the bathroom tiles in the apartment I had when I was nineteen.

My boyfriend Ben lived there with me. I remember taking a shower the night we moved in. I took my clothes off, turned the tap on, and stood with my hand under the running water. The showerhead made this shrill, screaming sound while I waited for the water to get hot. It splattered on the floor of the bath, and my body involuntarily flinched when ricochets of cold drops pelted my skin. I cranked the tap to the hottest setting, waited several more minutes, but the water never turned hot.

It was like that the whole time we lived there. The water heated to the temperature of an abandoned cup of coffee, right at the point where it could still be stomached, but it was unpleasant. It always felt like someone else had just taken a long shower and drained the contents of the water heater tank.

I like taking showers so hot they turn my skin red. I want

to exit the room in a cloud of steam, like a boiled lobster. I want dermatologists to warn me, *This is bad for your skin.* I've read plumbers put apparatuses on faucets to prevent the water from scalding. I think it was set too cautiously in that apartment. In retrospect, it's bizarre I tolerated it for so long. These days, I would call someone to fix it. I would even fix it myself.

I used to be someone different. Around age twenty-three, I split in two like a cell. One version of me is frozen at twenty-three. She's a coy, dependent girl who doesn't really know herself and doesn't want to burden anyone. She's dating Ben. They plan to get married, adopt a golden doodle, and have a baby. She wears uncomfortable clothing; shirts that cling to her abdomen, jeans she has to suck in to zip up. She speaks in a high pitch, laughs at jokes that aren't funny, follows rules, and apologizes too much. She endures lukewarm showers.

The other version is me now. I'm thirty-two. I'm a more honest, self-reliant person. I have a wife named Joy, two cats, and no desire to become a parent. All my clothing is loose-fitting and breathable. I speak in a lower, more natural pitch, and I don't laugh unless a joke is funny. I'm still inclined to follow rules, and I have an instinct to apologize too much, but I try to resist. My showers would boil a lobster.

A mirror faced the bathtub in that apartment. My reflection startled me the night we moved in. I didn't recognize myself. For a fleeting moment, I thought a strange naked lady was in our bathroom, gawking at me. The lighting in that room was harsh, like a doctor's office. I could see cellulite on my thighs I wasn't aware of. A shadow cast under the pouch of my stomach. Lines where my body folded when sitting, due to my ghoulish posture.

I missed the mirror in my last apartment. It was small, and round, and hung on the wall of my cramped, dimly lit bathroom. I could never see myself fully in it. The year prior, I still lived with my parents. I don't remember seeing myself in that bathroom mirror, but I do remember being rushed out by my mom, and always being afraid she might barge in. She didn't value privacy. I did my makeup in a compact mirror, looking only at small segments of my face at a time. One eye. My mouth. An eyebrow. I rarely saw myself completely.

I remember standing in that bathroom at nineteen, feeling the tepid water hit my fingertips, looking at my reflection as if I didn't occupy my own body. It was like I was looking at a strange drawing of an uncomfortable naked woman. It didn't feel like I was looking at myself.

I frowned at my reflection until I noticed a small black dot moving behind me. It was a spider. She was in the corner of the shower, where the ceiling met the tiled wall. She moved the way spiders do; unpredictably and scattered. Tilting my head up, I wondered what kind of spider she was. *What bugs did she eat? How did she get in?* After several moments of watching her, I wrapped myself in a towel and shouted, "Ben! There's a spider! Help!"

Ben rushed into the bathroom, grabbed a wad of toilet paper, and laughed at me for being scared. He crushed the spider's body into the ceiling, leaving a dark smudge that stayed there until I moved out. After he dropped her remains in the toilet, he kissed me and said, "You're safe now, dove."

He always called me "dove." That was his pet name for me.

I looked down at the spider's crushed, floating body, and said, "You saved me." But the truth is, I was never truly afraid of that spider. I just felt compelled to pretend I was so I could play the part of a meek, frightened girl, and Ben the part of a strong, brave man.

After he left the bathroom, I stepped into the lukewarm shower and told myself it was fine.

I'm still staring at the email I wrote two months ago. I'm glad I wrote it, but I wish I'd dedicated the millisecond required to review my spelling before I hit send. This typo-riddled email suggests I'm an unreliable employee who cancels last-minute, and I sent it directly to my boss.

I close my eyes. I wish I could go back in time and undo all the stupid mistakes I've made.

Joy would probably assure me this email doesn't make me come off as unreliable. *You had a medical issue. Who would think badly of you for that?* She would say that this is just a job, and while I care about my job, it isn't my whole life. The grass is going to keep growing. The stars aren't going to burn out. At the end of the day, I'm standing here telling people to mute their porn. Nothing is so serious.

I bet Joy is wondering how my first day back is going. She sat up with me last night while I groaned about this interview that I couldn't remember declining, worrying about all the people and questions I might have to face. She listened to me spiral, reassured me everything would be all right, and joked that we could move away. Change our names. Live in a cave.

I should call her. I'm sure she'll be delighted to hear my morning has been fraught with weird men watching poorly labeled lesbian porn.

"Did you think someone was having sex?"

I'm calling Joy from the break room while I watch the white bean soup she made us for dinner last night revolve in the microwave.

"No, it was obviously porn. The actresses' performances were overly theatrical." The microwave beeps. "I've had to deal with people hooking up in the stacks before, though. I've actually suggested we rearrange the shelves. There's a spot that's hidden where I've found multiple couples—"

"Is it always couples?"

I reach into the microwave to stir the soup, making sure to keep it away from my face. Sometimes soups heated in microwaves explode if you stick spoons in them haphazardly. Whenever I microwave liquids, or any food with a high water content, I'm cautious. I've had a few traumatic experiences, and I'm trying to learn from my mistakes. A reheated cup of coffee once severely burned one of my eyelids. Another time, I accidentally detonated a potato.

"What do you mean, *is it always couples*?" I ask. "Are you wondering if I've ever found people having group sex in the library?"

She snorts. "No, no, I meant—"

"The answer is obviously no, and I think exhibitionist

threesomes are rare, honey. That's got to be too much for most people, right? You're either having public sex, or a threesome. To do both would be over-the-top—"

She laughs. "I was thinking more like one person. I meant, like, do you ever find one person masturbating?"

"Oh. Yes. Of course. We get that all the time."

Some people do atrocious things in libraries. Get into fistfights. Film content for their OnlyFans. Urinate in the elevators.

She says, "You have a difficult job. Hey, why haven't *we* ever had sex in the library?"

I put the soup back into the microwave. "Because it's unsanitary, and I'd get fired. Plus, I know the guys who watch our security footage, and we'd have to move away. Change our names. Live in a cave."

She snorts. "Okay. Fair. Besides this porn incident, how's your morning been? How are you feeling?"

"Good." I watch the soup turn. "My coworkers got me tulips, and I checked my outbox and saw I did decline that second interview."

"Did you? That's great news," she says.

"Mhm. I'm relieved I didn't just not show up, but the email had typos. It makes me look like a flake. I doubt there's any chance I get that job now."

I speak too quickly when I feel anxious. I can feel myself gaining speed now.

She asks, "Why would that make you look like a flake? They know you were off sick."

Joy wouldn't think negatively of someone for missing a

meeting due to illness, but she always assumes the best in people. Whenever I voice worries I have about how others might negatively perceive me, she's always baffled. *Why would anyone think that? How do these thoughts even occur to you?*

The timer on the microwave is almost up. "I just wish I'd handled it differently—"

"I'm sorry this is making you feel bad, but I don't think you should beat yourself up. I know that job mattered to you, but regardless of what happens, everything's okay."

I knew she would say something like this, and she's probably right. It doesn't really matter. I did want that job, but I don't need to dwell on it. I have this tendency to get hung up on things that are outside my control.

I inhale. "Yeah. Everything's okay. It's not like this is life or death—"

My stomach drops. The microwave beeps. *Why did I mention death?*

"It's okay." She senses I've accidentally set myself off.

All the hairs on my body are standing up. The microwave beeps again. I'm picturing his name in the newspaper.

Joy's voice cuts through that image. "Hey, I miss you skulking around the house."

She's trying to distract me. I close my eyes tight. I'm picturing his hands.

She says, "There's no one around to interrupt my work. I'm getting way too much done."

I clench my eyes closed tighter. BEEP. I try to picture Joy working. She runs a bookbinding business out of a workshop on our property.

"You can come home if you need to, you know," she says quietly.

I'm picturing her wearing her canvas apron. BEEP. She has her hair tied up. She's gluing paper. Holding pages up to the light. BEE—

I open the microwave and the beeping stops.

It's not my fault he died, my therapist told me to remind myself.

I'm not the reason he died.

I say, "Sorry. I'm okay."

My chest feels heavy.

"Are you sure?" Her voice is shaky. She's never good at hiding her concern.

"Yes, I'm okay," I repeat, partly to convince myself. "Why don't you tell me about your morning?"

I want her to distract me.

"My morning? Sure. Uh. It's been fine." Her voice is quiet. I can tell she's worried about me. "Sophie called. She's going on leave tomorrow because she's too pregnant to work. Her doctor wrote her a note."

Sophie is Joy's sister. Her baby is due in a week.

"Is she happy to go on leave?" I ask while I take the soup out of the microwave. I place it down quickly, and hiss as the heat singes my fingertips. The bowl was too hot to touch. I'm flustered and not thinking clearly. I should have let it sit a minute.

"What happened? Are you okay?" she asks.

She's always worried about me hurting myself. She gasps as if I've been shot when I stub a toe, or trip slightly.

In an attempt to lighten the mood, I tease her. "No, I'm

not okay. That porn-watching guy just barged into the break room and attacked me!"

She gasps. "*What?*"

I laugh nervously. "I'm kidding. I'm fine. I just touched something hot."

"Please don't joke about masturbating men attacking you."

I look at my fingertips. They're flushed from touching the hot bowl. "He wasn't masturbating. He was just watching porn."

"Oh, weird. So, would you be allowed to kick him out if he was masturbating?"

"Yes, I'd be allowed to, but I probably wouldn't."

"Why not?"

I grab some paper towels from the dispenser by the sink. "I don't get paid enough."

She laughs.

"I have to go now, honey," I say as I sit down. "I'm about to eat that soup you packed for me."

"Did you see I put some rosemary focaccia in there?"

"Did you?" I look into my lunch bag. I notice a pouch of tinfoil and realize it's the bread. I peel the foil off and see it's flecked with coarse sea salt and rosemary sprigs. It's gold and shiny from olive oil. I say, "Wow, this looks beautiful. Thank you."

"No problem. Be safe, okay? I love you."

She always tells me to be safe.

"I will. I love you too. Bye."

"It's none of my business why you were away. Absolutely none of my business, but you're well enough to return, right? I hope you haven't rushed back, have you?"

Mordecai is in the break room. He doesn't know what caused my sick leave and has made it apparent that he's curious.

"Yes," I say. "I'm feeling much better, thank you."

"That's great to hear. Boy, was I worried about you. We all were. Brenda told us you were going to be out for a while, and I thought, *My God, I hope she's okay.* They didn't give us any more information than that, you know. Just, *poof!* Darcy's gone."

Rather than take the hint and reveal what afflicted me, I say, "Thank you so much for your concern, Mordecai. That's very kind of you. I appreciate it."

"We got you those tulips because I remembered your favorite color is yellow. I wasn't sure if that applied to flowers, but I told everyone that was your favorite color, so we just went with it. I hope that was the right call."

"I love the flowers. Thank you so much," I say, while a substantial drop of soup falls from my spoon to my chest. It burns the skin beneath my linen shirt.

I get up and walk to the sink. I soak a fistful of paper towels in cold water.

"Oh, damn. Do you think that'll stain?" he asks.

"I don't know." I blot the spot.

It's white soup on a white shirt. You'd think that wouldn't be the end of the world, but I don't know much about laundry. I can never predict when something will stain.

"That looks like a nice shirt," he says. "Rats. I bet that's the last thing you need right now. You come back to work after being sick and immediately wreck a good work shirt."

I close my eyes while pressing the paper towel to my chest. Mordecai is too talkative. I'm often exasperated by him. I don't dislike him; he's kindhearted, he remembers things like my favorite color, and he's good at his job. He talks too much, though. He's always prying. Unfortunately, my tolerance for him is low right now after being away for two months. Somewhat like taking a shot after a long bout of sobriety, I feel knocked out by him. I also think he's chattier than usual because we haven't seen each other in a while, so he's eager to talk. He seems to be speaking more rapidly than normal.

Generally, I try to appease him. I smile and nod. Today, I can't seem to listen to him. I keep tuning him out. I'm facing the sink. Closing my eyes.

Ben did our laundry when we lived together. He lugged it in a rucksack to a laundromat four blocks away from our apartment. He used fabric softener and dryer sheets branded with teddy bears that made our clothes smell like baby pajamas. I remember he regularly took all our curtains down to wash them, which I found interesting.

I appreciated that he wanted to clean our curtains, but not because I actually valued having clean drapery. Whether our curtains were dusty or not meant nothing to me. I valued his intention. I appreciated that he was doing a chore for us, despite finding his choice of chore perplexing. Our priorities weren't aligned. If he and I were on the same page, he might cook or do the dishes. But he never did that. He washed the curtains.

I've always been a tidy, organized person. As a kid, I put my toys away when I finished playing. I put my crayons back in the box. I couldn't stand having dirty hands. My mom used to say I was the only toddler without sticky fingers. As an adult, I can't relax unless my house is clean. I make our bed every morning. I wipe down the counters and run the dishwasher before we go to sleep. Joy and I deep clean the house every Saturday morning. We mop. Vacuum. Scrub the bathrooms. Wipe down the kitchen cabinets, clean out the fridge. That said, I've never been one for laundry. I forget to check for things in pockets. I don't care if I turn my white clothes gray or pink.

Ben and I didn't have a washing machine in our apartment. There was a closet that could be hooked up to one, but we couldn't afford to buy a machine, and our landlord would sooner die than supply one. He rented out several buildings and didn't care about his tenants. The heat rarely worked. We had mice, and there was this enormous crack in the plaster ceiling in our bedroom. Every email we sent that landlord went unanswered, yet he persistently wrote us about our utility bills being exorbitant—

Actually, I should say, *he wrote Ben.* He addressed all his emails to Ben, even though my name was on the lease too. He wrote DEAR BENJAMIN, as if Ben owned the home and I was his pet gerbil. A fragile, twitchy creature he took care of.

It was a grungy, unpleasant place to live, but it was nice that I didn't have to go deeper into student debt to live there. The unit was in a secure building, in a low-crime area. I felt safe there. Before we moved in together, I lived alone in a studio apartment where my packages were stolen and I was frequently catcalled on the street.

I haven't thought about that apartment in a long time. I don't usually forget things, but I can't fully picture it anymore. I remember the bathroom, but I don't remember what number our unit was. I can't remember which direction our windows faced.

For a long time, I wouldn't let myself think about the time I spent with Ben. Now all my memories of that period are muddled.

Mordecai is still talking. "You don't dress the same way for work as you do out in the real world, do you? I don't. Sure, we can dress pretty casually here, but most of my real clothes are, like, band merch."

I wouldn't care if Mordecai came to work every day dressed as a hot dog.

"I'd feel a little unprofessional wearing a band shirt or a graphic tee at work," he says. "I know Sue wears them all the time, but I prefer to wear a knit sweater, or something with buttons. I might make an exception if I were leading a themed children's program, or something for teens, of course. But you know what I mean, right? I've got a collection of work shirts I cycle through, and I never wear cardigans or collared shirts outside the library."

He continues to ramble while I stand at the sink, holding the wet wad of paper towels to my shirt. I'm trying to recall a time when Joy and I washed our curtains. I don't think we ever have. I'm not sure I know how to wash curtains. Can they just be tossed into a regular machine? Do they need a more heavy-duty cycle, or something gentler? We have white drapes over our front windows, and in our bedroom. They're lightweight and sheer. Our cats are always basking in the sunlight that breaks through them. We bought our house six years ago, and I don't think we've ever washed those curtains.

"Can I ask you a question?"

A man in an ill-fitting suit is hovering by the reference desk. I minimize the website open on my screen. I was looking up how to wash curtains.

There's a prominent sign suspended above my head labeled QUESTIONS?, and I'm wearing a sizeable pin on my vest that reads, ASK ME ANYTHING.

I smile. It's important to control your body language when you man the reference desk. People should feel welcomed and comfortable approaching me. Even when someone asks a nonsensical or obvious question, I need to present as interested and gracious.

I nod. "Yes, of course you can."

"Can I record it?" he asks, holding out his phone.

"Sure."

Sometimes people like to record conversations. This is especially true of people with anxiety, attention deficit disorder, as well as some other disabilities. I always say yes.

"Wonderful." He hits record. "I'm a correspondent with *Liberty Lately*. We're doing a story about your pornography policy. A distraught woman contacted me today voicing her distress when a local degenerate was spotted watching pornography on the public library computers this morning. She said she spoke to the librarian on duty. Was that you, miss?"

I nod. It seems I've misread this man. He isn't a patron with ADD. He's a reporter. Though I guess he could be both.

"Can you please answer verbally, for the recording?" He taps on his phone.

I lean toward his phone. "Yes, that was me, and I'm actually a Mrs."

Joy and I have been married for six months now.

"Can you explain why you would allow the public library, which is funded by citizens like that woman, to devolve into a godless sex hole?"

I stifle an urge to laugh. It's important not to laugh at patrons. It's impolite, and it can be off-putting, depending on the context.

"The library is not a godless sex hole." I lean toward the phone. "The public library is actually a democratic institution. For democracies to work, citizens need to be able to freely educate themselves. Anyone without home internet or a device can come here to access information. You don't have to pay for books, or for subscriptions, or even for personalized research. Public libraries are sometimes referred to as "the last free space" because we're one of the last places that exist in the public domain without the expectation of spending money. I'd be happy to recommend some books about the history of—"

"In what twisted, debauched universe is a publicly bankrolled space, where creeps can binge-watch porno, a democratic institution? Perhaps you're confusing democracy with fascism."

I consider the suggestion, then say, "No, definitely not. Fascism is a system of government led by a dictator who usually rules by forcefully and often violently suppressing opposition—"

"You're forcefully and violently subjecting innocent women to deviants watching depraved sex acts."

I'm tempted to comment that the sex acts weren't really *that* depraved, but instead I say, "Respectfully, sir, I think that's a misrepresentation. While of course it's unpleasant to be in the vicinity of someone engaging with it, people can technically watch porn anywhere. I was just on the bus last week when a man was watching—"

"We pay for the library," he interrupts me. "We pay the electricity bill. We pay your salary. We're paying for that perv's access to porno—"

"The bus is also subsidized by taxpayers."

I notice he's clenching his fists, and his neck is turning purple. His body language suggests he's restraining himself.

I lean back. "You're a reporter?"

I want to create more space between us.

"Yes." He leans forward.

I lean back more. "A journalist?"

He inches closer. "Yes."

"Where did you go to journalism school?"

His face flushes.

I don't think I phrased myself politely enough. He looks offended by my question.

He raises his voice. "You don't have to go to journalism school to be a journalist. I'm not interested in being indoctrinated by biased, money-grubbing liberal colleges. I'm with the non-mainstream media. I'm self-educated."

Recognizing I've accidentally insulted him, I apologize. "I'm sorry, sir. The reason I ask is because I'm a librarian, and like journalists, there are professional ethics associated with my job. Librarians aren't in the business of policing what content people consume. It has to do with intellectual freedom. If we prevent people from accessing certain websites, what's to stop us from restricting their access to anything? For example, if I personally didn't like your reporting, I could censor your website at the library, and then no one—"

"You're going to censor my website?" he shouts.

Patrons at the computers look at us.

"No, it was a hypothetical—"

"You made a powerful enemy today, lady." He thumps a fist on the desk. "You're a sexual deviant yourself, aren't you? Do you get off on creeps watching porno at your library? You're sick too, aren't you, miss?"

I'm tempted to remind him I'm a Mrs., but instead I say nothing.

He scowls at me. "You've got blue hair. I've got you figured out."

Joy dyed my hair blue on a whim last month. She was trying to cheer me up. She said it looked cool.

I frown. "What do you mean? What's wrong with my hair?"

"Are you an atheist?" he asks. He's looking right into my eyes.

I'm not supposed to answer personal questions about my

beliefs. I need to be neutral, a-religious, and nonpartisan. Rather than respond directly, I try to politely redirect. I say, "I can recommend some excellent philosophy or theology books if you're interested in exploring the question of God—"

"You should pray," he says before picking up his phone and exiting the library.

I've written an email to Brenda, my director, alerting her to the pornography incident, as well as the visit from *Liberty Lately*. I'm supposed to tell her when there's been a confrontation that could potentially escalate. That's the protocol. I'm also required to inform her because I interpreted the man's suggestion that "I should pray" as a possible threat, and our rules stipulate that employees must record those sorts of intimidations.

I want to include an apology for bailing on the branch manager interview, but I won't. Both Joy and my therapist would tell me I shouldn't apologize. *It's not your fault you were sick.* Besides, I'm sure Brenda has more important things on her plate than dealing with my failed job application. Mentioning it could be perceived as me fishing to be reconsidered.

Before I send the email, I read it over and imagine I am the recipient. I do this to ensure there's no unintended tone, accidental implications, or rudeness.

While signing off on the email, I receive an incoming message to the reference desk inbox. It's titled DO GROUSES EAT BUGS?

Before replying, I need to consult at least three credible

sources. In order for a source to be credible, it must be published by an authoritative body, such as an accredited university. Its purpose should also be considered. Does it exist to make the author a profit? Who is its intended audience? Was it peer-reviewed, or published by a scholarly source, such as an academic journal? Is it relevant and up-to-date? Does it cite other credible sources?

I find two good digital sources through an ornithology database, as well as a handbook about birds. After consulting and citing all three, I write, YES, THEY DO. THEY ALSO EAT LEAVES, BUDS, AND FLOWERS. IF YOU HAVE ANY FOLLOW-UP QUESTIONS, PLEASE FEEL FREE TO REACH OUT TO US AGAIN. WE ARE HAPPY TO HELP.

While researching this answer, I found a photo of a sage grouse. He has plumes around his neck that look like a fur scarf, and feathers growing from his shoulders in a style that reminds me of the coat Joy wore on our first date.

We went to a Mexican restaurant. Joy chatted with the waitress while she led us to our table. They were laughing. They interacted with this comfortable familiarity, like old friends. When the waitress left us to look at our menus, I asked Joy if they knew each other. She said no, they just met.

Joy speaks to strangers with the same candor she has with her friends. Customer service representatives always lose their fake, formal tone when they talk to her. They use their real voices.

I remember glancing at her across our table that night. The lighting was soft and reddish. Her plumy, ostentatious coat was hanging off the back of her chair. There were chips and salsa in front of us, and she ate them with no reservation. Her hand dipped in and out of the basket. Crumbs fell on her shirt.

I was the type of person who counted how many chips I ate to make sure I wasn't taking too many or eating faster than my date. I neurotically dabbed my face with my napkin and covered my mouth when I chewed. I spent the majority of my time on first dates attempting to follow an unspoken social script. *Ask them questions. Don't talk too much. Offer to pay.* I ate for the performance of eating. I spoke for the performance of conversation.

Joy and I had only interacted briefly prior to this dinner. I didn't really know her yet. I felt apprehensive about going out with her, and almost canceled. I thought of first dates like job interviews. They were tedious and exhausting. I prepared prior to the date like I would for a test. I primed topics we could chat about and practiced my phony laugh.

When Joy laughs, her chin juts into her neck, and she makes this throaty, choking sound. She doesn't restrain it. It reminds me of a baby's laugh. It's her natural, unpolished bodily reaction. It's never been refined by insecurity. It's this raw, precious laugh.

I felt disarmed by her. She exuded this unguarded authenticity. I found her refreshing and endearing. I still find her that way. It's never a performance for her. If she likes something, she says, "I like this." If she's worried about something, she says, "I'm worried." She smiles when she's happy and she frowns when she's sad. She wears whatever clothes she wants, regardless of what's in style, and she says what she thinks. There's no artifice. She's an honest person.

I felt a weight lift in her presence. We didn't discuss any of the topics I prepped, and I never used my phony laugh. I watched her eat tortilla chips, listened to her chortle like a baby playing peekaboo, and fell in love.

CHAPTER
TWO

Opening the back door with my foot proves to be difficult. My hands are full, I have a poor sense of balance, and I overestimated my dexterity.

"What are you doing?" Joy asks.

My foot is raised. I'm trying to use my big toe to hook the doorknob.

"I trapped a spider," I explain. It was crawling across our kitchen counter, so I caught it under a teacup. I slid a sheet of newspaper under the lip to trap it so I could free it outside.

Joy opens the door for me.

"Thank you." I carry the cup toward the

dock. That's where I always free spiders. There are lots of them weaving their webs by the water. They catch the midges, flies, mosquitoes, and grow to be very fat.

After placing the cup down and removing the newspaper, the spider remains motionless, assessing her surroundings. I watch her until she feels safe enough to run from the cup and scurry between a gap in the wood.

I stay at the end of the swaying dock, holding my empty teacup, looking out at the moving water. The wet wood beneath me groans and creaks. The air smells like algae and damp grass. The lake is thawing from winter. We'll be swimming in a few months.

I went about a decade without swimming. I didn't like how I looked in a bathing suit. I was insecure about my weight. I was very thin, but I didn't see myself that way; I only see it now in old photos. My gaunt face. My knobby, angular legs. There was a sickliness to my skin. I looked tired.

I used to weigh all my food and track my calories. I would make stir fries or salads for dinner, serve Ben's with meat and carbs, and plate myself lettuce, bell peppers, and broccoli. Back then, I claimed pickles were my favorite food, but they were just low calorie. I subsisted on pickles, Diet Coke, sugar-free Jell-O, and zucchini noodles, until I lapsed and binge ate.

My mom was always fixated on weight. In middle school, I hadn't grown to my full height, and there was a two-year period when I was, as my mother would say, "chunky." By high school I'd thinned out, but my mom always referred to my middle school body as my natural state. Mom said I'd inherited my "weight issues" from her, and I'd need to stay on top of my diet or I'd become fat. We weighed ourselves together every morning.

I never acknowledged binge eating to my mom, or to Ben. It was a secret. I did it privately. I shoved wrappers into the bowels of our garbage cans, claiming I had no clue what happened to the missing food, or that it had rotted so I'd tossed it. I remember feeling my stomach distend, spending days after with this nagging voice in my head calling me fat and ugly.

I used to think that wanting to be thin was about wanting to be beautiful, but I know better now. When I realized I wasn't straight, I became privy to something. I know the secret. I know how it feels to be attracted to women. There's nothing unattractive about women having fat on their bodies. There's also nothing unattractive about women having asymmetrical features, wrinkles, broad shoulders, cellulite, or any of the other qualities I'd been led to believe were ugly. Gay women know something, this secret, that dissolves some of the toxic, oppressive lens girls are taught to see the world through. The truth is that everyone is actually very beautiful.

I wasn't conscious of it, but I wanted to be skinny for the same reasons I wanted to have a boyfriend.

Joy is shouting at me from the back door. The water is too loud. I can't hear her clearly.

"What'd you say?" I yell.

"Sophie's in labor!"

I spread butter over sourdough bread. Joy is lying down in the next room, watching her phone for updates from her sister. I've got the kettle on. I'm making us tea and toast.

I look down at the butter melting into the crevices in the bread. A voice in my mind begins tallying the calories, as well as the calories in the honey I'll spoon into our tea, and the pear I've cut into quarters. I haven't intentionally counted calories in years, but there's still the voice in my mind that does it against my will.

I feel a twinge of guilt whenever I eat anything. I know this isn't logical, that there's nothing wrong with eating. I have to eat. I'm a living organism. It's healthy to eat. But this voice has been wired into me. I hear it on my birthday when I eat cake. *That's bad for you.* I hear it when I pack a lunch for work. *That's seven hundred calories.* I bite an apple. *Good, that's not too bad for you.* I eat another. *Too much sugar today.* I worry I'm going to be an old lady clocking the calories in prune juice, unable to eat anything without feeling slightly bad about it.

The kettle is whistling. I pour hot water over loose valerian root tea, hover over our mugs and watch the water darken as the tea steeps.

I hear that same voice when I think of Ben. The expectations I used to have for myself are so ingrained in me that I can't mute them now. There's this relic in the back of my mind of who I used to be, who is so disappointed in me. She wants me to be a thin lady with a sweet husband who counts the almonds she eats, owns an SUV, and questions why homosexuals need a parade. I hear her when I'm filling out medical forms that ask for my husband's name. When a hairstylist asks me what my husband does for work. When I'm in the card aisle of a store, and see the section titled FOR HIM, or when I visit my Catholic family.

I know I shouldn't feel guilty about being gay, but I can't turn it off, and it's intermingled with more complicated feelings I have for Ben.

Ben was a nice person. He had hopes and dreams for his life. I told him I wanted the same things he did, then pulled the rug out from under him. I know I shouldn't feel guilty about putting butter on bread, or honey in tea, but I think I should feel guilty about Ben.

When I grip onto Joy, my fingers make indents in her flesh like she's made of warmed beeswax. She looks like a neoclassical stone sculpture, or a painting of Venus.

The first time I had sex with a guy, I laid on my back solely because it made my stomach look flatter. When I had sex with men, I made movements as if I were being filmed. I felt disconnected from my body. I had this sense that there was a harsh, gremlin-like spectator in the room. He was there to point out my imperfections, and for some reason, I wanted him to like me.

I often flinched when men touched me, not because I was a closeted lesbian, but because I was worried the fat on my body would yield unflatteringly, or they might notice a missed patch of hair on the back of my calves, or a scar.

I don't think about how I look when I have sex with Joy. There's no gremlin in the room, and if he were there, I'd tell him to get lost. We don't move together like we're being filmed. We move together like we're present and comfortable in our weird human bodies. We're often fumbling, complimenting everything about each other, and laughing. I have never looked at her and thought anything negative about her appearance, and I would stomp on a gremlin if he suggested there was something wrong with how she looked.

Still, when Joy and I have sex, I feel this twinge of guilt. It's like when I eat.

"The baby is missing fingers."

Sophie gave birth. Joy has her on speakerphone. She and I are in bed. We just got out of the shower. Our bodies are red and radiating heat.

Joy grips my knee. "What? Is the baby okay? Are you okay?"

Joy's been anxious about Sophie since she told us she was pregnant. Joy is always worried about everyone's health. She fusses when I have chills or a headache. I take ibuprofen the way a person harboring a secret pill addiction might; behind a locked door with a bottle that I keep hidden under our bathroom sink.

Joy recently had a rash, and it consumed her. Not physically, it was localized to a small area by her elbow, but mentally, it engulfed her. Our house was teeming with ointments and lotions. She went to the doctor repeatedly. She took pictures of the rash to track how it was healing. She made me look at the photos and give her reassurance. She sent me so many pictures, my iPhone keeps generating curated slideshows of the rash paired with piano music, titled MEMORIES.

Joy phoned Sophie chronically throughout her pregnancy to ask how she was feeling. Whenever Sophie mentioned she felt nauseous, her ankles were swollen, her muscles were sore, there was a metallic taste in her mouth, Joy googled what it meant.

"Does she have gestational diabetes?"

"What if she's anemic?"

"We're okay," Sophie says. "They said it's some congenital limb malformation. They didn't see it in the anatomy scan, but the baby only has three fingers."

"Total?" I ask.

Joy nudges me.

"No, on the left hand. The right hand has all five."

I look at my hands and consider which fingers would be the most inconvenient to lose. The thumb, probably. Is that considered a finger? If not, the pointer finger would be the biggest loss. Though I think the middle finger could take over the pointer finger's job if it were missing.

"Which fingers are missing?" I ask.

Joy nudges me again. Her eyes are wide with concern. "What's the baby's name?"

I put a hand on her head. She finds it calming when I play with her hair so I let strands fall between my fingers.

"We haven't named her yet," Sophie says. "We have a few names picked out, but none of them really suit her."

"It's a girl?" Joy asks.

"Yes."

I smile. Joy wanted it to be a girl.

She squeezes my arm, happy. "That's exciting. I thought she would be a girl. Remember I said—"

"I had an emergency C-section," Sophie interrupts.

"Oh my God." Joy winces as if she just witnessed a violent attack. "Are you okay?"

I'm glad she didn't know about that until it was over. She would have been beside herself.

Sophie says, "Yes. I'm okay."

I want to ask more about the baby's fingers, but instead I ask, "How much does she weigh?"

I don't actually have any interest in knowing how much the baby weighs, but new parents usually tell people that information, so I think it's polite to ask. Joy doesn't nudge me, so it must have been a decent question. I know Joy, so I'm just trying to make sure we don't dwell on the C-section.

"Seven pounds and six ounces."

"That's good, right?" I ask. "Is that big?"

I have no frame of reference. I don't know how much babies usually weigh.

"It's normal," she says.

Joy pulls several sweaters out of our closet. She's going to stay with Sophie.

I keep our closet meticulously organized. Heavy knitwear and jeans are folded on the shelves at the back. Blazers, jackets, trousers, and delicate fabrics like silks and satins are hung on hangers. I sort Joys clothes to the left, and mine to the right.

She's steamrolling through everything, unfolding the sweaters, knocking shirts off their hangers. Little piles of fabric are accumulating on the floor. She's demolishing the organizational system. Two of the sweaters she's taken out of the closet are mine. She notoriously steals my clothing. I don't think she remembers what belongs to her, and what belongs to me, even though it's obvious. It's organized.

Given the sensitive context, I'm not going to complain about the theft or the havoc she's wreaking on the closet. I know she feels anxious right now. She's worried about her sister and the baby.

Sophie lives over five hours away. Joy wasn't planning to visit until the baby was about a month old. She wanted to give them time alone to settle in, but on the phone earlier, Sophie asked her if she could come now. Joy said, "Of course I can."

"She sounded strange, didn't she?" Joy says.

Her luggage is open on our bed. Our cats, Lou and Toulouse, are sitting inside it like two loaves of bread.

"She might just be a bit shaken after everything," I say. "She's probably just hopped-up on drugs. And the whole missing-fingers thing may have surprised her a bit, but it sounds like everything's okay—"

"She sounded off," she says. "Maybe she has postpartum depression. It's upsetting that the baby is missing fingers. She's probably struggling with it."

Their mom had postpartum depression after she had Sophie. It was so severe she left their family for a full year. Joy was only four, but she remembers. She talks about that time often. Her dad moved them into his mom's house. He worked a lot, so Joy's grandma took care of her and Sophie. It was hard on her grandma. She lived off a measly pension, and she had health problems, including COPD. She used an oxygen machine.

When we visit Joy's family in her hometown, we often drive by her grandma's old place. It's a redbrick bungalow with a chain-link fence around the front yard. Joy would point at the windows and say, "That was my grandma's bedroom. And that was the living room . . . "

When her mom came back, she rented an apartment near Joy's grandma's place. Joy and I drive by that building when we visit too. It's a shoddy-looking, brutalist apartment building. She says it looks the same as it did when she was a kid.

When we drive by that apartment, she typically tells me about the day her mom came back, how her hair was shorter and she looked older. It's one of the stories she repeats that I pretend I haven't heard before. Her mom cried when she saw Joy and Sophie.

Joy said, "It's hard to tell why an adult is crying when you're a kid. My mom was happy to see us, but I felt scared. She held Sophie really tight, like she'd just saved her from drowning. She had tears streaming down her cheeks. She reached her hand out for me, but I was afraid of her, so I didn't get closer."

I called Joy's mom during my recent mental health crisis to ask about her own. She's texted me several times since to ask how I'm doing.

Postpartum depression makes a lot of sense to me. There are so many hormones and chemicals involved during pregnancy. After people give birth, there's this rapid drop in estrogen and progesterone. It's a physical, bodily experience. It's not surprising that it affects brain chemistry. Actually, I'm surprised more people don't struggle with postpartum depression.

What I find strange is that our brains are capable of misfiring without experiencing something physical or bodily, like pregnancy or childbirth. We can lose our minds after simply reading something, like an obituary.

Joy is sitting on our bed. She's worked up a sweat obliterating our closet.

I touch her hair. She's winded. I don't know how to help her right now.

"Are you expecting any book drop-offs this week?" I ask.

"No. I don't have any scheduled," she says.

I wish she did. That way I could help her. I'm not a book binder, but I can do admin tasks like paperwork.

"I can write invoices, if you need, or help with your ads. Or I could clean up the shop," I offer. "And I'll book you a train ticket right now, while you pack, okay?"

She looks at me. She has dark brown eyes like a deer. "Okay. Thank you. But what about you? Will you be all right if I leave?"

I nod. "Yes, of course I'll be all right."

She frowns. "I'm worried about leaving you alone."

"I'll be fine, honey," I say. "My medication is working now, and I have my job. I'm basically back to normal."

She doesn't look convinced.

"I'll be all right, really," I say. "Don't worry."

Two months ago, Joy dragged me inside our house after she found me standing naked on our dock. I was having a panic attack. I'd never had a panic attack before, and in my desperate, frantic state, I thought my clothes were constricting my breathing. I ran outside because I rationalized that the air indoors was too hard to inhale.

It was mid-January. The lake was frozen. I was standing in the snow in flimsy slippers made of memory foam and cotton. Joy elbowed me back into the house, forced me into clothes, and drove me to the emergency room. I made her unroll all the windows in the car as we drove, despite the fact that it was well below freezing. I couldn't breathe. I thought maybe I was having an asthma attack or was in anaphylactic shock.

Following that humbling incident, I spent one week in a psychiatric ward, where I was fed antipsychotics, and forced to sleep on a crunchy bed in a room with my door open. There I confessed my deepest fears to medical professionals. That I'm unworthy of happiness, and that anyone who loves me is worse off for it. They told me it's normal to have a dissociative response when someone you care about dies.

Joy is snoring and babbling in her sleep. The only coherent words I can make out are, "I bought these peaches, lady. Get away from me." I think she must be having an argument with someone in her dream.

I close my eyes. Joy exudes a tremendous amount of body heat when she's sleeping. It gets caught beneath our quilt and attracts the cats. They always sleep on top of her. The window above our bed is open. It's the beginning of spring, and the air outside is cold. I can hear frogs croaking by the lake, and water lapping against the shore.

Joy snores, then says, "And if they bruise, I'll scream."

I roll on my side. My pillowcase smells like lavender. Joy spritzes this linen spray on our bedding. It's supposed to help us sleep. It isn't working right now, sadly. I've been lying here for hours. I was prescribed sleeping pills, but I'm worried it's too late to take them. I have to get up for work in the morning. Plus, I don't like taking them. They give me migraines, fuzzy vision, and dry mouth.

I close my eyes. I can't remember what it was like sleeping next to Ben. We slept in the same bed every night for five years, but it's been ten years since we broke up. It feels like I was a different person then.

I remember that we slept on a mattress on the ground because we couldn't afford a bedframe. There was that crack in the ceiling above us, a central fracture down the middle, flanked by raised plaster. It sort of resembled a vulva.

I think Ben was a quiet sleeper. I don't remember him snoring or talking in his sleep. I do remember that once in a while, I woke up to him crying.

I can picture myself consoling him. His large body curled into me like a baby. His scratchy face pressed into my neck. I'd never seen a man cry before I lived with him. I felt bad for him and wanted to make him feel better. Usually, he was crying about his mom. She died when he was a teenager. Other times, he cried about things like fights he had with his dad, or worries he had at the time. I don't think he was emotionally vulnerable with anyone else in his life, and I remember feeling like I was responsible for absorbing his sadness.

I open my eyes and look at Joy. Her face is scrunched, like she's in pain. Her dream must be upsetting her. Maybe it's a nightmare.

"It's okay." I touch her hair. "You're just dreaming."

Her face relaxes.

I put my hand on Joy's leg. I'm driving her to the train station on my way to work.

"I feel so anxious," she says, while biting her fingernails and looking out the window. The radio is playing a song I know she likes, so I turn it up.

She looks at her phone. "Oh, Sophie texted me. She says they named the baby."

"Did they? What did they go with?"

"I'm not sure yet. It says she's typing— Oh! They named her January."

"January?" I frown. "But it's March."

She breathes air out of her nose. "She's not named after the month she's born, honey. They must just like the name. It's a nice name, don't you think? I like it."

I shake my head. "That doesn't seem right. I feel like you need to be born in January to be named—"

"Oh my God. I forgot my toothbrush," she interrupts me. "It's too late to go back home, isn't it? Fuck. I'll miss the train if I go back, won't I? I'm going to get gingivitis—"

"Just buy a new toothbrush there," I say. "Toothbrushes are cheap. I bet your sister has an extra one already."

She exhales. "You're right. I'm an idiot."

"You're not an idiot."

We pull up to the train station. I park the car and get out to help her with her bag.

We face each other with her bag between us.

"All set?" I ask.

She nods. "Yes. Be safe, okay?"

I say, "I will. Don't worry."

Is This a Cry for Help?

We hug goodbye before she rushes through the automatic doors. We never kiss in public.

Brenda replied to my email about the porn incident yesterday. I'm reading her response while sipping my morning coffee.

DARCY,

THANK YOU SO MUCH FOR KEEPING ME POSTED ABOUT THESE CONCERNING INCIDENTS. THE BEHAVIOR OF THE *LIBERTY LATELY* REPRESENTATIVE IS UNACCEPTABLE. IF POSSIBLE, PLEASE LET ME KNOW IF YOU'RE ABLE TO FIND OUT WHAT HIS NAME IS. THANK YOU FOR REPORTING THIS.

I sip my thermos and google *Liberty Lately*. I scour the results to see if I can unearth the man's name. I quickly discover he's already written and posted an article about the pornography incident.

LIBRARIES ARE TURNING INTO COMMUNIST SEX DENS

LIBRARIES, WHICH WERE ONCE SANCTUARIES OF SCHOLARLY PURSUIT AND INTELLECTUAL REPOSE, ARE NO LONGER SAFE. THE OLD LADIES WHO ONCE MAINTAINED DECORUM AND ORDER HAVE BEEN REPLACED BY BLUE-HAIRED LIBERAL RADICALS WHO HAVE ABANDONED ALL SEMBLANCE OF PROPRIETY, AND WHO BLITHELY ALLOW

PERVERTS TO WATCH DEPRAVED SEX ACTS NEXT TO OUR CHILDREN AND GRANDMOTHERS . . .

I snort, almost spitting coffee onto my keyboard. I put a hand to my chest, close my eyes, and try to muster the Zen required to swallow the swig of coffee in my mouth without cackling.

I finally gulp it down. I let myself look at the article again.

Sex dens. What a hysterical way to refer to the library. It's obvious the folks at *Liberty Lately* have never been to a real sex den, communist or otherwise. I find the term "communist" hilarious too, remembering the reporter called us "fascists" yesterday.

The post goes on. I scroll down to see if there's a byline. There is, and it's even accompanied by a photo. *Declan Turner.* A thin, weaselly-looking white man with blond hair and no eyebrows. That's our guy. His name is hyperlinked. I click it. I'm directed to the About Us section of *Liberty Lately*, where I discover the site is owned and operated by Declan. I copy his name to send it to Brenda, then continue scrolling. Beneath the post, there are comments.

> YET ANOTHER EXAMPLE OF THE FAILURE OF OUR RADICAL LEFT LEADERSHIP.

> WE NEED POLICE IN LIBRARIES.

> DEFUND LIBRARIES!

"What's so funny over there?" Patty asks. She's working at a desk nearby.

"I'm sorry, it's not actually funny," I say, still laughing. "It's really sort of appalling. It's just the verbiage. But I'll send you a link."

She waits at her computer, clicks, then reads. She starts giggling. "Oh my God. Did you read the comments?"

She throws her head back and laughs so hard she doesn't make noise.

I look at Declan's photo, trying to guess how old he is. He's dressed like a middle-class suburban grandfather. He's tucked his red golf shirt into his disheveled, baggy khakis, fashioned with a phone belt; however, he appears to be someone much younger than his clothes suggest. *Is he my age?*

Patty sighs, "Oh, we shouldn't laugh. This is actually quite troubling, isn't it? I thought we'd left these attitudes in the past."

I squint. I think Declan might be in his thirties. That throws me off. That means we grew up exposed to the same school curriculum, news, and pop culture. I'm disturbed to think we followed the same steps, in the same world, in the same timeline, and he turned out like this.

"It is troubling," I say, still examining his photo.

CHAPTER
THREE

"Are you in there, Darcy?" Mordecai shouts into the women's washroom.

I'm crying in a stall. I was feeling fine earlier, but then a man who resembled Ben came into the library. He was returning board books. He had a baby and a golden retriever puppy with him. People were cooing over the puppy and the baby. The man was grinning. Proud.

"Hello? Darcy? Are you in there?"

It's not my fault he died, I remind myself. *I'm not the reason he died.*

"Hello?"

I'm trying to do my therapy exercises, and my medication *is* helping, but there are still these moments when I feel so intensely anguished, I worry I'm going to lose my mind.

"Hello?"

I found out Ben died two months ago. Actually, he died six months ago, but I learned about it two months ago. I was here at the library, looking up an obituary for a patron, when I stumbled on his picture and froze.

I hadn't spoken to him in years. When I broke up with him, I wanted to stay friends, but he didn't take the breakup well. He bombarded me with calls, and left me long, rambling messages about being in love with me. It was awful. I eventually blocked his number and deleted him off social media because I couldn't handle it.

"Darcy?"

It was selfish of me to ignore him like that. It must have been confusing for his live-in girlfriend of five years to suddenly flip a switch, and leave. I imagine he felt insane.

"Can you hear me, Darcy?"

I thought I dreamed the obituary at first. I didn't feel lucid.

I wish I'd slept last night. I should have taken a sleeping pill. I feel fragile when I don't sleep. I'm unsteady and easier to rattle.

"Darcy?"

"Yes?" I answer finally, annoyed to be shouted at in the sanctity of a public washroom stall. I chose to cry here, rather than in a staff bathroom, specifically so I could avoid my coworkers discovering me in this compromising state.

"Oh, thank God you're there. Um. There's a bit of a situation out here. Are you, um, busy?"

I exit the washroom expecting to find the library on fire, but instead I see Mordecai clutching a large orange cat.

"I'm so sorry for bothering you in the bathroom. I know you've just been sick. I don't know if you went in there to take medicine or something. But if so, please forgive me. I heard you breathing loudly. Is your medical issue related to your lungs? Sorry. None of my business. Not the point. Anyway, again, so sorry for disrupting you in the bathroom, I just didn't know what to do. This animal just came right in." He's holding the cat away from his torso. He looks like he's never held a cat before. The cat's body has stretched. He's elongated and looks tube-like.

Mordecai has many good qualities. He's creative, tech-savvy, and knowledgeable about manga. He is, however, lacking in some other areas. I wouldn't recommend he interrupt someone using the bathroom to alert them to the presence of a cat.

"Did you try shooing him?" I ask.

"Yes, I tried that. It won't leave. It just keeps jumping into my lap. I thought maybe it needed help. Do cats do that thing dogs do, where they lead you to a kid stuck in a well? Do you think there's some sort of emergency? I haven't spent much time around cats. Or is it sick? Oh God. Should I be touching it? Should I put it down? Am I going to get rabies? Should we evacuate? Wait. Is this a domesticated cat? It's so big. Is it a fox? What should we do? Should I call someone?"

He rambles on with his questions while I smile and nod.

A lump from crying still lingers in my throat. My head hurts, and there's pressure behind my eyes.

I let the cat smell my hand before I pet him. I rub his chin and behind his ears. He closes his wide, amber eyes.

I say, "He's sweet."

"Oh, you think it's a he?" he asks.

"Most orange cats are male, I think. Maybe you should set him down. He looks kind of uncomfortable."

He places the cat on the ground.

"What are we supposed to do now?" he says, as if this is an emergency.

The cat is exposing his belly at our feet.

He's a good-looking cat. He has a masculine bone structure.

"He likes you." Mordecai smiles.

THANK YOU FOR THE HELPFUL INFORMATION YOU PROVIDED ABOUT GROUSE DIETS. I HAVE A FOLLOW-UP QUESTION. COULD YOU PLEASE TELL ME: WHAT WOULD HAPPEN IF EVERY GROUSE ON EARTH WENT EXTINCT? I'M ALSO INTERESTED IN KNOWING WHAT WOULD HAPPEN IF EVERY BIRD ON EARTH DIED OFF.

THANK YOU,
SAMMY

We don't generally get many requests like these. Most of the questions I field usually relate to technical troubleshooting. *How do I change my password? How do I print?* We do get questions relating to genealogy, law, taxes, financial aid, and that sort of thing, but generally, most people know how to google, and there's a lot of free information available nowadays. Rarely do we receive obscure research questions. I spend most of my time at the reference desk helping people find physical resources in the library or assisting patrons on the computers. I don't normally field repeated questions about birds.

While I begin preparing a response, I wonder what this patron will do with the answer. Usually, I try to probe reference questions to clarify their purpose. I ask things like, "Is this for school?," to dig a little into the question, narrow it down, and clarify exactly what they're looking for. It's a little more difficult to do that over email, though, and besides, this question is relatively clear enough.

The cat is sitting in my lap. Purring.

From my research, I learn that half of the world's bird population is on the decline. Over the last half century, almost three billion birds have disappeared across Europe and North America alone.

The cat is watching the screen as I scroll past pictures of birds.

birds have a significant impact on our ecosystems, I type. they disperse seeds. they're predators, scavengers, and pollinators. grouse birds, in particular, occupy an important role in many ecosystems, including grasslands, boreal forests, and tundra. if they died, there would be a domino effect on other creatures, like foxes and—

"How the fuck do you print on this thing?" a woman yells. I look up. She's pointing at the printer nearby. "I have something I need to print urgently. I'm so fucking annoyed by this stupid machine. It won't work. It's garbage."

I stand up to help her. After assessing the print job, I learn she sent it to the printer on the other side of the library. I explain that to her, but she scoffs. "Well, how the hell am I supposed to know that?"

Rather than point out it explicitly says so on the print job, I say, "I understand your frustration. Please let me know if I can do anything else to help you."

"I didn't have to help her. We don't have to help patrons who swear at us," I tell Joy. I'm sitting on a picnic table outside on my last break. "Our code of conduct stipulates you can't swear at us, among other things. I could have asked her to leave."

Someone has carved I HATE BRAD into the picnic table. I'm running my finger along the grooves in the wood. I wonder if Brad did something cruel to warrant this, or if he's just an unlikable person.

"Why didn't you ask her to leave?" Joy asks.

Maybe the person who carved this is unkind, and Brad's actually a nice guy.

"The code of conduct leaves it up to our discretion," I say. "Employees are supposed to use judgment when faced with belligerent patrons. I find sometimes it's more work to kick someone out than it is to just put up with them. Do you know what I mean?"

"Yeah, I get that. That's why I dated Ruth for two years." She laughs.

"Don't mention Ruth to me," I say, half-joking. We have this bit where I pretend Ruth is my enemy. I've only ever met her once, and she was perfectly nice to me. She and Joy broke up on good terms. Obviously, I don't like to picture Joy with someone else, but I'm mostly kidding.

"Fuck Ruth," I say.

She snorts. "Don't say that."

I feel something in my stomach squirm. Joy used to rib similarly about Ben, but I'm sure she won't do that anymore. She hasn't since we found out.

Ben was my first serious boyfriend. Our relationship shaped my understanding of how to be someone's girlfriend. I learned from the mistakes I made with him, but I had positive takeaways too. How to share a space with someone. That's who Ruth is to Joy too. She was her first live-in partner. Ruth and Ben are cornerstones in our relationship; our two big exes. I know Ruth taught Joy how to make bread. Joy knows Ben bought me the brass dove I keep on a bookshelf in our living room.

I dealt with my feelings about Ben by repressing them. I don't keep things from Joy. I tell her how I feel without hesitation; however, I rarely let myself dwell on him. I felt so bad about what happened between us. Because of that, I never really opened up to Joy about him. I couldn't even articulate my feelings to myself. I still can't, really. I know Joy has always understood that he is a sensitive topic and she's never pressed it. Instead, she made light of him the way I did with Ruth. We joked about them as if they were our enemies, both understanding without saying it that these were once very close, important people to us.

Moving past that thought, I say, "I forgot to tell you Mordecai found a cat. He waltzed right into the library."

"A cat? Is he a stray?" she asks.

"I think so. He doesn't have a collar, and he sort of looks like he's been through it. I picked burrs out of the fur on his stomach. I'm going to take him to the animal shelter after work to check for a microchip. He's cute. He's this big long-haired orange cat."

"Send me a picture of him."

"Okay. I'll take a picture after my break. Mordecai is watching him right now. He's still fishing to find out why I was away."

She tuts. "Oh, Mordecai."

She's never met him, but I talk about work enough for her to know who the main players are.

I say, "He's so nosy. It's uncomfortable. I was thinking maybe I should pretend I was sick with something else just to shut him up."

She asks, "Like what?"

"I don't know. Like, syphilis?"

She laughs. "You'd be less embarrassed to say you have syphilis than to admit you had a psychological breakdown?"

"I'm not embarrassed. I just—" I pause. "I don't know."

I hear a lot of lip service about mental health at my job. Leadership preaches about the importance of mental health in staff meetings ad nauseam. We're often reminded about our employee support resources, and how important it is to reach out and get help. There are posters about managing stress on the back of the doors in the staff washrooms. But ultimately, the topic is discussed at arm's length, as something significant, yet impersonal, and anonymous.

I worry if I said I was off work because I had an acute stress reaction, people would see me as an unreliable and less competent employee. I think when really faced with it, my coworkers would be unlikely to consider my sickness a legitimate medical condition. At best, people would see me as a dramatic faker, and at worst, as someone fragile and inept.

Joy says, "I'd prefer you not tell people you have syphilis, if that's cool."

I laugh. "Okay, fair. I won't. How much longer will you be on your train?"

"A little over an hour." She's speaking quietly so she doesn't bother other passengers. "I'm worried about Sophie, but I'm excited to see the baby."

I'm still running my finger over the I HATE BRAD carving.

"I'm excited for you to see her too," I say.

When I hang up with Joy, I see my mom left me a voicemail.

"*Hi, Darcy. I'm just calling to say I'm disappointed to learn you didn't call your Aunt Cathy on her birthday—*"

I wince. My mom cares a lot about social graces. She taught me to call relatives on their birthdays. To remember the anniversaries of any couple whose wedding I've attended. To keep track if they divorce. To send thank-you notes after receiving any gift, no matter how trivial. *Thank you for this opened box of dryer sheets. Thank you for this rusted frying pan.*

Despite believing this is unreasonable, I try my best to accommodate her expectations. I can't help but feel like a disappointment to her in many ways, and I'm willing to make minor concessions in certain areas, such as manners, to appease her. Last year I called Cathy—a woman who I haven't seen in roughly a decade—to awkwardly wish her a happy birthday. I also called my Great-Uncle Jed; our old neighbors, the Watsons; and a slew of other distant relatives and acquaintances. Unfortunately, I spent the last two months incapable of working, temporarily sequestered to in-patient care, and adjusting to my new antipsychotics—so I forgot to call Cathy.

"*Now, I understand that you're a grown woman with your own opinions regarding how you operate in this world, but I raised you to be polite, and I occasionally worry that you don't look outside yourself enough—*"

I don't look outside myself enough? That's funny. My therapist told me I have dissociative tendencies, that I find it hard to look inside myself. My mom's diagnosis contradicts my doctor's. Maybe I should get a third opinion.

"*It's important for you to consider other people, and while I understand that you think you need to exist in this world as unapologetically yourself, it would behoove you to take a touch of advice from me. Believe it or not, I do know a few things.*"

I make the same face I would if I'd just swigged curdled milk. I'd like to meet the version of me my mom thinks I am. I have a feeling she and I have very little in common.

I feel terrible about the negative ways I've impacted people. Even now, listening to this voicemail, I feel sorry. Did Cathy wait for my call? She must have told my mom I didn't call. Was she upset?

My mom doesn't see me as the person I truly am. For

instance, she thinks I went to college to assert myself as better than her. That I think I'm a higher-class lady. Uppity. That I think I'm so smart. That I rejected the life she wanted for me, the one that looked more like hers, because I think I'm better than her. I chose to live far away, become a lesbian, marry a woman, and have no children because I'm selfish.

It would never occur to her that I didn't call Cathy because I was mentally incapacitated. She doesn't understand that I went to college because I wanted to learn something. I'm a lesbian because that's the hand I was dealt. She has no idea that I considered her, and other people, so much that I deluded myself for years, sacrificed a significant portion of my life, just to win her and other people's approval.

I worry she's witnessed some snippet of a Pride parade, associated it with me, and decided I must be operating in this world how she imagines the kinkiest parade participants do—with no apologies. Shamelessly. I have no care for anyone but my own primal desire to have sex with people of the same gender. I do things like go to college, marry Joy, and gain weight because I'm just living for me.

I think it's unreasonable that she expects me to call Cathy, and I think this voicemail is over the line, but nonetheless, I wish I'd called. I wish I were someone who didn't disappoint my mom. I'm never deliberately trying to disappoint her. Unfortunately, disappointing her is one of the unavoidable side effects of me existing. It troubles me that I can't find a way for her, me, and for everyone to be happy.

If my mom were a more reasonable person, I'd tell her that my consideration for her, and for everyone else, has tortured me. I'd explain that I do exist as myself, and I am living my life for me, but I'm not unapologetic about it. I am myself with many, many apologies.

Sadly, my mom isn't a reasonable person, and I've learned the only way to respond to this sort of message is to ignore it.

"*To replay this message, press seven. To delete it, press eight.*"

I press eight.

I'm crying in my car. The voicemail my mom left me, the man who came into the library, Joy being away, the baby missing fingers, my grief, and the fatigue of returning to work has all compounded, leaving me depleted and run-down.

The orange cat is sitting in my passenger seat watching me.

"I'm okay," I say to him. I know he probably doesn't understand, but he's staring intently at me, and I feel compelled to explain myself.

I look at my reflection in the rearview mirror and wipe the tears off my cheeks.

It's normal to cry. It doesn't mean I'm having a breakdown. I'm just exhausted. This is cathartic. Crying is healthy, I think.

I sniff. This isn't my first struggle with mental health, but it is my first time going to therapy or taking medicine. I was a depressed teenager. I dealt with a lot of conflict with my mom. She was unreasonably strict, and I was always getting in trouble for trivial things like hanging out with kids she didn't approve of or eating too much refined sugar. It really weighed on me that I wasn't the person she wanted me to be.

I felt similarly when I broke up with Ben. I wasn't the person he wanted me to be either. More importantly, I wasn't the person *I* wanted to be. The mess of our breakup left me feeling anxious and lost. There were no clear steps forward. I remember googling "how to be a lesbian." Unfortunately, the search results were all essentially porn.

I close my eyes. I was hoping the medicine and therapy would miraculously cure me, and that I would stop crying in public, but sadly, resolving my issues seems to require more effort.

I remember lying with my head in Ben's lap, feeling the rough pads of his fingertips touch my face while we talked about what we would name our hypothetical baby. If it was a girl, he wanted to name her Rosemary, after his mom. We liked Franklin, if it were a boy.

I open my eyes. The cat is still looking at me. I reach past him, open the glove compartment, and grab the wad of McDonald's napkins I've stowed away there.

I blow my nose. My recent breakdown felt different. This wasn't something I could push down into the soles of my boots, put on a brave face, and step out into the world. At one point, I found myself sobbing in the produce section of a grocery store while I dropped oranges on the tiles around me. I was disoriented and confused. I wasn't sleeping.

I've always carried this heaviness for Ben. For years I tried to repress my thoughts about him. When I learned he died, I felt like a rabid animal in my chest woke up and started thrashing, clawing at my insides, and foaming at the mouth. I felt anguished for him, his dad, and his friends. Intrusive images of his face kept flashing in my mind. He had these faint laugh lines by his eyes. Unkempt eyebrows. Calloused hands. I could hear his low voice calling me "dove."

I still feel that animal in my chest, but I'm trying to subdue it.

Before this happened, if someone told me they were off work on stress leave, I might have been judgmental too. Now I understand that issues intensify when we smash them down into our boots. If I could go back in time, I'd go to therapy sooner. I'd try to treat the issues I was compacting earlier, and then maybe I'd be more resilient.

"Big Red doesn't have a microchip," the animal shelter employee tells me. She puts the cat down on the counter between us. "And I'm afraid there's no room at the inn."

"What?" I ask.

"Unfortunately, there's no available space for this big guy," she clarifies. "We're completely full."

She's patting the cat's back. He's purring.

"So I can't leave him here?" I ask.

"Well, you could, but . . . uh."

I frown. "What would happen to him?"

She doesn't look at me.

"What would happen to him?" I ask again, quietly.

I shut the door to Joy's workshop. I've secured Big Red inside. I'm in a rush. I have to go to therapy. I can't put him in the house because properly introducing cats to each other requires careful preparation. There's a whole procedure to it. Cats are territorial, and they need to acclimate to each other.

I've put a pillow on the ground, a box of cat litter in the

corner, and served him a can of Fancy Feast with a bowl of water. I've covered Joy's workstations in a protective tarp and secured all the books she's repaired in closed storage.

"I'll be back in about an hour," I tell him.

"Be safe, please," I add.

He looks at me.

"How have you been feeling since our last session?" Dr. Jeong asks.

I'm sitting on a couch in my therapist's office. There's a bowl of mints and a tabletop water fountain in front of me. The fountain makes a babbling sound.

"Better," I say.

"You're back to work? How's that going?"

"Yes. Today was my second day back. It's going well so far."

Should I tell her I cried in my car and in the bathroom this morning?

"And you've still noticed a positive change since taking your medication?"

I nod. "Yes. It's helped a lot, I think. I'm still not totally feeling like myself, but I'm on the mend for sure."

"Good. I'm glad to hear that. And are you sleeping through the night?"

"I didn't sleep very well last night," I admit. "I should have taken a sleeping pill, but I waited too long. I didn't want to take it in the middle of the night and knock myself out when I had to work in the morning."

She writes something down. "You should take one tonight, okay? Lack of sleep has a significant impact on you."

In a previous session, she told me that sleep deprivation disrupts our neurotransmitters. When Joy found me naked on the dock, I hadn't slept in three days.

"Shall we do some grounding work to get started?" She hands me a red-and-white peppermint from her candy dish.

I put it in the palm of my hand.

"How does it feel?" she asks.

I'm terrible at these exercises. I have a hard time taking them seriously.

"It feels like a mint," I say.

"Go on."

"Uh, it's a hard mint. I guess it feels like a rock." I grip it. "The plastic wrapper on it makes a crunching sound."

"Open it. How does it smell?"

I unwrap it and hold it to my nose. "Fresh."

"If you're comfortable doing so, please close your eyes, and take a few deep breaths."

I don't feel comfortable, but I close my eyes anyway. I don't want to be difficult. I want to be a good sport. A lot of therapy feels hokey to me, but I'm trying to take it seriously because I want to get better.

When I was a kid, I wanted my teachers to like me. I was the student they sat next to the troublesome, unruly kids because of my good influence. I listened, raised my hand, and kept my desk neat. My report cards were glowing. I was a pleasure to have in class.

I feel a compulsion to behave similarly in these sessions. I want to be Dr. Jeong's star patient. I want to earn an A+ in therapy.

"If you're open to it, I'd like us to practice imaginal revisiting," she says.

She introduced me to this in our last session. She sent me home with a printout about it. It's a form of treatment that's supposed to help me process memories and emotions.

I nod. "Yes. Sure."

"All right, I'd like you to think of a specific memory from your relationship with Ben. It could be any memory that stands out to you."

I say, "I'm sorry. My memory is foggy when it comes to Ben. I'm not sure I remember much."

"You don't have to recall it perfectly. Take your time."

All my memories of Ben are vague. I was eighteen when he and I met. Twenty-three when we broke up. I'm thirty-two now. Memories fade when you neglect them. Ever since I broke up with Ben, I've spent most of the time actively trying not to think of him.

"I sort of remember the day we met," I say.

"Can you try to describe where you were? How it looked and felt?"

I think for a moment, then say, "We were at a call center. We'd both just been hired to sell cruise line tickets. We were in orientation in this training room. It was like a computer lab. There were fluorescent lights. I think I felt nervous to start the job."

"What do you remember about your interaction with Ben that day?"

My eyes are still closed. I'm trying to remember Ben's face. Of course, I know what he looked like. We were together for years. We lived together. I know he had hazel eyes and a big mouth. The structure of his face is jumbled now, though. I can't fully picture him. I can see the puzzle pieces that make him up, but I can't put them together.

"I was having a hard time remembering the phonetic alphabet," I say. "They made us learn it, and this script. We had to memorize all these lines. There was a test we had to take at the end of the shift. I was worried I'd fail it. Ben and I chatted during our lunch break. He was nice. I told him I was nervous for the test. He said not to worry and sat beside me later. When the instructor wasn't looking, he let me cheat off him."

"How did that make you feel?"

"Relieved," I say. "I felt appreciative. I think I may have also sensed that he liked me, so I felt kind of awkward and flattered."

"What else do you remember?"

I still can't really picture Ben's face. I'm trying to think of his teeth. Were they crooked? I don't remember. When we were together, I recognized his shadow. I could pick his hands out of a lineup. I knew his nailbeds.

"It was nighttime at the end of our shift," I say. "He and I walked out together. I think it was July. I'm not sure. Maybe it was August. He walked me to my bus stop and waited with me, even though he wasn't taking the bus. He lived nearby, so he was going to walk home. But it was dark out, and the call center was in sort of a rough area. I appreciated him waiting there with me. We talked. I don't remember what about. I was certain he liked me at this point, though. He was smiling, making eye contact."

"How did you feel about Ben liking you?"

I had just moved out of my parents' house. I left at the

beginning of the summer, months before college started, because I wanted to escape. My mom was as controlling as ever, and we were fighting a lot. My parents didn't approve, and my mom was so angry she didn't speak to me until October that year.

When I first moved out, I was worried my mom was right. It took a while to find that job, and I didn't have much money. I remember sitting alone in my apartment, cross-legged on my twin-size bed, feeling like I was a lost kid pretending to be a grown-up. I thought maybe I'd made a big mistake.

Ben appeared right when I needed someone. I felt a spotlight cast on me when he looked at me. I thought it was so nice of him to like me.

"I felt happy," I say. "I thought he was really nice. I appreciated that he wanted me to be safe getting home. I thought maybe I liked him back. It was hard for me to tell the difference between being flattered and liking someone, back then."

I was never truly attracted to Ben, but I could see why someone would be. As a kid, I used to pick guys to have crushes on. I wasn't aware I was doing it. I thought everyone's crush was a calculated choice. I based who I liked on criteria like: Does he like me? Would other girls think he's good-looking? Would I pick him to be my friend? When I met Ben, my answer to all those questions was yes.

"Okay, good. When you're ready, please open your eyes."

I open them immediately.

"How did you feel revisiting that memory? Have any insights emerged for you?"

I don't know how she wants me to answer. I open my

mouth and ramble. "When Ben and I were together, I thought of that day as sort of sweet. Now, I wonder why he liked me. I was really insecure and quiet. And he was ten years older than me. I felt safe with him walking to the bus stop, but he was a stranger then. In retrospect, it's bizarre that I felt protected by a strange older man walking with me in the dark."

She's writing something down. I squint at her paper in an attempt to read what she's scribbling, but I'm too far away.

To help her with her notes, I add, "I think I used to be overly focused on other people's feelings, and out of touch with my own. I think maybe I was taught not to trust my own gut and was sort of hyper-keyed into the feelings and objectives of others. So I did things like wait for a bus at night with a man I'd just met because I'd muted my own instincts, and was too focused on putting myself in his shoes. Does that help with your notes?"

She pauses. Her pen hovers over her paper. "Do you notice that you're focused on my perspective before your own right now?"

The cat is asleep on his pillow. I texted Joy about bringing him home and setting him up in her workshop. She wrote back, WHAT SHOULD WE NAME HIM?

I replied, WE'RE NOT KEEPING HIM. WE CAN'T HAVE THREE CATS.

She said, I WANT TO NAME HIM GARFIELD.

WE'RE NOT NAMING HIM GARFIELD.

THOMAS O'MALLEY?

Is This a Cry for Help?

NO.

WHAT ABOUT KYLE?

MAYBE.

I put my face underwater. I'm in the bath. I lit a candle. The bathroom smells like vanilla and patchouli.

Dr. Jeong told me to treat myself the way I'd treat a loved one. This applies always; however, it's especially relevant when I'm not feeling well. She says things like, "Consider what you might feed someone you love, and prepare that food for yourself."

I unearthed a bag of navel oranges in the back of the fridge, and force-fed them to myself. I should have just eaten one, but I consumed several. I now have heartburn, and my mouth feels irritated by the citric acid. I don't know why I did this to myself. I would never feed someone I love seven oranges.

In an attempt to course correct, I've drawn myself a bath. If I knew Joy didn't sleep last night, cried at work, got sworn at, almost accidentally euthanized Kyle, suffered through an unpleasant therapy session, then binge ate oranges, I might put her in the tub.

I drop a bath bomb in the water. I watch it fizzle and start to dissolve. It's black with glitter in it. It's turning the water purple. It's swirling and mesmerizing, like a galaxy. I find it calming, so I take a picture of it and post it to my Instagram story.

"I'm holding January," Joy whispers.

We're on the phone. I'm still in the bath. I have a cold washcloth on my forehead.

"I'm glad you got there safe. How is January?"

She says, "She's perfect."

"And where's Sophie? How's she doing?"

"She's sleeping. She's okay, I think. I'm glad I came, though. She's recovering."

It's shocking how quickly people return home from the hospital after giving birth. Sophie had a C-section and was still out of there in less than two days. I stayed in the hospital for a week after my breakdown. I can't imagine pushing a human person out of my body, then being sent packing soon after.

"How was therapy?" she asks.

"It was fine," I say. "But I'd rather talk about January."

"She has a lot of hair. She's a little bigger than I thought she'd be. She looks healthy. She's wearing a pink onesie right now. It has little ears on the hood, and a twirly tail on the butt, to make her look like a piglet."

"That's adorable. Send me a picture."

"I will."

"Does she look anything like you?"

"Maybe a little."

"She must be cute."

Joy laughs.

"Does Kearney mind you being there?" I ask.

Kearney is Sophie's husband. Joy hates him. He cheated on Sophie before their wedding. Sophie has forgiven him, but Joy hasn't. She's civil with him, but cold. Joy always assumes the best in others, so when people behave badly, she finds it shocking.

"He's barely been here," she says. "He's working. Thank God."

I can tell she's rocking January because she keeps saying "coo coo" to her.

"Coo coo," she whispers.

I'm thinking about my session with Dr. Jeong earlier today.

I'm still in the bathtub. The water is tepid. I'm inspecting my pruning fingertips, ruminating about what I told her. I regret how I talked about Ben. I need to think before I speak. I rambled. I didn't put enough thought into what I said, and how she might interpret it—

Wait. No, I shouldn't do that. She'd say that's not how I'm supposed to approach our sessions. I shouldn't be thinking about her perspective. I should be more focused on mine.

It's just that I made him sound like he was a predator. I wish I hadn't done that. What I was trying to say was that in retrospect, I was naive, and my eighteen-year-old judgment was questionable. What I said was more about me than it was about him. Yes, it's odd that I felt safe with a guy I'd just met. But that's all. I didn't mean to suggest that Ben himself wasn't a safe person, or that it was a mistake to trust him specifically. He and I dated for five years. He was trustworthy. The problem was me.

He used to text me on the nights we spent apart: ARE YOU HOME SAFE, DOVE? He met me after my night classes so I wouldn't have to walk across campus alone in the dark. When we went out drinking with my girlfriends, he intervened when men made them uncomfortable, and he always made sure they had a safe way home.

I loved him. When you're with someone for a long time, living in a shared space, drinking from the same coffee-stained mugs, you feel familial. For a long time, I knew Ben as well as I knew my family members. I didn't love him in that romantic, passionate way a girlfriend is supposed to love her boyfriend, but I did love him.

I might have married him if I were straight. I felt demonic breaking up with him. I considered staying with him until I was dead, rather than endure the guilt I felt for wasting years of his life, abandoning him. He and I talked about dying together—

I wince. There it is again. *Ben is dead.*

My face tightens. Tears well in my eyes.

I wake up with my hair matted to the back of my head. I didn't comb it after my bath last night. I crawled from the tub to my bed like that cursed girl from *The Ring*, took a sleeping pill, and passed out.

I don't know what time it is now. I think it's morning. Lou and Toulouse are both on my chest. I look at my phone.

There are six replies to my Instagram story. That's odd.

WE CAN SEE YOUR NAKED REFLECTION IN THE TAP.

Is This a Cry for Help?

HEY, JUST LETTING YOU KNOW THERE'S A
REFLECTION IN THE TAP.

I open the story and there it is. My contorted nude body holding my phone out to take a picture of my bath bomb. Three hundred and thirty-two people have viewed the picture.

CHAPTER
FOUR

WHICH BIRD SPECIES HAS THE BIGGEST ECOLOGICAL IMPACT ON EARTH? I'D LIKE TO KNOW WHICH SPECIES, ABOVE ALL OTHER BIRDS, WOULD HAVE THE MOST SUBSTANTIAL EFFECT ON OUR PLANET IF THEY ALL SUDDENLY DISAPPEARED.

THANK YOU,
SAMMY

When we get recurrent requests from one patron, we're supposed to be mindful of ensuring that person doesn't view us as a de facto personal assistant. Occasionally, people expect more than is reasonable from library staff. We have to set boundaries. Personally, I always try to help. I give myself up to thirty minutes per question, as long as there are no other patrons waiting, and provided I don't have something else critical to do.

After scanning through several sources, I learn that eastern barn owls are often named as being very valuable; however, that's mostly due to economic reasons. They help keep rodents and other predators that impact crops and spread diseases at bay. I'm not sure there's a definitive answer to this question. It seems you could make a good argument for several species. Honey buzzards control insect populations. Crows are critical in dispersing seeds.

In cases like this, when the answer isn't well-defined, I usually recommend resources rather than provide a direct answer.

"Excuse me." A woman approaches my desk. "I'm looking for a purple book."

I smile at her. "Of course. Is it a particular purple book you're after? Or are we looking for any old purple book today?"

"It's a particular one," she says. She's an older woman with a short gray perm.

"All right. I'm happy to help. Can you describe it any further, please?"

I minimize the bird content, pull up the catalog, and turn my monitor toward her.

"It was a romance." She folds her hands.

"A romance, okay. Do you remember anything else about the cover, or what the story was about?"

"Yes. It was about a young, widowed astronaut who falls in love with an older woman living in an old, dilapidated Tudor house."

"Sounds interesting," I say as I use the advanced search to narrow down the results.

"Is it this?" I ask.

There's a purple book titled *Celestial Love* on the screen.

"No, I'm afraid not," she says.

"What about this one?" I point at another, titled *Orbiting Ethel*.

"That's it!" She grins. "Is it available?"

I check, then say, "No, I'm sorry, but I can put it on hold for you."

WE'RE IN THE NEWS.

Brenda emailed me. That's the subject line of her message. The body says, HEADS UP. WE HAVE THIS ON OUR PLATES NOW. YOU'VE HANDLED THIS WELL SO FAR. THANK YOU. PLEASE LET ME KNOW IF THIS COMES UP AGAIN.

The link isn't from Declan Turner, or *Liberty Lately*. It's from a mainstream local newspaper from the closest city to our town. *The Pert City Times*. I guess they caught wind of the incident. I click it and read:

PORNOGRAPHY IN THE LIBRARY SPARKS OUTRAGE

HICKORY LIBRARY, A SMALL BRANCH NORTH OF PERT CITY, HAS COME UNDER FIRE AFTER A MAN WAS SPOTTED

WATCHING EXPLICIT PORNOGRAPHY IN PLAIN VIEW ON THE LIBRARY COMPUTERS.

PATRICIA FELLOWS, A CONCERNED LOCAL LIBRARY CUSTOMER, REPORTED THE INCIDENT ON MONDAY, STATING: "I WENT TO THE LIBRARY TO FIND THE NEWEST E.E. FAIRVIEW NOVEL AND WAS SHOCKED AND DISMAYED TO WITNESS A MAN SURFING PORNOGRAPHY. WHAT IF I'D BROUGHT MY GRANDCHILDREN WITH ME?"

FELLOWS WAS DISTURBED TO LEARN THE LIBRARY POLICY ON PORNOGRAPHY ACTUALLY PERMITS THIS BEHAVIOR. RHONDA WHEELER, LIBRARY CEO, SAID, "WE RESPECT OUR PATRONS' INTELLECTUAL FREEDOM. WE DO NOT CENSOR LEGAL CONTENT AT THE LIBRARY." WHEELER ALSO NOTED, "THERE ARE PRIVACY SCREENS ON ALL OF OUR COMPUTERS."

I minimize the news and exhale.

People regularly abandon their children in this library as if this is a day care. Why isn't that in the news? I frequently get questions about where the local shelters are, and we're currently planning programs like "How to Eat on a Budget" to combat the cost-of-living crisis. Where are the headlines about that?

My coworker Patty is roaming the shelves with a preteen girl, collecting books about Greek and Norse mythology. Mordecai is in our workshop room, working with a crowd of new immigrants on their résumés. Randall, a regular who comes here almost every day, who I know does not have stable housing, is sitting in a comfortable chair contentedly reading a magazine about woodworking. Jill went to a senior center this morning to lead a yoga and wellness program that we've been told has been "life-changing" for the residents, and our teen volunteer program is so active, we've had other branches book meetings with us to copy our approach. Why isn't any of that newsworthy?

I find it grating when attention is focused on seedy, unconstructive things, while so little focus is put on all that's good.

"Ben got up early on the days I had eight a.m. classes to put on a pot of coffee for me while I showered," I tell Dr. Jeong. "When I was sick, he made me chicken noodle soup, and this drink his mom made him when he was a kid. I don't know what was in it, but it was neon yellow, and it did seem to help."

I came here prepared to say this. I regret how I described Ben in our last session. I cast a bad light on him. I want her to know he wasn't a terrible guy.

"I appreciate you sharing these positive memories of him with me," she says. "It's clear your relationship had moments of kindness and warmth."

I feel out of breath for some reason. "Yes. It did. And Ben himself was kind. He was very generous. And he loved animals. He talked about wanting to move somewhere with a lawn someday so we could get a dog."

She's nodding. "I understand it's important to you that I know positive things about Ben."

That sounds like she still thinks he's a bad person but wants to validate that I don't.

"He called his grandma weekly," I add quickly. "And he regularly woke up in the night crying about missing his mom."

I remember his wet, sobbing face in my neck. His shoulders shaking.

I feel tears form in my eyes. "And he had this infectious laugh. It was really loud. He was generally quiet, so it startled people sometimes. I liked to watch their surprised faces. It was this big, booming laugh." The memory still stirs something happy in me, until I blink and realize I'm crying.

She hands me tissues. "I'm sorry, Darcy."

"Oh, it's okay," I say as a reflex, immediately realizing it's strange of me to deflect my therapist's condolences during our grief consoling session. Muscle memory often makes me deflect people's apologies. It's clearly not okay.

"Sorry. I mean, thank you," I correct myself.

I think I'm bad at therapy.

I came home the day I found out Ben had died, and Joy told me my face looked strange. I said, "I know. It's because I'm dreaming. My face always looks strange in dreams."

She looked worried. "No, honey, you're not dreaming."

I said, "Yes, I am. I read Ben died."

She said, "*What?* Are you serious?"

I stood stiff and still like a scarecrow while she wrapped her arms around my torso, engulfed me like a swarm of crows, and said, "I'm so sorry."

She made us pumpkin soup for dinner that night, but I couldn't eat it. I kept pinching my arms, trying to wake myself up. When I accepted that I *was* awake, I thought I must be sick. I felt off. I sat on the tile in front of our toilet, waiting to throw up, but I couldn't.

I had my fingers down my throat when she knocked on the door to check on me. I took them out and told her to come in. When I looked up, she jumped back slightly, like she was startled by my face. In the moment, I interpreted her alarm as her seeing me differently. I thought some light had shifted, and she'd realized I was wearing the skin of the person she thought I was, but beneath it I was really monstrous.

Joy's since told me I looked disturbed. Wide-eyed, tense, and drained, like an abandoned baby tottering out of the wilderness.

Ben weighed on me like this anchor I couldn't lift. I blew his life up when I broke up with him. He made plans with me, and I jilted him. Once in a while, I'd look him up on social media, and it never seemed like he was doing well. I wanted to see a picture of him laughing. I wanted him to have a new girlfriend, to travel, make new friends, get a job he liked, be happy.

Since then, I'd never heard of him having another girlfriend. He looked unhealthy. He seemed to drink more. He had the same friends he had when we were together, and they were grim, smarmy men. When we were dating, they made constant offhand derogatory comments and smoked weed in excess every day. A few of them had kids they'd abandoned.

They constantly complained about their child support payments, and their ex-wives, or ex-girlfriends. After Ben and I ended things, I got messages from some of them. One asked me to hang out, one called me a bitch, and another asked to borrow twenty dollars.

I felt like I'd abandoned Ben, propelled him into a deep depression, and left him to live a miserable life among miserable men. I'd prioritized my own happiness over his and pushed him into this dark pit, where he ultimately died.

While I was heaving into the toilet, Joy said, "I'm so sorry Ben died."

I felt this heavy brick in my chest. I put both my hands over my heart and winced. I said, "Oh my God, don't say that."

I didn't want to hear anyone say *Ben died.*

She was crying. She said, "What can I do? How can I help you?"

I said, "Please double-check that it's true."

She found his obituary.

"Did he kill himself?" I asked. I was still on the bathroom floor. I was leaning against our bathtub. My face felt swollen. I couldn't breathe in through my nose.

I hadn't read his obituary in full at the library. I just saw his picture and his birthday. He was born July 13.

"It doesn't say," she said. "But normally when that happens, they ask for donations for something related to mental health, right? His doesn't mention anything like that."

"What donations does it ask for?"

She looked then said, "The humane society."

I felt the pang again. I thought I was going to throw up, so I leaned into the toilet, but still I couldn't, so I cried. Joy tried to hold my hair back, but I swatted her away, so she just stood at a distance.

I barely slept for days. I spent those nights lying down in various areas of our house. For some reason, I thought lying on the tile at the front door would help me sleep. I tried sleeping on the floor in our closet. For several hours, I lay with a pillow in our empty bathtub. Drops of water from our leaky faucet soaked the ankles of my pajamas.

I kept apologizing to Joy. I knew I was freaking her out, because I'm usually a composed person.

I wasn't myself.

"January is breathing weird. We're going to the emergency room."

Joy is on the phone, crying.

I'm standing in the kitchen frying zucchini. I step away from the stove. I say calmly, "It's okay, honey. Can you describe her breathing?"

Her voice cracks. "Sophie is just g-getting the keys. I-I'm in the car beside January. She's, like, rapidly breathing."

I say, "Okay. But she can breathe, right? There's nothing blocking her airway?"

I look over my shoulder at the zucchini and see that

somehow it has caught on fire. I make no indication of that to Joy. I hurry to turn the burner off and quietly cover the flames with a baking sheet.

She sniffs. "Yes, she's breathing. We looked in her mouth and nose. It's just weird breathing. It's, like, quick."

"Okay. I understand that's scary, honey, but it's okay. You're doing everything you need to do. Breathe and try to be calm for Sophie, okay?"

"Okay," she sniffs.

"Can I stay on the phone with you while you drive to the hospital?"

I know that she finds talking to someone helpful when she feels panicked. It distracts her.

"Yes," she says.

"Okay. Tell me what's happening."

"Sophie's running to the car," she says.

"Is Sophie going to drive?" I ask.

"Yes. She's in the car now. You're on speaker."

"Hi, Sophie," I say. "Will Joy go into the hospital with January while you park?"

"Yeah," Sophie says. Her voice sounds panicked too. "Because I know how the parking works, so we figured that would be fastest."

"That's smart," I say. "You live close to the hospital, don't you?"

"Yeah," she says. "It's only like two minutes away."

"Good. What's January doing now, Joy?" I ask.

"She's breathing. She's looking at me."

I say, "You guys are doing everything right."

Sophie says, "We're almost there now. I'm just turning."
I say, "Okay, good."
I hear seat belts unbuckle.
"All right, I'm bringing her in," Joy says.
"Okay, good work."
"I'm going to hang up now, okay?" she says.
"Okay. Keep me posted."
"We will."
Sophie says, "Thanks, Darcy."

Ben was a fat baby. His dad used to show me pictures. His mom dressed him in overalls, and for years he wore a wooden train whistle on a chain around his neck. He loved *Thomas the Tank Engine*. I remember sitting in his dad's living room with their family photo albums open on my lap, chatting about what a sweet, happy baby he was.

"He had to get eye surgery when he was two," his dad told me. "I remember his mother and I were waving goodbye to him as they led him on a gurney to the operating room. We were smiling, acting brave, but the second they rolled him around that corner, we were hysterical. It's terrible having a baby in the hospital."

I feel the weight in my chest get heavier. I put both my hands over my face. I feel like there's a *Thomas the Tank Engine* toy wedged in my throat.

It's not my fault he died.
I'm not the reason he died.

I start envisioning a reality where I stayed with him. We

have a fat baby that looks like him. I think of that baby and me sitting on the floor of his dad's living room, calling him papaw, playing with trains.

I still don't know if Ben killed himself.

"Hi, buddy," I say. Kyle is looking up at me through the window in the door to Joy's workshop. The glass is aged and murky, and the paint on the window frame is peeling. I've come to visit him to distract myself while I wait to get an update from Joy. I unlock the door and flip the light switch on. A soft, yellow light spills across the cluttered, dusty room.

I'm scratching Kyle behind his ears while glancing around the shop at all the material, tools, and books Joy's amassed. It's a mess in here. Joy says it's organized chaos, but I don't think there is any order or structure in this room.

When we were house hunting, this place stood out partly because of the shop. Joy's work creates a significant mess, and I find it hard to exist in a chaotic environment. Having this separate space where Joy can be messy was a nice compromise.

There are volumes of encyclopedias stacked beside me. They're burgundy with gold embossing on the spine. Joy works on encyclopedias a lot. They're sentimental to people. Before the internet, they were an important part of a lot of people's homes.

I flip through one of the volumes. It has marbled endpapers. It's the *X* volume. I pause to admire a picture of Xiphias, a genus of large, predatory fish.

The shop smells like paper, leather, and wood. The

light casts long shadows on the floor. Dust motes are floating in the air. Kyle meows and leans his body against my ankles.

I watch the light in the room flicker while I pet him. Sometimes, when I look at light bulbs, I think about how I'd never be able to discover electricity. If someone hadn't experimented with lightening, or whatever they did, I wouldn't have thought to. When I use a phone, turn on the TV, or browse the internet, it often occurs to me that I benefit from these inventions I never would have dreamed up if I relied solely on my own devices. I doubt I'd think to grind grains to make bread. I couldn't invent fabric. A compass. Medicine.

Sometimes people talk about humans today as if we're more advanced than everyone in history, but we aren't really individually more advanced. Collectively, because we exist on the shoulders of everyone who came before us, we've developed. We benefit from the information the people before us gathered, applied, and made easier to find.

Kyle is purring.

I wish I knew what I know now when I was younger. I would have done a lot of things differently.

Kyle sneezes.

"Bless you," I say.

I'm glad to live in a time when people can bring their babies to hospitals and get help. I assume the only reason we can do that is because someone's baby struggled to breathe or spiked a fever in the past, though. We benefit from the struggle of the people before us.

I look down at my phone. I wish Joy would text me. I don't like picturing her in a hospital. She hates hospitals.

When Joy and I first started dating, we took the bus to meet up with our friends Matthew and Marco for dinner. This was before we moved in together, when we both lived downtown in Pert. We were in the beginning stages of our relationship. I felt a buzz in my chest when I was around her. We had a few drinks at her apartment before leaving, and we were laughing on the bus. She kept kissing me—quick, small kisses, like the ones you might involuntarily give a baby animal. Her mouth tasted like white wine and vanilla chap stick.

I kissed her back the same way, and felt bright, happy, and endeared to her. I've always felt this lightness around her. We were holding hands.

There was a man on the bus we noticed was watching us.

There had been other times before when people would stare if we kissed or held hands. We'd endured it in previous relationships too. I usually interpreted those looks as judgmental. In some cases, with some men, the looks felt predatory, like they perversely enjoyed watching us. This time felt different, though. This man looked angry.

Without saying anything, we both dropped each other's hands. We looked out the bus window to avoid making eye contact with him. We reiterated things we had already discussed to appear occupied, and to offer each other a sense of reassurance and distraction from the man.

He shouted, "Oh, now you'll stop?"

We ignored him. We pretended we couldn't hear him. We continued to speak to each other, but Joy whispered that she was scared. She kept fidgeting with her hands.

"Can you hear me?" the man yelled. "Lesbians? Can you hear me?"

There was only one other person riding the bus, and they had headphones on. It was an accordion bus, and we were sitting at the back. The driver was far away, out of view. It felt like we were trapped alone with the man in a narrow, confined space—like an isolated boat at sea, or a spaceship. It was just us, and him.

When the bus stopped, the man stood up. Joy stopped fidgeting. She froze.

I sat up straight. I tried to look bigger.

I hoped he would just exit the bus, but instead he came right up to us. He said, "Are you two deaf? I'm talking to you."

Neither of us replied. We were scared. I didn't know what to do.

"I'm talking to you!" He jabbed a finger into the groove of Joy's shoulder.

"Don't touch her," I said.

He punched me in the face, then immediately got off the bus. I covered my face with my hands. I think Joy screamed because the driver turned the bus off. She rushed toward us. When I took my hands off my face, there was blood in my palms. I thought he'd cracked something in my nose.

The driver drove us to the emergency room. I kept saying how it was so nice of her to stray from her route, but Joy barely replied. She was panicked. When we went inside the ER, she kept tapping her chest with her fist.

I asked, "Are you okay?"

She said, frazzled, "No, I'm not, but nobody punched *me* in the face, so I should really be asking you that."

She looked pale and frantic. She was breathing in and out really hard.

I was touching her hair when the doctor told me my nose wasn't broken. Joy exhaled loudly, and some color returned to her face. The doctor said noses are just delicate parts of our bodies. They have a lot of blood supply. Trauma breaks the blood vessels.

"But she'll be okay?" Joy asked.

"Yes," the doctor said.

Joy and I looked at each other. The fear we felt regarding my nose and the angry man dissipated, but it left us with the awareness that we weren't safe, and we needed to be more cautious.

I wonder what it would feel like to be a man with a girlfriend and to know that I had the capacity to protect her, to really punch back. I remember play fighting with Ben and realizing how much stronger he was than me. I'm aware I'm not a match for most men.

If Joy and I were born a few hundred years prior, or in a different part of the world, I might suggest we take husbands for the sake of our safety. She and I could meet in secret. Convince our husbands that our families should live together. I wonder how many women have done that. It's sad to think of a woman living with, sleeping with, and devoting her life to a man she doesn't really love to stay safe, and it's also sad to think of her husband, unloved, and unaware.

While it's depressing that Joy and I aren't comfortable kissing in public, it's nice to know that she and I aren't together just because we can provide for or protect each other. In *Pride and Prejudice*, Charlotte marries Mr. Collins because she's twenty-seven years old, has no money, no prospects, and *she's frightened.* While of course women today don't have to get married for the exact same reasons the ladies in 1813 did, the residue of those reasons is pervasive, and it impacts heterosexual relationships. I wasn't consciously aware of what motivated me to be with Ben, and it was very hard for me to recognize that I was with him for the wrong reasons.

It's nice to know that Joy and I are together just because we want to be.

"She has a respiratory infection," Joy says. "They gave us these saline drops for her nose, and we have to use a humidifier, and elevate her head."

I exhale, relieved. "Oh, thank God. So she's okay?"

"Yes. She's okay," she says.

I put a hand on my heart. "I'm so glad."

She sighs. "Me too. I'm sorry for the panic earlier. I worried it was, like, an obstruction in her airway, or a sign of some underlying medical condition. I googled it, and it listed congenital heart defects and underdeveloped lungs. And we haven't gotten all of her test results back, and she's missing fingers, so I worried maybe it was something awful. I—"

"It's okay. I'm just happy she's all right. Though I'm sorry she has a respiratory infection."

I feel bad for babies when they're sick. It must be so confusing. They don't understand.

She says, "I know. It's hard to see a baby sic k. She's never been sick before. She's probably confused."

"I was just thinking that. She's in good hands, though. She's got you and Sophie taking care of her," I say.

"Yeah." She laughs feebly. "We're figuring it out. How are you doing there without me?"

I'm in bed, wearing her sweater because I feel lonely.

"I'm doing well, thank you," I say. "The house is extremely tidy. No one's left tea bags in the sink or created little doom piles of miscellaneous items on the coffee table. And there's much less hair on the tile in the shower. I usually get to interpret this abstract art made of long human hair—"

"Wow," she interrupts me. "So, you don't miss me at all, do you?"

I laugh. "No, I do."

"How are our cats?" she asks.

"They're good."

"Even Kyle?"

"Kyle isn't our cat," I say, "but he's a good guest. He's enjoying your workshop. I don't want to keep him cooped up in there too long, though."

"Maybe you could try introducing him to the girls tomorrow?"

"I need to take him to the vet first to get his vaccines," I say.

"Oh, that's smart. I knew there was a reason I married you."

"Ha ha," I say tonelessly.

She laughs. "I miss you."

"I miss you too. When are you coming home?"

"I need to stay a little while, I think. Sophie would have lost it if she had to deal with that breathing thing alone.

Kearney is useless. She needs help, and she seems really worried that I'll leave soon. She keeps asking me with terror in her voice how long I plan to stay."

"Are you sure she's not hinting that she wants you to leave?" I joke.

She laughs. "No, definitely not. Me being here is the only reason she's able to sleep or shower. She can't move quickly or lift anything heavy because of the C-section, and now January is sick. Is it okay with you if I stay a while, though? Do you mind?"

"Of course, yeah, that's okay," I say.

"Have you been feeling okay?"

"Yeah. I'm feeling fine."

"You're safe?"

"Yes. I'm safe."

CHAPTER FIVE

WHAT IS ANTING IN RELATION TO BLUE JAYS?

I've received yet another bird request. It's unusual for someone to continue asking questions like these. I wonder why they aren't just googling the answers for themselves. I think sometimes people ask questions simply for a bit of human interaction. I get the impression that a lot of people are lonely and looking for connection.

I look up the definition of the word "anting" in a dictionary on my desk. I then google the word and find another definition. I read two articles about blue jays and anting, specifically.

> ANTING IS BIRD BEHAVIOR THAT INVOLVES BIRDS RUBBING ANTS ON THEIR FEATHERS TO DRAIN THEM OF CHEMICALS, SUCH AS FORMIC ACID. BLUE JAYS EXHIBIT THIS BEHAVIOR. SOME SCIENTISTS THINK THIS MIGHT HELP PREVENT PARASITES. IT'S ALSO POSSIBLE THAT BIRDS LIKE BLUE JAYS FIND ANTS TASTE BETTER WITHOUT THE ACID AND ARE SIMPLY RUBBING OFF A BITTER TASTE.

At the bottom of my email, I add, HERE ARE SOME RECOMMENDED RESOURCES FOR ANY FUTURE QUESTIONS YOU MIGHT HAVE ABOUT BIRDS, and I list several resources for the patron.

"What the hell is going on here?" a man shouts.

We're watching a performer named Ms. Mother Goose read *Frog and Toad* to a horde of toddlers.

"What the hell is this?" the man yells.

I stand up and position myself between him and the children. Mordecai and Patty both hurry to stand with me. A concerned mother accompanies us.

"This is the children's section, sir," I say, hoping he's lost.

His face is red.

"Let me walk you out—" Mordecai says.

"Why the hell is a drag queen reading books to children?" the man yells.

Ms. Mother Goose isn't a drag queen. She's an elderly woman who wears a synthetic wig.

"Sir"—Patty points at the exit—"you need to leave now."

The parents in the room are scooping up their babies. Ms. Mother Goose has closed her book.

"I have to leave for calling this shit out? Really? This is the place where you also let perverts watch porn, right?"

One of the toddlers is crying, upsetting the other toddlers. They progressively join in, and soon, every toddler is crying.

I feel like crying.

"Time to leave, man," I say. "Sir, I mean."

"This is sick!" the man shouts, while Mordecai directs him toward the exit.

I'm on the phone with Brenda. I told her about the story-time incident.

My hands are shaking slightly. I feel rattled by the confrontation.

She says, "I'm so sorry that happened. Thank you for letting me know."

"I'll write up a report," I say. It's part of the protocol established in the "Violation" appendix of our Patron Code of Conduct Policy.

I don't know what happens to incident reports after they're submitted. The policy doesn't say. It should. If I were writing it, I'd outline what happens next. When people are given directions to follow without understanding why, it's hard to trust that they're taking the right steps. I like having a process to follow, but I don't like following steps that make no sense or lead nowhere.

I want to ask her what will happen with my report, and

what our organization plans to do in response to this. If I were a manager, I'd have more say. I could influence this policy, review our processes, equip staff with training and with clearer messaging on safety. I could do a lot more.

I'm not sure if it's appropriate for me to speak frankly with Brenda about this, or to ask her many questions, though I want to.

I take a breath. "This is the second person I've had to confront in this branch in a week. I'm concerned. What are we going to do about this?"

She's quiet. Maybe I shouldn't have asked.

She sighs. "I know. I'm concerned too. I brought the previous article about the pornography incident to the board. So you know, in addition to that, and to these incidents you've shared, there have been similar incidents at our other branches, as well as an influx of targeted messages about this to the mayor's office, and other city officials. The messages aren't just about the pornography case, though. They also wrote about material in our collection they want removed, and voiced complaints about our programming. In response, we're likely going to conduct a review of our related policies."

I exhale. Declan and his cronies are inundating the city with their complaints. It's taxing how much time, effort, and money is spent on these issues. Critical matters always take the back burner, like our high staffing turnover rate and our crumbling infrastructure, just to name a few.

I ask, "What material do they want removed?"

I'm sure I can guess the answer.

She takes a breath. "It's a long list. Mostly children's material."

Surprise, surprise.

I say, "Right. Well, thanks for sharing that with me."

"Of course, Darcy. And you know, I'd like to chat with you more about your thoughts on how we approach this. I really value your insight."

My stomach churns. Brenda is who encouraged me to apply to that branch manager position. She sent me the job posting in an email with a note that said, CONSIDER APPLYING FOR THIS. I'D RECOMMEND YOU TO THE PANEL. WE'D BE LUCKY TO HAVE YOU IN THIS ROLE.

I don't know if she sincerely wants to chat with me about how we approach this, or if she's just trying to be nice. I'm sure her impression of me has changed after I bailed on the second interview and disappeared from my job for months.

"Thank you," I say quietly.

I'm embarrassed I blew that interview. I probably made her look bad.

She says, "Maybe we could meet next week to discuss this. Are you available on Tuesday at 1:30 p.m.?"

I open my calendar.

"Yes, I'm free," I say.

"Wonderful. I'll stop by your branch, then. How are you doing, by the way?"

"Oh, we're doing well here. There's lots of great initiatives coming up—"

"No, I meant how are *you* doing. How are you feeling? How's the return to work?"

"Oh," I say.

I feel tension in my neck.

"I'm doing well, thank you. I'm on the mend."

"I'm so glad to hear that. We're happy to have you back."

"He walked me home one night the first week we worked together," I tell Dr. Jeong. I have my eyes closed. We're practicing imaginal revisiting again. She asked me to revisit when Ben and I first started dating. "The bus wasn't running. We'd worked a late shift, it was midnight, and I didn't want to pay for a cab."

"Tell me about the walk," she says.

I try to picture it. It was late in the summer. Ben was wearing a blue anorak. My hair was in a ponytail.

"He said I shouldn't walk home alone in the dark. It was dangerous. I thought that was, I don't know, *gallant* of him, I guess. It was like a forty-minute walk. On the way, we talked about how much our job sucked. It really was an awful job. He joked about our managers and coworkers. He said he used to work in restaurants, and it was bad there too. It was him talking mostly, and me responding with, like, hesitant bursts of laughter. And he kept complimenting me. I remember feeling both embarrassed and sort of drunk off the attention. When we got to my building, he asked if he could come up to my apartment. I wanted to say sure, I thought it would be off-putting if I said no, but my apartment was full of boxes because I'd just moved in. It was a tiny studio. It had room for a twin bed and a small desk. I told Ben there wasn't enough room to hang out up there, and he said that it was okay."

I pause. I remember something else, but I don't want to

say it out loud. It grosses me out. He asked if he could have a hug before I went upstairs. That sounds creepy in retrospect. I didn't find it creepy at the time, though. I do now. I thought it was a normal request when it happened, so I hugged him.

I skip that part and continue, "Then he asked if he could get my number. I gave it to him, and he texted me that night. I remember he wrote 'I have a crush on you.'"

"How did that make you feel?" she asks.

"At the time? I felt like I had a crush on him too. And I did, sort of. I'd just moved there. I didn't really know anyone yet. I felt kind of scared, living somewhere alone for the first time. I was nervous for school. It was nice to meet someone who liked me. It made me feel good about myself. I wanted him to like me."

She says, "Okay. You can open your eyes now."

I open my eyes.

She says, "Can you please tell me how you feel about that night now, today?"

I inhale. "Okay. Um. I think I was insecure and looking for validation. I wanted to be affirmed as a likable girl. In retrospect, Ben and I didn't really have anything in common. He was in a different stage of life. We didn't have similar interests. I think I liked that he liked me, more than anything. And he was nice to me. I shouldn't have been dating him when I was just starting college. I should have been around people my age who were having the same experiences as me. I feel kind of robbed of that, I guess. But I also feel guilty for thinking that way now, given everything. I still appreciate Ben as a person. He was sweet. I do think he was too old for me, and I was inexperienced and naive, but it's not like he was trying to take advantage of me. I guess maybe he was, a little. But I think he was just looking for someone to love."

She makes a humming noise that implies she hears me and understands. She says, "It sounds like you feel regret, but also compassion for Ben."

"Yes. I regret how our relationship negatively impacted him. I wish things were different. I wish I'd met him, but we never dated, and were just friends, or something."

She looks at me. "Do you think you two would be friends if he were alive and you met him today?"

I wince. *If he were alive.*

"Yes," I say. "That was part of why I liked him initially. I remember meeting him and thinking that I'd like to be his friend."

She tilts her head. "You mentioned you two didn't have anything in common. And he was in a different stage of life, and considerably older. I wonder, do you recall why you thought you'd like to be his friend?"

I look at her. I can't think of an answer.

"Um. I don't know. I guess I thought he was . . . nice? He made me feel like I was interesting."

I pause. That's a narcissistic reason to want to be friends with someone.

She says, "It's normal to seek out validation from other people, especially when you're young. Can I ask, as the person you are now, what motivates you to become friends with someone?"

I think of my friends. "I guess the first thing that comes to mind is having things in common—like shared experiences, interests, or senses of humor. But to be honest, I think the main thing for me is that I feel like I'm on the same page as them. Like we're on the same wavelength. Do you know what I mean? Sometimes I'll meet someone and feel like we get each other. Does that make sense? I have to feel understood, and like I understand them, to really want to become friends with someone. And then on top of that, I also have to, you know, trust them and enjoy being around them."

She hums. "Yes. That makes sense. And so, I take from that, you can meet someone whom you think positively of, and have good things to say about, and still not be well matched as friends. Right?"

I sit up straighter. "Right."

"Okay. Now, I want you to reflect a bit more on the relationship you had with Ben, by asking again, if you met Ben *today*, as the person you are now, do you think you would want to be friends?"

I clench my toes in my shoes.

Ben and I didn't have similar interests. We didn't like the same TV shows, or music. I was interested in school. I liked reading. He was working. He liked fishing. Video games.

I picture the two of us standing next to each other. Him in his anorak. Me with my ponytail.

Would I want to be friends with a twenty-eight-year-old man dating an eighteen-year-old girl?

I look at her. "No," I say quietly.

"I don't really like guys our age," I told my old friend Haley. We were drinking vodka sugar-free Red Bulls around her coffee table. She lived in a basement apartment next to our college with three other girls. We met in our first-year Women's Studies class.

The table had an ashtray shaped like cupped hands, half a gram of weed, and tarot cards on it. It was covered in people's signatures and little notes, like the end pages in a yearbook. Haley was wearing a bedazzled push-up bra, and she'd bonded wispy fake eyelashes to her eyelids. I was taking pictures of her.

"And Ben doesn't really look that much older," she said while posing for the photo. "I couldn't tell he was twenty-eight. Plus, you're pretty mature for your age."

She had just ended things with a guy she'd been seeing, so we were taking hot pictures of her to post for him to see.

I told her, "Look happier. You want him to think you're having fun."

She smiled wide with teeth.

Later that night, Haley made out with a stranger at the bar while I drank four vodka Diet Cokes, swayed in a crowd of damp people, and texted Ben: WISH YOU WERE HERE.

COME SAVE ME..

Ben was waiting outside the bar after last call. He was chatting with the bouncer at the door. He paid for Haley's cab home, and he and I walked to his place.

He said, "I'll always come save you, dove."

"I hate to say it, but it is kind of weird that you let people watch porn in the library," Hodan says. She puts both her hands up as if I'll arrest her for saying so.

I invited her and her partner Ada over. I wanted company in Joy's absence, and I hadn't seen them in a while. The four of us hang out regularly, and Ada and Joy have been friends for over a decade. She and Hodan were already dating when Joy and I met.

They brought Korean food, and we're watching a movie titled *But I'm a Cheerleader*.

I say, "Don't get me started, Hodan."

She saw the article in the newspaper and asked me about it.

She says, "Well, I mean, come on. No one wants to witness some guy cranking his hog at the library."

Ada chokes on her tteokbokki. "Oh my God. Why did you phrase it like that?"

"He wasn't cranking anything." I laugh. "He was just watching porn. And believe me, if the rules were based on what I prefer to witness people do, he'd be given the boot. I'd spend my days just watching polite people silently read. But that's not how it works, tragically."

"Wait, I thought that's what you did. Don't librarians just sit around and read all day?" Ada ribs.

I roll my eyes.

"You could make a case that it's sexual harassment, though, couldn't you?" Hodan asks. She's opening a few bottles of beer with the church key she keeps on her carabiner. "I think it could be considered an indecent act."

"You'd know better than me," I say. She's a lawyer. "I don't know. I didn't make up the policy. I'm just a lowly librarian, following the rules."

"Do you think it's a good policy, though? Would you make that rule if you were in charge?"

She hands me a beer. I say, "If I were in charge, the entire system would be overhauled. The root cause of why we have so many people watching porn and behaving badly in our libraries is because of the erosion of our social services—"

"Oh no, here we go," Hodan says while I climb on my soapbox.

I continue, "Our health care system has been gutted, and there's widespread disregard for mental illness, poverty, and humanity in general. It's hard to pluck one policy out of that wider context and say whether I support it. I know some libraries don't let people watch porn. Not every public library system has the same policy we do. But do I support censorship?"

"I bet she doesn't." Hodan nudges Ada.

"No, I don't," I continue. "And that's a core value of librarianship. Because, let me ask *you* a question. What is porn?"

"What do you mean 'what is porn'?" Ada asks.

"I mean what's the definition of porn? Because I'd argue it's a difficult word to define. Some people would consider a lot of Baroque and Renaissance art pornographic. Flashing an ankle is porn to some folks. There are some religious groups who think the Twilight books are porn. What makes something pornographic depends on cultural context, subjective sensibilities—"

"What porn was this guy watching?" Hodan asks.

I sip my beer. "A lesbian threesome from the seventies."

She throws her head back. "Is there any mistaking that with Baroque art?"

"Okay. Let's think about it another way." I lean forward. "Do you think porn should only be accessible to people who can afford home internet, or people who own devices? Should poor people never be able to see porn? Porn is privileged content, only for those who can afford it?"

"I don't think that specifically, no, but I don't see why anyone would *need* access to porn—"

"So, you think libraries should only allow people access to things they *need*. We should burn all the comic books and romance novels?"

"No, but I think porn is a little different from comic books and romance novels—"

"Then you haven't read much romance," I say.

She laughs.

"And this stuff snowballs, right?" Ada says. "Today it's porn, but tomorrow it's someone asking you to burn *Heather Has Two Mommies* or *Why the Caged Bird Sings*, right?"

I nod. "Yes. It's censorship. Most of the books in this room would be banned."

The room we're in is surrounded by bookshelves. Joy and I have amassed a large home library. I studied English Literature before getting my master's in library science. Joy was a women's studies major—so our shelves are full of feminist theory, classics, and literary criticism. Joy also collects a large number of old picture books and fairy tales. We both like to read queer fiction, poetry, and memoirs.

If I hadn't read these books, or studied what I did, I'd be a different person. It's hard to question things, or expand the way you think, without being exposed to new information, or different perspectives. I wonder who I'd be if I didn't have access to the books and information I've read, and I wonder who I'd be if I had more information when I was younger.

Hodan crosses her legs on the couch and looks around. "I just love your place. There's such a warm, cozy ambiance here."

"Thank you. That's nice of you to say." I sense she's tired of hearing me preach about libraries.

Ada nods with her mouth full. "It feels like a retreat. It's a tranquil escape."

Joy collects art from thrift stores; she likes oil paintings of flowers and fruit, and I like anything that features grumpy-looking women. Our cats have beds in every room. There's two in this room in front of the fireplace. Lou and Toulouse are sleeping in them now. Joy likes to dry flowers by hanging them upside down with twine from the windows, and she collects rocks and crystals. All the windowsills have pebbles lining them. She's worried that kids will visit and find the place boring, so she's strung rainbow fabric triangle garland around the house, collected children's books, and filled baskets full of peculiar stuffed animals. In this room, we have a stuffed octopus and a snail.

"I feel like we haven't seen you in forever." Hodan sips her beer.

They don't know about my mental breakdown.

"Have you guys been busy? What's been going on?"

"Yeah. We've been really busy," I say. "Things have been hectic with work and family stuff. What about you two? What have you been up to?"

"Well, we're thinking about getting a dog," Ada says. "But we're worried about all the responsibility. You know we like to travel and not be so anchored to our condo. Plus, we can't agree on what kind of dog to get."

"I want a big dog," Hodan says. "But this lady here wants a little dachshund."

"I'm open-minded about big dogs. I just like the long-haired dachshunds that have those little beards," Ada says. "They look like little old men."

"Joy and I can always dog sit if you go away," I offer.

"Ah, that's nice of you." Ada takes a bite of a kimchi pancake. "When does Joy come back?"

"She hasn't booked a return ticket," I say. "Sophie's recovering from her C-section, and the baby has a respiratory infection. I think it's helping a lot for Sophie to have Joy there. It's hard to adjust with no sleep, the baby crying, breastfeeding, the psychological torment of becoming a mother, and all that."

"What's Sophie's husband doing?" Ada asks.

I give her a look. We've all discussed Kearney at length. None of us are fans.

"Off sleeping with Susan, or whoever he's cheating on Sophie with now?" Hodan jeers.

"Can you imagine?" I say.

"Their relationship really doesn't help negate my theory that all straight women are just masochists," Ada says.

Hodan nudges her. "Don't say that."

"Why not?" Ada looks over her shoulder. "Are there straight people here I don't know about?"

We've chatted about Ada's theory before. A lot of her thinking stems from our experiences dating men, which were colored by our lesbianism. Before realizing we were gay, we all used to believe that every woman considered having sex with men a form of self-harm. The theory aligned with the messages we received from pop culture, our friends, and general society. Women were prey. Men were hunters. When we had sex with them, it was bound to be damaging. That was no reason to make us question whether we were straight. All women were like slain deer.

Hodan, Ada, and I are now eating and watching our movie quietly. Megan, the gay cheerleader who stars in the film, has just arrived at conversion camp. In this scene, it's dawning on her that she's a homosexual.

It was hard for me to realize I was gay. A lot of my lesbian friends found it similarly tricky. Most lesbians don't realize they're gay until they're older, because of compulsory heterosexuality. Heterosexuality is pushed on everyone. It's assumed that all women are wired to like men, but we aren't. That preference is socially scripted.

It's hard to recognize you're a lesbian because of that social script, and because most women have some unpleasant experiences with men. As a teenager, I didn't notice a big difference between how I experienced sex with men and how straight girls did. I wasn't notably more put off than any of them were. Most of our experiences ranged from okay to revolting. Most of the guys my friends and I dated had limited sexual experience and were influenced by porn, which catered to a narrow, male-centered perspective. There was often an ignorant or undignified undercurrent to the sex we had as teenagers.

Every time I had sex with Ben it felt like I was feeding my pet lizard. It was a chore I had to do. It was part of the terms and conditions of having a gecko, or a boyfriend. I understood it was important. You must feed your lizard. It was generally unpleasant, of course, lizards eat bugs; however, it was my duty. It was fine. It was something I had to do for the health of my pet.

I never revealed I felt this way to Ben, of course. In fact, I'm sure he had no idea. I gave him no reason to suspect I was unhappy. When we had sex, I acted the way I understood men wanted women to act. I acted the way, I have reason to believe, many straight women do.

I had secret sex rules for myself. They included faking it before five minutes passed, only allowing myself to cry in the bathroom for a single minute afterward, and never refusing him when he initiated it. I never initiated it because I thought guys considered that too aggressive, and besides, I didn't genuinely want to; however, every single time he initiated it, I'd do it. I even complied when I was sick. I remember once I was delirious. I had strep throat.

Something moves in my chest. The image of my sick nineteen-year-old face flashes in my mind's eye. I see myself feverish, run-down, and coughing into my pillow. *Why would Ben want to have sex with me when I was sick?* Who looks at their girlfriend, weak, fever-ridden, nauseated, and wants to fuck her?

Ada and Hodan laugh at something in the movie. I wasn't paying attention, but I pretend I was and laugh too.

After they leave, I go outside to the workshop to give Kyle wet food and company. He's nuzzling his head on my chin. I brought one of Lou and Toulouse's beds out here for him. He had a pillow to sleep on already, but this bed smells like them. I'm introducing their scents to each other.

"I'm sorry you didn't have much company today, buddy," I tell him.

His vet appointment is in a couple days. I can't introduce him to our cats until he's been checked out.

Joy texted me several photos of January. She's swaddled and sleeping in most of them, but in one her eyes are open. She's alert. She has dark, cloudy eyes. We can't tell what color they'll be yet.

In one photo, January's hands are showing. I zoom in to inspect which fingers are missing. It's hard to tell which fingers are which when some are absent. I see she has a thumb, and I think she has a pointer and a pinky. I believe she's missing her middle and ring fingers. That's good, I think. She can't flip people off with her left hand, but she can just use her right hand for that. That's not the end of the world.

I look at my left hand. I have a gold wedding band on my finger.

I guess not having a ring finger might cause her grief when she's older. Which finger will she use for her wedding ring? Though, of course, maybe she won't get married at all. Maybe it's a nonissue. Not everyone wants to get married or wears a ring. And even if she does, does it really matter which finger she uses? Maybe she won't care.

I used to care a lot about getting married. I watched shows like *Say Yes to the Dress* and envisioned myself in a popular Pnina Tornai gown. I had a Pinterest board titled BIG DAY. I wanted to look how I believed all brides aspired to look. Worryingly thin. Almost sickly. I'd bleach my teeth so bright they'd glow in black light. I'd get just enough muscle definition in my arms to look trim, but not too much that I looked masculine, or strong. I'd purchase an elaborate push-up bra. I'd spend countless hours carefully selecting decorative trash for the evening, and ultimately, for the landfills.

My dad would walk me down the aisle, despite the fact that we barely speak, to stage that we're a traditional, typical family. Ben would wear a suit. I'd warn him that he had to tear up as I walked toward him or people might not think he really loved me. I might even tuck a safety pin into his pocket to poke himself with, to ensure his eyes welled up. We'd pay thousands of dollars to feed distant relatives dry, unseasoned chicken and we'd take photos with big fake smiles in our kitschy wedding regalia, like clowns. I'd post the photos on social media annually to assert how inspirationally normal I was.

It was like I was an actor preparing for a play. I didn't recognize that at the time, but it was for show. I had this compulsion to prove that I was capable of living the life I was told every girl dreamed of.

I had no idea I was gay, and the way I viewed weddings and marriage didn't tip me off. I think there are a lot of straight women who want to get married for the same reasons I did. We're all trained in overt and subconscious ways to associate our worth with how much men value us. Getting married to a man feels like something girls have to do to prove we matter. In order to assert that we are desirable, respectable ladies, we're told we have to do things like marry men.

I think some straight women operate in their relationships with men the same way cloistered lesbians do. That's part of what makes it difficult for lesbians to recognize they're lesbians. Women aren't driven to have relationships with men solely by their sexual attraction, or by their goal of finding love. Women are drawn to men for other reasons relating to power, privilege, and safety. Love and attraction are tenuous terms; it's hard to recognize whether you're really attracted to someone, or whether you really love them, when there are other factors influencing your desire to be with them.

I like weddings. I think it's sweet to witness a couple commit to loving each other forever. It's nice when they're surrounded by people who support and care about them. Weddings suit people who enjoy throwing big parties. They're fun when they genuinely make the couple feel happy, and when the event feels truly aligned to the couples' authentic wishes. I don't think all weddings reflect some horrible performative compulsion to prove something, but I do think that some do.

Some weddings feel staged. You can sense it when you're at them. There's this inauthentic, synthetic feeling. The vows sound trite and hollow. The groom has barely been involved in any of the planning, and the bride seems frazzled, and excessively concerned about how she looks. It's awful to witness that kind of wedding. It feels like watching a sad, tired play, except its real people's lives.

Joy and I got married at city hall in September. I wore a patterned jumpsuit that reminded me of wallpaper, and Joy wore a dark red dress.

Neither of us like big events or being the center of attention. We're quiet, introverted people. We didn't want to speak in front of a crowd, or deal with the cost and logistics of planning or throwing an event. We just wanted to make sure we'd be admitted into each other's hospital rooms if one of us got in a car accident. I wanted to make sure that if I die, my insurance will go to her.

We signed our marriage license, then we went out for pizza and ice cream. We wrote each other vows on pieces of paper and read them while we ate. Joy's said:

> Dear Darcy,
> I vow to:
> Be your best friend
> Love and care for you, sweet Lou, and Toulouse (and anyone else who joins our family) unconditionally
> Take care of you when you're sick
> Take you anywhere you want to go
> Cheer you on
> Keep it tight
> & Be your girl.
> Til death,
> Joy

Mine said:

> Dear Joy,
> Here are things I like about you:
> When we're driving in the car and you're singing
> How much you love our cats
> How you snore and talk in your sleep

Your face when you're making someone laugh
I find the things you don't like about yourself endearing (i.e., snoring)
I think you could do anything you set your mind to
You won't like this one, and you probably didn't like that snoring one either, but I find you precious, interesting, and special.
I promise to support you. I will always want the best for you; for you to be happy, to be the best you can be, and to have a good life. If you are ever sick or having a hard time, I will take care of you. I love you and promise I always will.
Darcy

CHAPTER
SIX

I couldn't sleep, so I decided to reorganize our home library. It's nice to have a project to keep me occupied while I'm alone. I've organized our books alphabetically by author before, but we've added a lot to our collection, and I've noticed Joy struggles with that system. She rarely puts books where they belong.

I also need to dust the shelves, rotate the books so none get prolonged sun exposure, and make sure they aren't overcrowded—which can compress and warp books. I also need to weed. I want to get rid of worn-out books that we wouldn't read again and didn't love enough to warrant Joy repairing. Sometimes, duplicate books find their way into the house. I occasionally get sent advance review copies of new books for collection development and readers' advisory at the library. I keep some of those, but not all of them. I'll donate our spares.

I pick up a warped, water damaged copy of *Lolita*. I've had this since university. I remember lying in the bathtub the night before an exam while Ben read it to me. He was helping me study. I told him I needed to finish the book and was too busy to shower, so he said he'd read to me.

I open the book. I read the line, *Perhaps, somewhere, some day, at a less miserable time, we may see each other again.*

I close it.

I'm going to take every book off these shelves. I'm going to place them in piles around the room, and I'm going to put them away in a logical order that works for us.

Joy often puts dried flowers in vases in the blank spots on the shelves, so I'm brushing dusty, dried rose petals into a compost bag. Lou and Toulouse have jumped into the empty spaces in the shelves, entertained by the change in their environment, and the new spots to perch.

I pause when I get to the shelf where I keep my brass dove.

"Put that book down, Josie. You won't like that one. It's for little boys," a woman tells her daughter. They're standing in front of a book display in the children's section. The theme of the display is "Mighty Machines." All the books are about trucks, planes, and construction vehicles.

The little girl is about two years old. She's wearing a headband with wigtails, or fake hair affixed to it to mimic pigtails. She doesn't have enough hair naturally to wear it in pigtails. I assume the hairpiece is meant to assert the child's gender; God forbid anyone assume she's a boy. She's clutching a yellow board book with a backhoe loader pictured on the front.

"Let's pick a book for girls," the mom says, taking the book from her child's hands.

I fight an impulse to say something.

When I was about six, before I was conscious of social norms and the expectations of my mother, I used to beg my parents to buy me little boy clothes. I preferred the iconography ascribed to them. Dinosaurs. Pirate ships. Bugs.

I remember sitting crossed-legged on the carpet in my elementary school library, leafing through a book about a little blue spider. It was my favorite, but I knew I couldn't check it out because my mom would think it was weird that I picked a book about a spider.

Our librarian's name was Ms. Carol. I remember her buying more books in the little blue spider series, which she set aside for me. I was astounded that she'd noticed I read those books, and felt seen and touched by the gesture.

I had to write a letter of intent when I applied to library school, and I wrote about Ms. Carol. I said I wanted to become a librarian because of her. I wrote about how she sparked my love of reading. I wanted to have a meaningful impact on other people like she did.

I can't go tell that mother not to snatch books about trucks from her kid, but I can make sure our reading lists, book displays, and recommendations challenge gendered stereotypes. I can make resources about diverse reading that outline why letting kids explore all types of books is good for them. I can hand books about bugs to little girls, and ones about ponies to little boys.

I look at my monitor. Tomorrow is Tuesday, which is when I'm meeting with Brenda. I've got a blank document open to brainstorm what I'd like to talk to her about. So far, I've written:

- Come to the meeting with ideas and proposed solutions.
- Emphasize our role in community education.
- What can we do to bolster awareness and understanding?
- Think of program ideas . . .
- Look ahead.

"Excuse me?"

An older man with a mustache and long gray hair is standing in front of my desk. He's holding a stack of books about Vietnam.

I smile. "Yes? How can I help you?"

"What's that pin mean?" he asks, gesturing to my vest.

My smile wanes. I have a trans flag pin on.

Please don't tell me I have to deal with yet another confrontational patron.

I take a shallow breath. If this guy gets angry at me for wearing this pin, I'm not going to take it lying down. I've had enough. Why do people keep picking me to hash out their grievances? Is there something about my face that suggests I deserve to bear the brunt of everyone's animosity?

Is This a Cry for Help?

I sit up straight. I don't deserve this. I've come to work today to do my job. I have good intentions. I'm trying.

I look him in the eyes. "This is a pin I wear to demonstrate my support for the transgender community, and to signal that the library is a safe space for them."

I brace for the backlash.

"Oh, groovy." He smiles. "I like the colors."

I blink.

He remains where he is, still smiling.

"Thank you," I say, my heart racing.

I really thought he was going to yell at me.

"I like the colors too," I add, which is a lie. The pin is pink and blue, which are my least favorite colors, and they're pastel. I prefer vibrant palettes. Yellows, reds, and greens.

"I *love* the colors, actually," I say, so relieved by this man's lack of anger that I feel compelled to be excessively positive.

An email notification pops up on the side of my screen.

COULD YOU PLEASE RECOMMEND SOME BOOKS, ARTICLES, OR ONLINE RESOURCES THAT EXPLORE HOMOSEXUALITY IN BIRD SPECIES?

THANKS,
SAMMY

I squint. They want resources on gay birds? Is this person messing with me?

I'm going to wait a little while before I respond. I've given them a little too much of my time, I think. I can't allot hours of my capacity to one person. There are other questions in the reference email inbox. I want to spend the time I have today between helping people at the desk and preparing for my meeting with Brenda. I also need to create a better sign about how to connect to the Wi-Fi, in the hopes that we receive fewer questions—

"Darcy?"

I look up. A woman is standing at the desk.

"Hello," I say.

"Do you remember me?"

She has dark skin, a nose ring, and long braids. I don't remember her name. I open my mouth, hoping it will come to me, but it doesn't.

"We went out once," she says. She's sort of smirking.

I don't know what to say. I'm surprised to see her here. We met once in Montreal, which is hours away.

"You don't remember me, do you?" she says.

I do remember her, but I don't remember her name.

"I'm so sorry," I say. "I—uh. Your name is probably just escaping me out of context."

"I guess saying we went out once is a bit of a stretch," she says quietly. There's no one standing near us. In a quiet voice she says, "We hooked up once. You don't remember?"

I look at her. I do remember her.

She's sort of laughing. "It was a really long time ago. Like ten, thirteen years ago, maybe. It was just this one night. It's sort of brazen of me to mention it, I guess. I'm sorry. I just saw you and thought, *Wow, that's wild. It's her.* Are you from this area?"

I was dating Ben the night I met her.

"No," I say. "I lived in Pert for a while, but I moved to this area about six years ago."

"What a small world. This is where I grew up," she says. "I'll be honest, I'm a little disappointed you don't remember me. The night we met was memorable for me. It felt sort of cinematic. We were in Montreal. We met in a bar bathroom. I was crying. Does any of that jog your memory?"

"You were crying?" I say, but I remember. I've thought about her a lot. I always wondered if I'd ever run into her again.

"Yes," she says. "This girl I was sort of dating ended things, and I was sobbing in the bathroom. You came in, heard me, and asked me if I was all right. You consoled me."

"I consoled you?" I repeat.

It's interesting seeing her face. She looks the same.

She laughs. "Yes, you did. We made out in the bathroom and left together. Maybe it felt memorable to me because I was so sad that night, and you turned it around. We ran down Sainte-Catherine Street, under that canopy of pink plastic balls. It was an art installation. Do you remember?"

"Yes," I admit.

She has a bright smile. "It felt sort of like that movie with Ethan Hawke and Julie Delpy, where they meet on a train and spend twenty-four hours together. Have you seen that? I think it's called *Before Sunrise*, or *Before Sunset*, or something like that."

"I haven't seen it," I say.

"Well, it was a lot like that, except gay," she says. "We walked around Montreal until the sun came up. We told each other our life stories. You told me I was the first girl you'd ever kissed. I thought of you a lot after, and I wanted to look you up, but you only told me your first name. What's your situation like now? Are you with someone?"

"I'm married," I say.

"To a man?" she asks quietly.

"No."

She smiles. "Good."

"How about you?" I ask.

"My partner and I live about ten minutes up the road," she says. "We have two kids. Twin boys."

We look at each other for a beat with pursed smiles, our eyes scanning each other's faces.

"It's nice to see you again," she says. "I wondered what happened to you. I've thought of you and that night often. I'm sorry for coming up to you. This was weird of me, I guess, but I couldn't resist."

"I thought of you too," I say.

She smiles.

HI AGAIN,

I DON'T KNOW IF YOU GOT MY LAST EMAIL. ARE THERE ANY WEBSITES OR ONLINE RESOURCES WHERE I CAN LEARN ABOUT SAME-SEX RELATIONSHIPS IN BIRDS?

THANKS SO MUCH,
SAMMY

The bird patron has sent in another question. I haven't answered the prior question yet. I haven't really done anything since I spoke to that woman. A few people have asked me for help with the computers, but mostly I sat here, clicking, pretending to work.

I'm distracted. I'm thinking about that woman. I remember walking around Montreal with her. We walked from a bar on Sainte-Catherine Street, past the Notre Dame Basilica toward the St. Lawrence. I remember holding hands. We walked through a park, I think it was La Fontaine Park, through the Plateau, and eventually found ourselves standing outside of Leonard Cohen's old house. It was near her apartment. The sun was starting to rise by the time we went inside. I remember her bedding was pink, and there was this bright beam of sunlight that came through her window.

One night, years before I cheated on Ben with that girl, he and I were at a bar with some friends. The music was loud. A remix of that Katy Perry's "I Kissed a Girl" song was playing. The room was dim and humid. We were moving through a crowd. There were red laser beams flashing above us. Ben shouted in my ear, "Would you ever kiss a girl?"

At the time, I had no idea I was gay. Despite that, I answered, "Maybe," because I knew that was what he wanted me to say.

Later, he asked me if I would ever have a threesome with him and another girl. The guy I dated in high school asked me that question too. I considered it something men always asked women. Despite knowing I would never have a threesome with Ben, I answered, "Maybe," because I understood that was the response he wanted. I knew he fetishized women having sex with other women, and that it would be unattractive to deflate that fantasy. I wanted to be what he wanted. That's also why I rarely expressed when he upset me, and we hardly fought. I knew it wasn't attractive to nag or complain.

It depresses me now to think of myself then. I would prefer to be perceived as a bog monster today rather than entertain the sexual fantasies of a man, especially any fantasy rooted in sexualizing lesbians. I'd sooner defend the image of me as a hideous, withered hag, rather than the image of me as a coy, quiet, sexualized teenaged girl. It's appalling that I was trained to behave the way I was when I was younger, and I think of it as a societal betrayal, and a depraved way to treat girls.

I remember Ben doing things that bothered me. He left hair in the sink after shaving. He drank a lot. He had friends around I didn't like. I had to remember important dates for him, like his dad's birthday. Sometimes he made offhand, objectifying comments about women on TV. He did our laundry, but I did the rest of our household chores. I made the bed. I cooked. I did the dishes. I cleaned the bathrooms. I found him dismissive and patronizing when I voiced my opinions about topics like music. He regularly put movies and TV shows on that I didn't like. I sat in our living room, watching mindlessly, bored. I kept the vast majority of my complaints to myself.

When I did voice a complaint, it was calculated. There were times when we had issues that I had to confront, like when he let his friend Randy sleep on our couch for a week without asking me. But I also understood that being a total pushover would make me unattractive, so I had to demonstrate some degree of backbone. In those instances, I put on makeup before I confronted him. I put on clothes with his taste in mind. I never argued with him without brushing my hair first.

Ben and I slept beside each other, saw each other naked, and took care of each other when we were sick. He washed my hair in the shower. I worried for his safety when he was delayed coming home, and he worried about mine. When bad things happened to him, or to me, we both felt upset. There was a lot of comfort and intimacy between us. Still, there was also a divide. In many ways, I felt weak and unsafe in our relationship. I had my guard up.

I think I objectified myself and other women partly because Ben did, and because the rest of society seemed to. I didn't think of hooking up with that woman as cheating because I didn't consider her a person the same way I considered men people. I didn't consider myself a full person. I thought of us both as part object. Two plastic playthings pretending together.

Joy made a disaster in the kitchen last December when I was sick. She gets a lot of business in December. People restore old books as gifts for the holidays. She was overwhelmed with jobs, I was out of commission, and the kitchen got away from her. I emerged from our bedroom for the first time in days, like a raggedy bear out of hibernation. I ambled into the kitchen and saw dirty pots and pans piled on the stove. Tomato sauce smeared across the counter. The sink teeming with crusty dishes. An open bag of bread.

I had an ear infection as well as an allergic reaction to

the penicillin prescribed to me. My face was swollen and enflamed. My entire body was covered in bright pink hives. I hadn't showered in days.

I care that the kitchen is clean. I don't go to bed without wiping down the counters, running the dishwasher, scrubbing out the sink. That day, I was bothered by the state of the kitchen, so I stormed outside to Joy's workshop. I threw open the door, and I stood in front of her—hollow-eyed, grimy, and disheveled. I said, almost in tears, "The dirty kitchen makes me feel like you don't care about me."

It didn't occur to me to consider how I looked before I confronted her. It's never occurred to me that I should look in the mirror before I tell her I'm upset.

I don't consider if Joy will think I'm a nag, or find me unattractive, if I look bad when I tell her I'm upset. I speak to her openly. I don't weigh the pros and cons of expressing my honest thoughts and feelings to her. I'm not plotting what I do, say, and wear like I'm an actress in a play prepping for a scene. I'm not playing the part of her partner. I am her partner.

"I cheated on Ben once," I tell Dr. Jeong. "Ben was away on a trip with his friends. He was fishing, I think. I'd gone to a bar with some people from school and I met this girl in the bathroom."

I tell her about the woman who came to the library.

"I never told anyone about her. Ben never found out. I thought of it as this strange blip in time. I didn't know what to make of it, so I just sort of tucked it away."

Her head is tilted. "Why do you think you tucked it away?"

"I don't know. I remember telling myself it wasn't really cheating because it was with a girl. I feel gross recognizing that now. It's bizarre that I ever thought that way. And I feel guilty doing that to Ben, and to that woman. I don't know what I was thinking. It just happened. I was confused at the time. I didn't know how to talk about it, and I figured it was just this weird one-time thing. I told myself it didn't count as cheating, but maybe if I'd faced that properly I might have saved us all some grief. It happened a couple years before we broke up."

She says, "You were struggling with your identity, and you didn't have the tools you needed to explore that. It's good to acknowledge that you feel guilty, and to reflect on mistakes you made, but we also need to acknowledge you were in a difficult situation. How can we work toward you forgiving yourself?"

I squint at her. "Is that what I need to do? Forgive myself?"

"Well, how do you feel about that?"

I exhale. "I feel like I have no right to mourn Ben because I cheated on him. And when we broke up, I felt relieved. I was sad, but mostly I felt like it was the right thing to do. But he was so upset. He called me a lot. It was awful. Now I feel like I abandoned him, and I don't know if he ever got over that. I never heard about him dating anyone else after me. I wish he had. He stayed in that apartment we lived in for a long time. I don't know if he ever moved. I finished school and got my first job that paid more than minimum wage. I moved into a nicer place. I made new friends. I was single for a while but started dating people. I was happy. After a few years, I met Joy. We moved in together soon after, and I felt really content. But he was still sort of stuck and seemed depressed. And now he's . . . " I pause.

He's dead.

My face feels hot.

"You're allowed to mourn Ben even if you feel guilty, and even if your relationship was difficult. It's normal to have complicated feelings like this, and you shouldn't judge yourself so harshly. I know that you care about Ben. Let's take a breather from this, okay? Can we do some mindfulness exercises?"

I nod.

We gotta make a decision. Leave tonight or live and die this way.

I'm driving home. "Fast Car" by Tracy Chapman is playing on the radio. I have the windows rolled down. I'm gripping the steering wheel, looking at the lights that lay out before me.

I'm trying to remember moving out of the apartment I lived in with Ben. I know I packed my clothes in garbage bags. The only suitcase I owned was full of my books. I remember hauling my belongings out of that building, up and down the stairs, sweating, worrying I was making a mistake.

I'm at a red light.

I think that was the last time I ever saw Ben. He was sitting on our couch with his head in his hands. His hair was

Is This a Cry for Help?

hanging over his knuckles. I said goodbye to him from the doorframe. He wouldn't say bye back.

"Bye, Ben," I said.

"Bye?"

"Are you going to say goodbye to me?"

I turn up the radio. This song used to play in the grocery store when I was a kid. I remember hearing it while I rode on the end of my mom's cart. It always stood out to me as the best grocery store song. When I was a kid, I didn't really register the lyrics. I just liked how it sounded. The first time I absorbed the words I already knew them. I understood the lyrics as I sang along.

The song is about a person dreaming of having a better life. She has a difficult existence; she lives in poverty, and her dad is an alcoholic. She wants to escape with her partner to someplace better, but they don't escape. She's left to take care of their kids while her partner stays out drinking with his friends. She eventually realizes they aren't going anywhere.

In the last verse of the song, she changes the line to say, "*You* gotta make a decision." She said the word "We" before. At first, the dream was this collective hope for a better life, but by the end of the song, it's this solitary choice.

Someone honks at me. I look up. The light turned green.

"He's normally an angel," I tell the vet.

Kyle has pinned his ears, arched his back, and hisses at the vet.

"It's okay, buddy," I say to him. "You're okay."

He's crawled into the sink and is howling like a rabid skunk.

"Maybe he had a bad experience at the vet before," I say. I feel oddly insecure about his behavior. I feel like I'm at the principal's office watching my child throw a fit. "He's a stray. I don't know his history."

The vet tries to comfort Kyle, but he's afraid of her. He's stuffed his head into the corner of the stink, as if that hides him. His round orange butt is facing us.

"Why do they pin their ears back like that?" I ask. For some reason, I feel driven to make conversation. I want this vet to know that I'm a normal person. I'm not abusing Kyle. I don't know why he's behaving this way.

"I've read they're trying to look like snakes," she says.

"Really?"

He looks nothing like a snake.

I snort. "Cats must have a terrible read on other animals. When my other cats see birds, they make these bizarre noises. I imagine they must think it will lure the birds, but they just sound ridiculous."

Kyle is biting the vet.

"I'm so sorry." I grimace.

She gives him his vaccines in his legs. "It's okay. He's just scared."

He howls like he's being murdered.

Kyle is back in the workshop, resting after his traumatic evening. I'm standing in the living room, surveying the stacks of books I've taken off our shelves. I don't know how I should organize them.

If I lived alone, I might digitally catalog everything. I could use software and add all the books to a catalog. I'd track things like date acquired, reading status, and rating. I'd update the catalog every time I bought or read a new book; however, I think that would be too much for Joy. I need to use a system that works for both of us.

I could put all our unread books on one shelf and organize the rest by how we rate them. I could put all our favorite books together. Our least favorites could go on the bottom shelves.

I'm not sure Joy and I always agree on ratings, however. And what would we do with books one of us has read that the other hasn't? Or that one of us loved but the other didn't?

I think Joy would find it easiest to put things away if we organized books by color; however, that approach only works well when it comes to putting books away. It's less useful when it comes to finding them. I can't be sure I'd remember the color of a cover.

I have the windows open. I'm in bed. Lou and Toulouse are lying on Joy's side. I'm reading poetry, listening to the frogs croaking outside. A moment ago, I wrote a large block of text for Joy, but I erased it. In it, I planned to tell her about the woman who came to the library today. I didn't hit send because I've never really told Joy about that woman before. We have discussed everyone we've ever had sex with, and I did include that woman in the number of people I've slept with. It's seven.

1) Paul, who was a guy I regrettably dated briefly in high school.
2) Ben.
3) That woman.
4) A woman named Enid who I met on a dating app.
5) Zuri. We dated for about four months a couple years before I met Joy.
6) Georgia. We dated for about six months, roughly a year before I started dating Joy.
7) Joy.

I've never mentioned, however, *when* I hooked up with that woman. I never shared the details of the encounter. I think I've implied, in fact, that it happened after I broke up with Ben. I don't want Joy to know I've cheated on someone before. I'm worried it'll upset her. She might think of me differently.

I wish I could think of myself differently. Dr. Jeong said I should work toward forgiving myself. I should have asked her how to do that.

I've googled "how to forgive yourself."

The first result from a reputable source says: "Take responsibility. Face your guilt."

I scroll down.

"Telling yourself that you are a bad person is not

constructive, but feeling guilt can help you avoid repeating mistakes. Make Amends—"

I pause. *How do I make amends with someone who isn't alive?*

I scan the rest of the article.

It doesn't say.

CHAPTER
SEVEN

"Forgiveness doesn't have to involve making things right with the other person," Dr. Jeong says. "You can make amends by channeling your desire for healing into your current behavior and your existing relationships. To do that, can I ask you to try and articulate exactly what it is you want forgiveness for?"

"Okay," I say. "Um. I guess I want forgiveness for . . . hurting Ben? For messing up his life and abandoning him."

She hums. "Good. So, if you're a positive influence in other people's lives, and if you're there for other people—do you think that might help you forgive yourself?"

I consider the question. "Maybe."

I wish she would give me clearer direction. I want to be told exactly what to do. I want to be given instructions. I want concrete steps I can take.

I ask, "Do you have any ideas about how I could do that?"

She says, "You can apply it in your relationship with your wife, and with your friends, and your family. Your job also seems like a great venue to be a supportive, positive influence on other people. You interact with a lot of the community, right?"

I nod.

"Is there anything you could do at work that might feel connected to this? Is there anyone who you could be more present for, or have a more positive impact on?"

*

When I first decided I wanted to become a librarian, I envisioned myself reading *Where the Wild Things Are* to a pack of entertained toddlers. I thought of amiable middle-aged women at book clubs. Precocious teens who love reading.

The reality is I spend a lot of time around people who don't have stable housing, who struggle with substance abuse, or who have severe mental illnesses. A lot of people who come to the library are new immigrants, or refugees, or people from low-income families who are struggling. There are also people, like Declan, who I don't like or understand.

I'm surrounded by people who have perspectives I don't have, and who are living lives I don't relate to. I do want to be a more supportive, positive influence on other people, but I'm not sure I have the faculties to do that. I wish it were easier to pinpoint exactly what I could do to help people.

If Ben were still alive, and we met to clear the air, I don't know what I'd say to him. It would be hard to explain myself, and to give him the context needed to clarify what I'm so sorry about. If he were alive, and I were able to make amends with him directly, what would I need to do besides apologize?

I could have reached out to him when he was alive, but I didn't. I didn't explain myself when I broke up with him. After we broke up, I knew I'd morphed into a person he didn't really know, and it would be baffling for him to speak to a stranger through the face of the girl he'd lived with for years.

I think I'm sorry for more than abandoning him and messing up his life. I'm sorry that I pretended to be someone else when we were together. I'm sorry I wasn't honest with him, or myself. I wish we'd been on the same page.

*

I'm in a small, glass-walled workshop room in the library. I've written the words HUMAN LIBRARY on the whiteboard.

Human libraries involve having humans act as "books" who can be borrowed by patrons for a conversation. I'm brainstorming this as a potential program. It's something I could champion that might foster understanding. I also think it might be a constructive example of a program that promotes our library's values, and maybe it could push back a little against the bubbling division in our community.

The room I'm in has clear walls. People walking by can see inside.

I've written LESBIAN, FIREFIGHTER, SOMEONE LIVING WITH AIDS on the board.

People keep looking in and making faces.

IS THIS YOU?

I'm off desk duty, sitting at a computer in the back, writing Brenda a proposal to run the human library program. An email with the above subject line has popped up in the corner of my screen.

I click it and see there's an attachment. I hesitate to open it, concerned it might be a scam or a phishing attack, but the body of the email says, DARCY?

I preview the file. My stomach clenches as the image loads—it's a screenshot of my Instagram story where my naked body is reflected in the chrome tap. It's a close-up of the reflection.

What the fuck?

My chest tightens. *Who sent this?* I fumble to move the mouse and click to see the email address. It says: EaglesNest88@gmail.com.

"I don't want to tell Brenda," I tell Joy. I'm standing in a bathroom stall, panicking. "This is scary. And it's such horrible timing. I'm meeting with her in two hours. I wanted to propose this program idea and talk about what we can do better. I don't want to keep bringing her problems. I want to be helpful. I don't know what to do."

Joy says, "I think you just have to tell Brenda—"

I wince. "I don't want to tell her. What if she asks me to forward her the email? She'll see the photo."

"Who cares if she sees the photo? It's just a human body."

"That's easy for you to say. It's not your human body—"

"You're all contorted in the picture. You can't really see anything—"

"You can see nipple. And the photo isn't the point. It'll derail our whole meeting."

She exhales. "Then maybe just tell her about the email without showing her. You have to. I can't imagine why anyone would do this."

I don't want to involve Brenda, regardless of whether doing so entails showing her my naked body. It's embarrassing that I've accidently posted a nude on the internet. I don't think it reflects well on me as an information professional. I'd prefer my boss not to know about this humbling error, especially given the terrible impression I've given her lately. Furthermore, what's she going to do? She won't be able to do anything to help me.

"I'm not telling Brenda," I say quietly.

Joy sighs loudly. "I really want you to tell someone. Like, honestly, maybe even call the pigs. That's a frightening email. I'm worried—"

"I'm definitely not calling the pigs," I say. "Every time I call them it's a total waste of my time. I asked them to come here after that man bulldozed into our story time the other day, and they didn't even send anyone. And I know those officers from city events. I don't want to live in a world where any of them have seen me naked."

She's quiet. "All right, fine, but I don't like this. That's a chilling email. Why would someone send you that? Do you have any idea who it might be?"

I'm googling the email address as we speak, but there are no relevant results. I'm searching the name of the email in various social media platforms, hoping maybe the owner has created a YouTube channel or Reddit account using the same handle, but nothing is coming up.

"I don't know who this could be," I say. "Maybe it's just some asshole messing with me."

"Who would do that?" Joy asks.

My Instagram account is private. To get the photo at all, the person would have to be following me.

"I don't know," I say.

I scan through every person who follows me and ask myself: *Is this person capable of sending me an unprovoked, ominous email with my naked photo attached?* No names jump out to me.

I wonder, what could motivate anyone to send me that email? Is this some kind of power play? Is it a way to assert dominance, or to intimidate me? Or did the person who sent it think it would be funny? Sometimes people do strange things when they're trying to be funny. Maybe this is a misguided prank. Or is it revenge for something? Have

I slighted someone who wants to get back at me? Or is it a sexual gratification thing? Maybe the person who sent this is voyeuristic and likes to share naked photos of people without their consent. Is it just attention seeking? Someone looking for a reaction?

Maybe the person is naive and sent this because they saw it and didn't understand the implications. I could see my grandma doing something like that if she were still alive. Do I know anyone else who is simple-hearted like that?

I open the email and read it over.

My initial thought is to not respond. I hover my curser over the delete button. I consider blocking the sender; however, my instinct to be agreeable and passive has steered me wrong before. I'm starting to think it might be better to confront things.

Rather than ignore the email, I click respond.

I write, "Yes? How can I help you?"

After I hit send, an email notification pops up in the corner of my screen. I click it.

HELLO,

ARE YOU STILL GETTING THESE EMAILS?

IF POSSIBLE, COULD YOU PLEASE TELL ME, ARE THERE CERTAIN BIRD SPECIES THAT ARE MORE LIKELY TO DEMONSTRATE HOMOSEXUAL BEHAVIOR?

E.G., ARE VULTURES MORE LIKELY, WHEREAS GULLS TEND

TO BE HETEROSEXUAL? I'M TRYING TO UNDERSTAND MORE ABOUT HOW NATURAL IT IS IN BIRDS.

THANKS,
SAMMY

It's only been twenty-four hours, and this patron has sent three emails about gay birds. I wonder why they're so impatient—

Wait a minute. I go back to the email I received with my nude. The word "Eagle" is in that email address. Was that email from the same person who's been sending these bird questions?

I check the email address of the person sending bird requests.

No. It's not the same email address. The bird patron is SammyLeaf12@aol.com. Though something still feels suspicious. I got the nude email after not replying to the bird patron. Maybe they were mad that I didn't reply. But how would they get the picture? There's no way they follow me on Instagram.

I look at the clock at the bottom of my screen. It's time for my meeting with Brenda.

I'm ill prepared for the meeting. The naked photo email has rattled me, and the technology in this meeting room isn't working so I can't get my notes on the screen.

Brenda's a few minutes late. Maybe she won't show. Maybe she forgot we had this scheduled. She's a busy person.

Plus, she may have suggested this meeting solely to appease me and make me feel heard. It might not actually be a priority for her—

"Darcy?"

Brenda is standing in the doorframe.

"Hello," I say in a too-high voice.

She pulls out a chair. "Sorry I'm late. I underestimated the lunchtime traffic."

"No problem," I say, my voice still too high. "Um. Let me know if you have anything specific you want to discuss first, but I've come prepared with some ideas and suggestions."

"Have you?" she says while taking off her jacket. "You're always on top of things, aren't you?"

"No. Definitely not always," I say.

She laughs.

I take a breath. "Okay. So. We're talking about the complaints we've received regarding censorship. You mentioned that we're planning to review our related policies, and I know we have established procedures regarding how we address complaints related to our collections and programming. That all sounds good. I'd also like to suggest we consider training our staff on how to respond to this sort of conflict and aggression. I did my best in both of the recent instances, but I would have felt more confident if I'd been prepared with more specific messaging or direction."

I inhale. I'm speaking too quickly.

"Now, the main suggestion I have is that we consider these instances the same way we consider any rising issue in our community. In the same way we might plan programs or recommend resources on budgeting, or community assistance, when we notice our community is dealing with food and housing insecurity. I think now is the time to plan programs, develop our collection, and recommend resources about topics like intellectual freedom and community connection. I've been doing some research, and my understanding is that the behavior we've seen as of late is a symptom of deepening social and class division, and a significant number of sources suggest that one of the best ways to respond is to foster community and conversation."

I inhale again.

"So that all leads me to this recommended program, and I'd love to hear your thoughts. Of course, I don't think this is going to cure the problem—but I think it might be a small step toward connecting the work we do with these issues in a more constructive and positive way. Have you heard about human libraries before?"

She blinks. "No. I don't think so."

"It's a social program where people act as books and share their life stories with readers in one-on-one conversations. The objective is to promote connection, understanding, and challenge stereotypes, while fostering empathy. I thought maybe we could pilot one at this branch. I'm sorry I can't get the screen in this room to work, or I'd show you some examples. I have videos other libraries made. I can send you a follow-up email—"

"I love this idea," she says. "Let's do it."

"You do?" I say. "That's great."

I smile. I'm looking forward to telling Dr. Jeong that my therapy homework is on track.

I join my next meeting three minutes late. The other attendees are already talking.

"What are your most popular questions lately?" Annie asks. She's the meeting organizer.

This Zoom call includes reference librarians across our system. We meet on a quarterly basis to discuss our services. As part of this, we analyze the subject matter of our questions to identify areas where we might need to improve our collections, train staff, and so on. We also talk about work we can share, or complete together, like guides, or workshops.

Fiona, a librarian from a couple towns over, is talking about the reference work her branch has been doing. "We're getting legal questions. Questions about health. Tech support, of course. Job search assistance . . . the usual. Slight uptick in questions regarding social services."

The attendees can only see the top of my head, because I am making a list of people I think could have sent me my nude on a notepad. These are the suspects:

1) The patron sending me bird requests. The email address that sent me the nude is bird-themed, which is suspicious, and this patron obviously has my email address.

2) Ruth, Joy's ex-girlfriend. I don't know her very well, but she's on my social media, and while I'm mostly joking when I say negative things about her, the truth is I have no reason to trust her. Maybe she hates me. Maybe she's still in love with Joy and wants to fuck with me.

3) My cousin Tucker. He's an ignorant, overtly homophobic man who often makes me feel uncomfortable. I don't trust him.
4) Douglas, one of Ben's old friends. I only kept him on my social media because we had this interaction once that made me feel bad for him, but he's a lot like Tucker.
5) My mom. I don't know why she would screenshot my naked Instagram story and send it to my work email, but her behavior has always mystified me. I'm often flabbergasted by the choices she makes.

"Same here," says Aisha. "We had quite a few tax-related questions this quarter, as expected, but also quite a few questions relating to topics like affordable housing, food assistance, and financial aid."

"What about your branch, Darcy?" Annie asks.

I unmute my mic and look up at the camera. "Similar trends here."

I haven't actually assessed our data, so I'm lying. I barely worked this quarter. I've been away.

I mute my mic, look back down at my list of suspects and flip the page in my notebook. The next page is covered in notes about the human library.

I think of my earlier meeting with Brenda. Prior to her arrival, I'd been in the glass-walled room preparing my notes. People were looking in. Maybe someone who saw me in there, with the word "lesbian" written on the board and my trans flag pin on my vest, felt compelled to lash out at me. Maybe that's who sent me the picture. Maybe I upset someone.

But how would they get the picture?

I flip the page. I zero in on my first suspect, the bird emailer.

I unmute myself again. "I have noticed a slight uptick in questions about, um, wildlife. Birds, specifically. Has anyone else been getting those?"

"Pardon?" Annie says.

Why did I ask that? Am I losing it? Did I take my medication today?

"Bird questions," I repeat, having already dug this hole for myself. "Has anyone else been receiving questions about, uh, birds?"

"No," Fiona says.

Aisha turns on her mic. "No bird questions here."

"Hello," my mom says.

I'm home from work, sitting on the floor in Joy's workshop, petting Kyle.

"Hi, Mom," I say.

"Wow, hi. Is this my long-lost daughter? It's been a while since we've heard from you. I didn't know if you were dead or alive."

I feel myself revert slightly into the child I once was when I hear my mom's voice, especially when she sounds irritated. I remember being a little girl in that house with her. She did my hair every morning before school. She tied it into tight pigtails or French braids. I hated it. I used to pull them out at recess.

"I'm alive." I cringe. "How are you? How's Dad?"

"Beyond not hearing from my only child for months, I'm well. Thank you. Your father is all right. He has a sore hip, but we're managing. He's watching the game right now. He says hello. Why are you calling?"

"I'm just checking in."

I run my fingers against my scalp. My hair is down right now.

"For no reason?"

"Yeah, for no reason. I'm just calling to say hey. Is that all right?"

She huffs. "Whatever. You've always been good at keeping things close to your chest, that's for sure."

I frown. "What do you mean by that?"

I already know what she means. She considers me a secretive person because when I was a teenager I hid things from her, like eating, dating, and drinking. I behaved like a run-of-the-mill, standard teen; however, my mom never saw it that way. She thinks I'm dishonest because I'm gay. She has misconceptions about homosexuality and has interpreted my reluctance to come out to her as secretive behavior. I have reason to believe she also just considers gay people devious and untrustworthy in general. In fact, she doesn't believe I am truly gay. She thinks it's a choice I made to be defiant and alternative. Despite the fact that I'm married and in my thirties, she still views me as a rebellious child, driven by a bizarre and illogical motive to upset her for no good reason.

My head hurts. It feels like there are tight ribbons and elastic bands tied taut to my scalp.

She's always been like this. Before she griped about my lesbianism, she used to complain about my diet, my clothes, or about how I lived with Ben before marriage. She didn't think

I should go to university. It was too much money. It's always been something, and it'll always be something. She wants me to be someone I'm not. A modest, well-behaved, obedient, feminine, domestic, chaste, skinny heterosexual she can brag about to the ladies in her running club. Even if I were that person, I think she'd still complain. I doubt I could ever be who she wants me to be.

I don't tend to call her because she's difficult to speak to, and she rarely calls me. I live far away. I visit once every other year or so. I often feel upset by the fact that our relationship is strained, and I wish I could have an easier relationship with her and my dad, but I don't think it's in the cards for us. For the most part, I've accepted that.

My dad and I only speak through my mom. Once in a while he answers the phone when I call, we exchange pleasantries, then he hands me off to her. When I visit, he and I talk about baseball, despite the fact that I don't follow baseball.

She says, "I think there's a reason you're calling. Do you need something?"

She's not usually this confrontational right off the bat. Normally, when I call, she talks to me cordially, as if I'm an old acquaintance. I've established boundaries with her over the last decade, and she's usually not comfortable talking to me this way unless we've been around each other for more than a day.

She's probably mad at me because I didn't reply to her voicemail.

I'm offended by her asking if I need something. What could I possibly need from her? I've never asked her for anything as an adult. I've never borrowed money from her. I've never asked her to drive me to an airport, or to co-sign a loan. She's talking to me as if I'm someone who comes to her for help. I don't.

I close my eyes. I used to hide granola bars in my box spring, eat them in the middle of the night, and wake up terrified my mom might find the garbage.

I inhale and picture myself eating an enormous chocolate cake. I'm sitting on the floor. I've smeared the dark, rich icing all over my skin. It's around my mouth. Down my neck. In my hair. I've stained my boyish, dykey clothes.

"I just wanted to catch up with you," I lie. My voice is cold, and I'm sure she can tell I feel irked by her.

She says, "Oh, lovely. You're just bored? Well, I'm just dying to hear about whatever you've got going on after you've ignored me for months."

"Jesus, Mom, what's with the sour-ass attitude?" I ask.

She gasps. "Don't use words like that with me—"

"All right, never mind, you take care, Judy," I say. She hates it when I call her by her first name. "Tell Dad I said take care too, all right? Bye."

I hang up.

"Why do you sound so upset? Are you still freaking out over the disturbing email?"

Joy called to check in on me. I haven't recovered from the call with my mom.

"No. Well—yes. I just got off the phone with my mom."

"Ah. Why'd you call Judy when you're already worked up? She always upsets you."

I sigh. "I know. It was stupid of me. I just thought maybe it was her who sent that email."

"*What?* Why would you think that? I can't imagine any reason why your mom would send it. What would possibly motivate her to do that? And it didn't come from her email, right? There's no way your mom created a new email address just to send a screenshot of you. Does she even have your work email?"

"Yeah, you're right. I don't know what I was thinking. I have no idea why she would do that. The problem is, I don't know why *anyone* would do that."

"Can you see who viewed your Instagram story?"

"Yes, and she views all my stories," I say. "She's always watching everything I post. That's part of why I thought maybe it could be her."

I deleted her off Facebook because I rarely use it, and she relentlessly tagged me in memes. I left her on Instagram because she didn't seem to know how to use it beyond watching everything I did.

"I really don't think it was your mom," Joy says.

I sigh. "Yeah, you're right. Me either."

I have my list of suspects in front of me.

"What about Ruth?" I ask.

"*Ruth?*" she repeats. "Why the hell would Ruth—"

"I don't know. I'm grasping at straws here, babe. I just hate Ruth, so I assume maybe she could have—"

She snorts. "Ruth isn't a sociopath."

"All right, that's enough complimenting Ruth." I roll my eyes.

She laughs. "Saying she's not a sociopath isn't much of a compliment—"

"Well, actually, she is kind of a sociopath, because she followed me on Instagram after only meeting me that one time. So quit talking her up."

She laughs again. "All right, that was kind of weird of her, I'll give you that, but that was like four years ago. She's got a new partner. She's living in Spain."

I frown. "You're really keeping tabs on her, aren't you?"

She scoffs. "There's no way she's occupying her time sending you weird, creepy emails. Go ahead and cross her off the list."

"Fine," I say. "I guess I should just drop the whole thing entirely anyway. It's probably pointless. There's no way for me—"

She interrupts. "I'm so sorry, honey, I have to let you go. The baby is up."

I can hear January crying in the background.

"Okay, that's okay. Bye. I love you."

"Bye. Be safe. Love you."

There are some parts to life that we have to face on our own. When you have a partner, sometimes you can develop codependence, and find yourself operating in the world as if you are half of something. I'm not half of anything. I am Joy's partner, and glad to be, but I'm also a full person alone. I have my own thoughts, my own relationships, and my own problems. I am capable of handling things on my own.

I don't need Joy to help me find out who sent this creepy email. I can sort out this mess myself.

I've placed cans of chicken pâté on opposite sides of the living room. I've situated Lou and Toulouse on one side, and I'm about to bring Kyle to the other side. This will be their first meeting. The pâté is supposed to help foster a positive association. I've also scattered several cardboard boxes across the floor to act as cat panic rooms. The cats can hide in them if they feel overwhelmed. I plan to keep the interaction brief, and to supervise.

I carry Kyle from the workshop into the house. I feel his usually limp body become tense as we enter the new environment. He holds himself close to me.

The girls stop eating to look up at us. I carry Kyle to the other side of the room, place him down on the floor, and show him the cat food.

He does not look at the cat food. Instead, he stands still and stares at Lou and Toulouse. They're facing us, also standing stiff. All three cats stare at each other like statues, until a low, guttural noise starts to emerge from Kyle.

Toulouse hisses at him.

Lou hisses too.

They all start turning their bodies sideways, arching their backs, posturing. Their tails are puffing up, and they're all standing on their tiptoes. They begin making demonic, throaty cat noises. They're growling. Snarling. Spitting.

"All right, that's enough," I say.

I pick Kyle up and bring him back out to the workshop.

I'm having regrets about taking all our books off our shelves. I'm worried I've lost the ambition required to organize them.

I'm exhausted, lying limp on the couch next to mounds of books, questioning where I got the big, bright idea to put this room in shambles. I could have left everything as it was. It wasn't organized, but it wasn't total chaos. It looked okay, at least.

Maybe I should use the Dewey decimal system. I could teach Joy; I've taught pages and teen volunteers at the library how to shelve with it. I worry it might not be any easier than our previous alphabetical system, though. I'm also not a fan of Dewey. The system was developed for American libraries, and it shows. It's Eurocentric, homophobic, racist, and more. Within the religion class, which is the 200s, the notations 200–289 are designated to facets of Christianity. The notation 290 represents "other religions." So, for example, the notation 297 represents Islam. This means the notation for all of Islam is the same length as the notation for "Christian Sacred books." It's very biased.

That said, Joy and I don't own many religious books, so that particular issue wouldn't significantly impact us. It is symptomatic of larger problems in the classification system, though.

There are issues like this with most classification systems. Organizational systems are designed by humans, and most of us are limited and flawed.

I took a sleeping pill. I'm sprawled out in bed with Lou and Toulouse, who are still recovering from their hostile encounter with Kyle. They're both jumpy and tense. I'm waiting to drift off.

Sometimes, when I'm alone with my thoughts, I entertain my mom's ideas about me. I question if I'm really gay, for example. Am I actually a lesbian? Or am I bisexual? Am I demisexual? Am I pansexual? Or am I straight and confused?

I care about labels. Some people don't, but I do. I think there's value to categorizing things. We categorize fiction by genres so horror books can be grouped together. Nonfiction books are shelved by discipline, so philosophy books are grouped together. Categorizing books makes it easier to locate them, and it also makes it easier to discover new ones. Readers who like *Rosemary's Baby* are more likely to find *Misery* because a relationship between those stories was formed when they were categorized as horror. Relationships are created between all books once they've been categorized. We understand some of how *Charlotte's Web* and *Misery* relate to each other without having to read either story, because of their genres. Labeling and categorizing things can help us understand not only what they are, but how they relate to other things.

There are subcategories within genres too. While there are lots of readers who like horror in general, there are also people who only enjoy a specific subcategory of horror. Such as: horror monster fiction. Or even deeper than that: horror monster zombie fiction. There are even readers who prefer horror monster zombie *virus* fiction—as opposed to the horror monster zombie *undead* fiction.

To an outsider, if someone likes horror books, the nuance of their preference for monster zombie virus horror does not seem important. It seems needlessly complicated and specific; however, to a person who is seeking out books they like, the nuance matters.

We categorize sexual orientations for the same reason we categorize anything, to better understand what it is, and how it relates to other things. I don't think there's anything wrong with not liking labels. I understand that cataloging isn't widely considered a thrilling discipline, and it's true that categorizing people is restrictive and imperfect. Humans don't fit perfectly into boxes; however, I personally want the most accurate, specific labels for myself because I think it helps me better understand who I am and how I fit into the greater schema of humans.

For a while I thought I was bisexual. I think it was easier to recognize that I liked women than it was to recognize that I didn't like men. I'm pretty confident I'm a lesbian today, but it's hard to know for sure. I wish there were some way to check what I am, like a barcode on the sole of my foot. Though I guess that would introduce other issues. Being able to hide one's homosexuality has obviously served us through the years. Still, sometimes I wonder if I'm an imposter.

When I think of Ben, I don't just think of him as a person, I think of him as a life I rejected. He represents who I could have been if I'd carried on marking myself as straight. I'd be a book shelved in a different part of the library, connected to the rest of the collection differently.

In a strange way, the idea of marrying a man still feels comfortable to me. It's what I thought I wanted when I was a kid. It's what I was familiar with. I pictured myself growing up to be the mom character in all the cartoons I watched and the books I read. That image was so burned into me, the picture of my straight self feels nostalgic now.

Picturing myself married to Ben makes me feel similarly

to how I feel when I look at a childhood photo. Despite the fact that I see sadness in my face and would not trade places with that version of myself, I still feel strangely homesick for the picture.

I'd feel less awkward when I talk to strangers about my life if I had a husband. I'd feel more comfortable holding Joy's hand outside. Family events would feel less agonizing. When Joy and I bought our house, it was a seller's market, and our realtor told us to write the owners a letter. I wrote it and avoided using our pronouns, or acknowledging we're both women, in case the owners wouldn't pick us because we're gay.

In most ways, though, the picture of the life I could have had depresses me. I know what my life would have been like with Ben. I can see myself packing lunches, cleaning up after him and our kids, feeling strangely like a horror book shelved as poetry. When I envision that life, I see myself driving a minivan. I'm on my way to pick up the kids from school. I veer onto the highway, drive into the distance, and never come back. Or maybe I veer into a barricade, or off a cliff. I do think that I would be the one who wouldn't survive in that timeline.

CHAPTER EIGHT

"Here comes Karl Marx!" Declan Turner shouts at me as I approach the library. He and a crowd of a dozen people are protesting outside. They're standing at a distance from the front double doors. He's holding his phone in my face. The people with him are carrying signs that say:

PROTECT OUR CHILDREN!

DEFEND TRADITIONAL VALUES!

KEEP THE PERVERTS OUT
OF THE LIBRARY!

"Karl Marx?" I repeat. "*Really?*"

I push through the crowd like a disgraced celebrity fighting off a pack of aggressive paparazzi. I'm worried someone is going to hit me. They're all shouting. Taking my picture.

"I looked you up!" Declan says with his phone still in my face. "You thought you could hide it!"

Hide what?

"You're part of the gay agenda!" he says.

I look at him, baffled. "What does that have to do with anything? Are you suggesting I'm hiding that I'm gay?"

I'm wearing Birkenstocks and men's pants with a carabiner on my belt loop. I have a trans flag pinned to my lanyard, blue hair, and a wedding band on my finger with my wife's name engraved on the outside.

"I am not hiding anything," I say.

"We don't care that you're gay!" an angry woman shouts at me.

I make a face. "He brought it up—"

"We have no problem with homosexuals! Don't try to make this into us being anti-homosexual! This has nothing to do with that! Keep your sexual preferences in the bedroom!" she shouts.

"What?" I scowl. "That last thing you said sort of contradicts the prior—"

"And keep drag queens away from our kids! And porn out of the library! And if you disagree, you shouldn't be allowed anywhere near children! You should be in prison! Communist!"

Some people are shouting about puberty blockers for no good reason. I hear someone say something about vaccines and drinking unpasteurized milk.

"What are you all talking about?" I shout. "Get out of my way!"

Patty has the front door open for me. She's beckoning me inside. "Get in here, Darcy!"

"Hi, Brenda, we've got a bit of a situation on our hands over here."

I'm in the back room on the phone.

"I heard, yes. Mordecai called the police because they threatened him. I'm in touch with them as we speak. We've got two officers heading there right now. I'm sure they're almost there. Is everyone all right?"

"I think so," I say. "I'll send out an email to everyone working today to warn them. I'll tell them to use the back door to avoid the crowd out front."

"Thank you, Darcy."

"No problem."

She says, "Just to give you an update regarding the work the board is doing about this, and the complaints we're receiving, we've reviewed our policies with legal. Based on our review, we aren't recommending any changes at this point; however, the board has advised that we consult the community. So, we'll be hosting a public forum to review our related policies. I'm also bringing some of your suggestions, specifically about training, to the board. I'll keep you posted."

"Okay, thanks for keeping us in the loop. Didn't we review our policies with the community when they were updated last year?"

"Yes. They want us to do it again."

I can sense in her tone that she feels the same way I do about that.

"I see. Well, please let me know when that forum will be. I'd like to come."

"Of course, yes. I will."

I find Mordecai in the back room.

"Are you okay?" I ask.

He exhales. "Yes. I'm fine. Thank you for asking. Did someone mention that I phoned the police? I was in early and I decided to make an executive call. I figured if there's a swarm of people blocking the entrance, threatening employees and screaming that we're all pedophiles, that probably warrants a call to the police. Did you come to work through the front entrance where they're protesting, too?"

I nod. "I did."

"Did they scream at you as well? What did they call you?"

I nod again. "They called me Karl Marx."

He blinks. "I'm sorry, what?"

I laugh. "Don't ask. I heard they threatened you?"

"They did, yes. I was threatened. Were you? Or were you just referred to as a German political theorist? My insults were significantly less pretentious. They just kept calling me a pedophile. And I have to say, I'm considerably more dismayed about it now that I'm aware of the disparity in insults being tossed around. That is truly just rude. Isn't it? God. Well, in any case, I'm so sorry they yelled at you—even if they disrespected you more favorably. I wonder if they realize they were

Is This a Cry for Help?

screaming at someone dealing with your health issues."

I look at him.

He continues, "You know, I wasn't taught much about this in my Library Science program. We focused a lot on cataloging, collection development, community outreach, and that sort of thing. Very little time was spent on how to heave your way to work through a troop of angry extremists threatening to spit on you."

I sit down at the reference desk. I can hear the crowd outside. They're chanting, "Protect the kids!" I stare ahead. I can see the children's section from where I'm sitting. There's a mural painted on the wall. We commissioned it the year I started. It's of a yellow brick road weaving through forests and rolling hills. In the horizon, there's a castle, a dragon, a unicorn, and a hot-air balloon. In the corner of the mural, there's a group of kids reading books under a lemon tree.

I look at the computer monitor in front of me. It isn't turned on, so I can see my reflection in the dark screen. My hair ends at my shoulders. It used to be much longer, and blond. When I started my master's degree, it was almost at my waist.

I touch the reference desk. Someone's taped a little motivational note to a part of the desk that patrons can't see. It says, YOU DON'T HAVE TO HAVE ALL THE ANSWERS, YOU JUST HAVE TO KNOW WHERE TO LOOK, with a smiley face drawn on the end.

In my first class in library school, we talked about the height of desks in libraries. I remember my professor sharing an image from the movie *Matilda*, where the librarian looks down at Matilda from her tall, towering desk. The prof asked, "What's wrong with this image?"

We talked about why reference and circulation desks shouldn't be too tall. They should be a height that allows librarians to maintain eye contact with patrons without looking down at them. They need to be accessible for people of all heights. A person in a wheelchair shouldn't be blocked from view. A child shouldn't have to crane their neck upward as if approaching a judge on their bench. At the time, while this made sense to me, I thought it was strange that we spent our first lesson talking so much about furniture.

In my experience, a lot of being a librarian has to do with interacting with the public, paperwork, office bureaucracy, tech support, and emails. There is another element to the job, though. I think maybe that desk lecture spoke to that.

I remember reading stories in school about police demanding patron records, and librarians refusing to release them. There was one case, in the early 2000s, in Connecticut. Librarians were contacted by the FBI, who demanded to know what information specific patrons were accessing. The librarians challenged this in court, and the judge ruled in the librarians' favor. I remember learning that we have to defend our patrons' privacy for legal reasons, but also because people need to be free to explore information without fear of surveillance.

When I was a kid, I never kept a diary because I knew my mom would read it. She looked at the browsing history on our family computer. I never googled anything I wouldn't want her to see. There were subjects I would have benefited from investigating, like birth control. The first time I hooked up with a guy, we didn't use protection. I didn't know enough. I also would have benefited from reading about having an emotionally abusive mother. I would have benefited from being exposed to more content featuring lesbians too. I didn't read or watch anything that centered around lesbians until I was well into my twenties.

Beyond needing access to information for the sake of becoming informed, and exposing ourselves to different ideas, it's also important that we have access to information that represents different viewpoints—even viewpoints that are widely considered bad. Engaging with information that opposes our own opinions can open our minds up to new ideas, and it can help us get a deeper understanding of our own position. This is part of what justifies keeping or reading information that's hateful or ignorant. When we understand what we don't believe, we better understand what we do.

I remember sitting in class, talking about the moral panic that happens after horrible events, like school shootings. Metal music and video games are often blamed for making people do terrible things. There's no evidence that's true, and we shouldn't be afraid to read books, or play games, or listen to music because it could be used to prove we're criminals. There's a personal autonomy aspect to information privacy. We have the right to make our own choices about what art or information we consume.

The people outside are still chanting. I close my eyes.

Before public libraries existed, there were subscription libraries. You had to pay to access them. It used to be that information was only accessible to rich and powerful people.

"Protect the kids!"

Having free, uncensored, access to information is a fundamental human right. Even today, in a world where information is more accessible online, there are still barriers that libraries help resolve. People use the library. It's busy here.

"Protect the kids!"

I feel anxious. I put a hand to my chest. The crowd outside is making me uneasy. I pull at the collar of my shirt. I feel like I'm in the beginning stages of a panic attack. The last time I had a panic attack, I stood naked in the snow. That really wouldn't help my case with these protestors in my insistence that I'm not a pervert.

I stand up. There's no one to cover the desk, but I'm going to the bathroom anyway.

I'm sitting in a bathroom stall, folded over, with my head between my knees. I'm inhaling and exhaling loudly. If someone were to come in right now, they might think I'm giving birth.

There's a strange smell in the washroom. What is it? It's like basil, garlic, and meat. Why does the washroom smell like lasagna? I stand up and exit the stall. I examine my surroundings and see that in the corner of the sink, near the baby changing station, there's a Crock-Pot. I walk up to it, open the lid, and look down at a pile of warmed meatballs.

What the fuck?

I unplug the pot, pick it up, and exit the washroom.

"Whose meatballs are these?" I shout.

Patrons shoot me funny looks.

I haul the pot around the library. "Whose Crock-Pot is this?"

A woman near the children's section raises her hand. "That's mine!"

I approach her. "I'm sorry, but you can't use this in the library."

I place the pot down on the table in front of her.

She frowns. "Why not?"

I look into her pupils as if I'm looking at a *Brachiosaurus*. She has scaley, periscopic, dinosaur eyes. She and I are different creatures; we're both from earth, but I don't understand her, and she doesn't understand me.

I say, "You can't cook food in the library. It's a fire hazard, and the smell could affect the books. We have building codes. It's also a health and sanitation issue. Food shouldn't be prepared in a public bathroom."

She looks at me as if I've just said something ludicrous.

I look at her as if she has a thirty-foot-long neck.

I'm an adult. A woman in her thirties. I have free will. I could leave right now. I don't have to be here. I'm my own person, alive in this moment, enduring the mayhem inflicted on public librarians, when I could simply wash my hands of this and exit the building. Why did I choose this job? Why did I pursue this? Why didn't anyone warn me that I'd spend days telling people not to cook meat in the bathroom while hearing others chant from outside that I'm a pedophile? I just wanted to be around books and help people. I could go home right now, lie under the lavender comforter on my bed with my cats, and apply for a job in a law library or as a cataloger. I don't have to do this.

The woman has not left with her meatballs yet.

I say sternly, "Get these out of here."

I've returned to the desk with a glass of water. I open my email and see a response from EaglesNest88@gmail.com. It says:

> I DON'T THINK IT'S VERY PROFESSIONAL TO POST NAKED PHOTOS ON THE INTERNET.

I scowl, hit reply, and type fervently.

> WHAT KIND OF JOB DO YOU THINK I HAVE? DO YOU THINK YOU'RE EMAILING SOMEONE WHO WORKS SOME STRAIT-LACED, STATELY PROFESSION THAT PROHIBITS EMPLOYEES FROM ACCIDENTALLY POSTING THEIR NUDES ON THE INTERNET? I'M NOT A POLITICIAN. I'M NOT A PASTOR. I'M A PUBLIC LIBRARIAN. I JUST TOLD A LADY NOT TO COOK MEAT IN THE BATHROOM. WHO DO YOU THINK IS GOING TO GIVE A SHIT THAT I ACCIDENTALLY POSTED MY NAKED BODY ON THE INTERNET? WHO THE FUCK DO YOU THINK I AM, AND WHO THE FUCK ARE YOU?

I read my reply over. As I do, I feel the energy inside me dwindle. I hover my finger over the backspace key. I wrote this for the catharsis, but I won't send it because I *am* a professional.

I erase the email.

"Do you think EaglesNest88 is Declan?" Joy asks.

I called her, told her about the people outside, the Crock-Pot, and the email I received.

I say, "Maybe. But how would he get that picture of me? I have a private account. Declan Turner definitely doesn't follow me."

"Maybe he's got good tech skills and can break into accounts."

"I don't think he has good tech skills," I say. "I googled him, and he doesn't even know how to make his accounts private. He's got two Facebook albums that appear to be photos he accidentally took of grass up close. He's not breaking into my social media accounts."

She asks, "But then how did he know you're a lesbian this morning?"

"That's out there," I say. "I've done articles for the library sharing books for pride that mention I'm gay. You'd find it if you googled my name. I go to the Pride parade with the library float. I haven't hidden it. And I look like a lesbian."

"Right, right," she says.

"I'll add him to my list of suspects, though," I say.

"Who else is on there?" she asks.

"I've narrowed it down to my cousin Tucker, a guy named Douglas, and a patron who keeps sending me bird requests."

"How would a patron sending you bird requests get the photo if Declan couldn't?"

"I have no idea," I say. "I'm fishing in murky waters over here. And frankly, I'm burning out. I feel like quitting my job."

"You don't want to quit your job. You like your job," she says.

I exhale. "Not when I'm being harassed, and I'm surrounded by people cooking meat near toilets."

She snorts. "You aren't surrounded. That was just one lady. Look around, there's lots of people you like there. Where's that woodworking guy?"

Randall is asleep in a chair. He's got a magazine open on his chest. We're not supposed to let people sleep in the library, but I'm not waking him up. He looks comfortable.

I say, "He's sleeping, which is what I wish I was doing, but I have to get back to work now. I need to reply to the bird patron. I haven't responded to them for a while, and I'm on the clock right now. I'll talk to you later, okay? Tell Sophie and January I said hi."

"Okay, I will. Be safe. I love you."

"I will. Love you too."

I open up the emails from the bird patron. I spend about ten minutes gathering information, then reply.

DEAR SAMMY,

PLEASE NOTE OUR SERVICE DELIVERY TIME FOR REFERENCE QUESTIONS IS ONE WEEK. COMPLEX QUESTIONS MAY HAVE LONGER TURNAROUND TIME.

I HAVE ATTACHED SOME RECOMMENDED RESOURCES REGARDING HOMOSEXUALITY IN BIRDS.

THERE IS EVIDENCE OF SAME-SEX BEHAVIOR AND

Is This a Cry for Help?

RELATIONSHIPS IN VARIOUS ANIMALS, INCLUDING BIRD SPECIES. IT'S BEEN OBSERVED IN SWANS, WRENS, DUCKS, GEESE, SPARROWS, FLAMINGOS, ROBINS, RAVENS, HAWKS, FALCONS, EAGLES, OWLS, MAGPIES, DOVES, WARBLES, WOODPECKERS, STORKS, LOONS, BLUEBIRDS, GREBES, AND MORE.

IF YOU HAVE ANY FOLLOW-UP QUESTIONS, PLEASE REACH OUT TO US AGAIN. WE ARE HAPPY TO HELP.

"Did you see there's a group of anti-protestors out there now?" Mordecai says. He's standing at the window that faces the entrance. He has his hands on his hips.

I'm sitting at the reference desk nearby. I get up to look outside with him.

There were a dozen people with Declan when I arrived this morning. There are about thirty people outside now. The new people are holding signs that say things like:

I SUPPORT THE LIBRARY!
DON'T JUDGE, JUST READ!

Mordecai smiles. "Well, isn't that nice? Gosh, that is so encouraging, actually. I find it really uplifting to see so much of our community stand in solidarity with us, don't you?"

I look at the people outside.

He sighs. "Man, I'm going to be honest with you, I felt really disheartened earlier. You know, they shouted some really vile things at me. I've spent my entire morning feeling pretty down in the dumps. This new crowd of people has really turned things around. I feel so much better. Look at them!"

He grins and waves out the window.

Dr. Jeong and I are practicing imaginal revisiting again. I'm telling her about a time when Ben and I were dating, and I went away to a music festival with some friends.

"It was the August after my first year at university," I say. I have my eyes closed. "My friends and I rented an apartment for the week. I had my own room. I'd been living with Ben, so it was nice to have some privacy. This was the first time I spent days away from him, or slept alone, in over a year."

"How did being away from him make you feel?"

I consider the question. "I hadn't noticed it while I was with him, but in his absence, I remember realizing I hadn't been alone with my own thoughts in a long time. While I was lying alone in my bed, I felt like I was meeting myself for the first time in a year."

"Could you explain what you mean by that?" she says.

"Sure. Um. When I lived with Ben, I talked to him a lot, obviously. I told him my thoughts. His opinions influenced mine. We interpreted everything together. We lived in a small apartment, so we were always around each other. I was rarely alone with myself. Everything I thought and did was sort of influenced by him. I morphed into him, and the line between who he was and who I was, blurred."

"But you felt differently that week when you were away from him at a festival?" she asks.

"Yeah, that week, my thoughts weren't interrupted by his. I wasn't talking through my day with him, or hearing about his, or processing my thoughts with him. I was by myself. I was with friends, but before I went to sleep, I was alone. I felt sort of startled by how it felt to be alone. I realized I had been feeing disconnected from who I was for a long time. I'd become a stranger."

"Okay. When you're ready, please open your eyes."

I open them.

"How do you feel revisiting that memory? Do you have any other thoughts or reflections?"

I nod. "Yeah. I guess I'm thinking about how I learned some things about myself from my relationship with Ben. Like, because of that experience, I understand how important it is to check in on yourself, and to spend time alone, when you live with a partner. It's something I'm sure a lot of people learn after their first long-term relationship, or their first time living with someone. You can lose yourself."

"That's a good take away." She nods. "Your relationship with Ben taught you some valuable things."

I nod.

I feel like I'm inside a library after an earthquake. I've filled two sizable Rubbermaid bins with books I plan to toss or donate, but it looks like I've done nothing. I've barely made a dent in the mess. The living room is still piled with books. Anthologies. Box sets. Mass market paperbacks. They're stacked on the couch, the coffee table, and the floor. Several piles have been knocked over by the cats.

I hate being inside a chaotic, messy environment. Why did I do this to myself? I imagined it would be easier to put it all away. I thought I could take everything out, look at it, clean, and put the books back properly. I just want to feel comfortable here.

"Maybe you should come home," I tell Joy.

I'm lying on her side of the bed.

"Why? Are you okay?"

"Yes, I'm fine, but I think the cats miss you."

She laughs. "Oh, do they?"

"Yes," I say. "They told me if you don't come home soon, they might become depressed."

"Oh God, we wouldn't want that."

"No," I say. "Depressed cats are a nightmare."

"Have you tried introducing Kyle to them again?"

"No," I say. "That first time was a total disaster, so I'm giving it a little while longer. They despised each other."

"They were probably just a little nervous."

"Yeah, maybe," I say.

"I miss you," she says. I can tell by her voice that she's falling asleep.

"I miss you too."

I'm staring into the darkness of my bedroom, trying to sleep, thinking about my therapy session.

I don't feel out of tune with myself when Joy is away. I wish she were here, and I prefer being around her, but I don't feel like I've lost myself with her. The voice in my head right now, while she's gone, isn't a stranger to me.

I do think that when you live with someone, you take on parts of them. Even if you don't morph into each other and become a combined person, you change. I think that's why people often say, "You make me a better person," to their partners. When you're with someone who has good qualities, they rub off on you, and you're the better for it.

On the other hand, I've had friends who started dating people I didn't like, and part of why our friendship drifted is because my friend changed. They became more like the person they're with. They became, to me at least, worse.

I guess most people aren't fully good or fully bad. When you're susceptible to the people around you, both positive and negative things are bound to rub off on you. Regardless, you change. You aren't just yourself anymore. You become someone different.

Ben was generous. During our relationship, he worked at the call center, then for a lawn care business. He never made a lot of money. I was living off my student loans and my part-time paycheck. We were poor, yet he insisted on paying our rent. My money went to tuition, books, and my own expenses, but he covered our shared bills. He also paid when we went out. I never bought my own drinks, dinner, or a movie ticket. He liked to spend money on me.

He wasn't just generous with me, either. He often loaned his friends money. If he had it, he gave cash to people on the streets when they asked for it. He was generous with his time too. He often helped his friends move. He built a shed for his grandma.

He was also protective. Once, we walked downtown to meet some friends at a bar. On the way, Ben stopped at a corner store to get a bottle of water, and I waited outside. Two drunk men approached me. They said, "Who do we have here?" I told them I wasn't interested in talking, and they got annoyed. One of them touched my arm. Ben ran out of the store. He pushed the man who touched me, so hard he fell over.

There were other times when I went out without Ben, and I'd try to walk home alone, but he wouldn't let me. Even if he was sleeping, he'd wake up when the bars closed, come find me, and walk me home.

I do think he was protective and generous with me partly because he saw me as someone who needed protection. I was a girl, and he was ten years older than me. I think he thought I was vulnerable. I leaned into it, too, and felt frail when I was dating him because of that. I do think he sincerely cared that I was safe and taken care of, but still, I felt like a weaker person when we were together.

I'm not someone who needs somebody to take care of me. I'm a capable and driven person. I was the first person in my family to go to university. I went despite my mom discouraging me from going. I always got good grades. Teachers said I was capable and self-sufficient. I'm employed, and I get good performance evaluations. I know how to make a budget. I have an emergency fund and retirement savings. I recently built Joy and I a deck despite never having built anything before. The best version of me isn't someone who relies on someone else. Even though I think of Ben's generosity and protection as mostly good qualities, they weren't good for me.

We weren't well matched in that way.

I left that relationship understanding more about what makes two people a good match for each other. Some people complement each other; they rub off on the other in ways that make them both better people. But some people don't complement each other, and they make each other worse.

I think Joy makes me better. She's an honest, well-meaning person who operates in the world as herself. I've become truer to myself since meeting her. I like myself more.

Ben influenced the way I presented myself, the way I dressed, and the way I thought. He told me he didn't want me to get tattoos or to cut my hair too short. He preferred when I wore dresses. Today, I would never want to be with someone who controlled how I dressed. I felt compelled to look and behave in ways he liked. I was quieter than I am now. I was out of tune with who I was when I was with him. I was more passive, self-sacrificing, and insecure.

When we got together, looking back, I was impressionable. Ben had good qualities, but he also had flaws. In my opinion, he was ignorant. He didn't support abortion rights. He was friends with a group of unpleasant men, and while I don't think he was exactly like them, I do think there's something to be said about the company we keep.

If I met Ben today, in an alternate universe where he was still alive, it would be clear to me how we differ. I would know how my opinions clash with his. I would see who he was, and who I turned out to be, distinctly. When Ben and I were together, I didn't know who I was.

When I was with him, I used to dive out of people's way on the sidewalk. I'd step into traffic before brushing an arm against someone else's. I contorted myself to avoid people, to fit the spaces between them. I wouldn't use an umbrella in the rain if it took up too much space on the sidewalk. I'd sooner get soaked. I'd dart from empty space to empty space, twisting, hopping, going sideways. Saying excuse me. Forgive me. I'm sorry.

I used to pick my clothes, hairstyle, and all aspects of my appearance based on what I thought would be perceived best by Ben, and by men in general. I wasn't cognizant I was doing that, but I was. I packaged myself to be as likable and as unobjectionable as possible.

Now I wear what I want to wear. I have tattoos. My hair is shorter and blue. I do things like reply to people who send me creepy emails rather than ignore them. I walk straight. I take up space on the sidewalk. There have even been times when I've said, "Watch it!" to people who don't give me room.

CHAPTER NINE

PROTESTORS BLOCKADE HICKORY LIBRARY

A DOZEN PROTESTERS BLOCKED THE ENTRANCE TO HICKORY LIBRARY YESTERDAY IN RESPONSE TO A RECENT STORY-TIME EVENT, BOOK BANS, AND CONTROVERSY REGARDING PORN CONSUMPTION IN THE LIBRARY.

DECLAN TURNER, ONE OF THE PROTESTORS, TOLD *THE PERT CITY TIMES*, "WE JUST WANT TO KEEP CHILDREN

SAFE. WE DON'T SUPPORT DRAG QUEENS READING TO KIDS. WE ALSO DON'T SUPPORT PORN IN THE LIBRARY. THIS IS COMMON SENSE TO US, BUT WE'RE LIVING IN STRANGE TIMES."

DRAG STORY TIMES HAVE BECOME SOMEWHAT POPULAR EVENTS AMONG LIBRARIES, BOOKSTORES, AND SCHOOLS, BUT HAVE BEEN CRITICIZED BY MANY CONSERVATIVES AND RIGHT-WING MEDIA ACROSS THE COUNTRY. ANTI-LGBTQ+ THREATS HAVE BEEN REPORTED AT SOME PROTESTS, AS WELL AS VIOLENT CONFRONTATIONS.

"THERE WAS NO VIOLENCE," TURNER REPORTED. "IT WAS A PEACEFUL PROTEST."

A GROUP OF ANTI-PROTESTORS FORMED THROUGHOUT THE DAY. JUDE WALKER, ONE OF THE ANTI-PROTESTORS, STATED, "THESE PEOPLE CLAIM THEY WANT TO KEEP CHILDREN SAFE, BUT I SAW THEM SCREAMING AT PARENTS AND KIDS TRYING TO GO TO THE LIBRARY. THEY SHOUTED OBSCENITIES AT LIBRARY STAFF AND AT US. THE HYPOCRISY IS DUMBFOUNDING."

TURNER DENIES THESE CLAIMS, STATING, "WE'RE JUST CONCERNED CITIZENS WHO BELIEVE SEXUALIZED CONTENT SHOULDN'T BE AROUND CHILDREN."

"DRAG QUEENS AREN'T INHERENTLY SEXUAL," ALEX HASTE, A DRAG PERFORMER SHARED. "DRAG HAS ROOTS IN SHAKESPEARE. WE'RE NOT TALKING ABOUT BURLESQUE HERE; WE'RE TALKING ABOUT A STORYTELLER WEARING A COSTUME. IT'S THEATER. THE REASON DRAG IS DEEMED SEXUAL BY SOME IS BECAUSE FLOUTING GENDER NORMS ARE PERCEIVED AS SEXUALLY DEVIANT, BUT THERE ISN'T NECESSARILY ANYTHING SEXUAL ABOUT DRAG."

WHEN ASKED ABOUT THE STORY-TIME EVENT THAT SPURRED THIS PROTEST, RHONDA WHEELER, LIBRARY CEO, TOLD *THE PERT CITY TIMES*, "WE HAVE NEVER HOSTED A DRAG STORY TIME. THERE SEEMS TO BE SOME CONFUSION FROM THE PROTESTORS. NO SUCH EVENT HAS TAKEN PLACE AT THAT LIBRARY."

WHEN ASKED WHETHER THE LIBRARY WOULD HOST SUCH AN EVENT, SHE SAID, "IT'S POSSIBLE. OUR LIBRARY SUPPORTS INCLUSIVE PROGRAMMING, OFFERING A WIDE RANGE FOR CHILDREN AND ADULTS. OUR AIM IS TO SUPPORT LITERACY AND COMMUNITY. AT THIS TIME, HOWEVER, WE HAVE NEVER HOSTED A DRAG STORY TIME."

THE PROTESTERS REFUSED TO LEAVE THE ENTRANCE AFTER POLICE ISSUED A DISPERSAL ORDER, ACCORDING TO HASTE. "THEY DIDN'T MAKE ARRESTS, THOUGH," HASTE STATED. "THEY DIDN'T MAKE THE MOB OF PEOPLE MOVE. SHAME ON OUR POLICE. A GROUP OF FANATICS SHOULD NOT BE ALLOWED TO CONTROL WHO ENTERS OUR LIBRARIES."

The Pert City Times shared a link to the article on Facebook. That's where I found it. I scroll down and click to see who's shared it, and eventually find myself on the *Liberty Lately* Facebook page. They shared the article with the comment: BIAS LIBERAL MEDIA STRIKES AGAIN!

I scroll down and see that Douglas, an old friend of Ben's and one of my nude photo suspects, has liked this article.

I narrow my eyes. That doesn't bode well for him as someone on my list.

I click his profile.

I deleted all of Ben's friends off social media when we broke up, except for Doug. I wasn't close with any of Ben's friends. I felt out of place and timid around them. They were all Ben's age or older, and they rarely had other girls around. A group of them rented a house together. Sometimes I'd visit with Ben. The house always had an assortment of bongs on the coffee table, dirty dishes piled in the sink, and it smelled musty, like unwashed clothes. There were posters of *Fight Club* and *The Godfather* on the walls. I've never been inside a dirtier bathroom. The sink was encrusted in different colors of facial hair stubble. The floor, shower, and walls were coated in a thick layer of grime. I remember discreetly asking Ben to go back to our house rather than have to face peeing in that bathroom. In the fraught and harrowing instances when I did resort to using their toilet, I hovered over it and held my breath.

Whenever we were at that house, I sat quietly next to Ben. His friends often commented that I was shy. So I'd smile and make a remark here or there, but mostly I was mute. His friends were loud and aggressive, and when they drank, our visits almost always ended in a physical fight. They all made uncomfortable, sexual comments about women. I often felt insecure and unsafe around them. I never had a real conversation with any of them, except for one time with Douglas.

It was around midnight on a weekday. Ben had fallen asleep on their couch. The other guys had retreated to their bedrooms. Doug and I were the only ones left awake.

He asked, "Do you want to watch *Sleeping Beauty*?"

I said, "Like, the princess cartoon?"

He nodded. "Yeah. Have you seen it?"

At this time, Doug was a gruff almost-thirty-year-old man. He hadn't changed or showered since finishing his workday in construction. He was wearing a high-visibility vest, he had mud on his face, and black dirt embedded beneath his fingernails.

I said, "I've seen it, yeah. Have you?"

At first, I thought maybe he was making fun of me. I thought he was asking me if I wanted to watch a children's cartoon because I was nineteen.

He said, "Yeah. It was me and my sister's favorite growing up. I've seen it like, a thousand times. I like Merryweather best."

I said, "Who is Merryweather?"

He was already trying to get the movie on the TV. "You don't know who Merryweather is? She's one of Aurora's fairy godmothers. She's the one who wears blue. She's hilarious."

He grinned as the movie started playing. His eyes were bright, and his face looked animated, innocent. I remember thinking I could tell what he looked like when he was a little boy. He was in his late twenties, he was still young, but he smoked and drank a lot. He had a receding hairline, a physically taxing job, and he looked tired, worn-out, and old. That night, I could see his features soften, his skin become smooth, and his facial hair disappear.

I said, "I always liked *The Lion King* best."

"Oh yeah, that's a good one too," he said.

As the movie progressed, I noticed his face dimmed. By

the halfway point, his eyes were watery. He looked like he might cry.

I asked, "Are you okay?"

He rubbed his eyes. "Yeah. I'm just thinking about my sister."

I asked, "Why is that making you sad?"

"We don't really talk anymore." He wasn't looking at me.

"Oh, I'm sorry," I said.

He asked, "Do you have siblings?"

I said, "No. I always wanted one, though."

"When I was a kid, I always didn't want one." He was still rubbing his eyes. I could tell he was trying to hide that he was crying.

I asked, "What happened between you and your sister?"

"She doesn't like that I drink," he said.

At the time, I was naive and didn't understand that likely meant he had a drinking problem. I thought his sister must be oddly puritanical or anti-alcohol.

"I should probably stop drinking," he added.

I said, "Yeah, why not? If that would help you stay close with your sister. Who needs to drink, anyway? I don't even like drinking, honestly. And if it makes you feel sad not to talk to your sister, why not quit?"

"You're right," he said. He was looking at me now. His eyes were wet. I don't know if I'd ever made direct eye contact with him before. He said, "I'm glad Ben's dating you. It's nice having you around."

He still drank throughout my relationship with Ben. I remember he got a DUI the year before we broke up, and I've seen from his social media that he still drinks. There are cans of beer in the background of his pictures. Photos of him out with a pint on the table.

The night we watched *Sleeping Beauty* endeared me to him, but Douglas still isn't someone I would trust with a naked picture of me.

I can feel sympathy for someone and still not trust them.

I open his profile. I scroll down through his posts. He mostly reposts political memes mocking liberal politicians. There are a few photos of him with friends, drinking.

I keep scrolling until I see Ben's face. I pause.

It's a picture of the two of them in the back seat of a car. They have cigarettes hanging from their mouths. They're both grinning. The picture is captioned: BENNY BOY.

After Ben and I broke up, I couldn't look at pictures of him for a long time. I tried to ignore my feelings about him, quash them down, and forge ahead. I've always thought of myself as the villain in Ben's story, and I do still think I made mistakes, but now that I'm letting myself really think about him, I realize he made mistakes too.

I used to think that if I weren't gay, Ben and I would still be together, but I don't think so anymore. Ben wasn't the uncomplicated victim I thought he was. I was too young for him. We weren't equals. When we got together, he inundated me with attention and compliments. It was manipulative. I tried to play the part of his girlfriend, and to be who he wanted me to be. A coy, shy, helpless girl. It's clear he didn't really know me. I disappeared in our relationship. How did he not notice? I was really young and inexperienced, but he wasn't.

I feel sympathy for him, and I regret that I hurt him, but if I'd faced my feelings about this earlier, when he was alive, maybe he'd say that he regretted things too.

"That is suspicious that he follows *Liberty Lately*," Joy says. "He probably took a screenshot of your nude and sent it to Declan."

"Yeah, that's what I'm thinking too," I say.

"What an asshole. What are you going to do?"

"I'm going to call him out on it," I say. "I'm going to contact him."

"And say what?"

"Fuck you."

She laughs. "What's the point of doing that?"

"Fine, I won't do that. I'm going to find a naked picture of him and send it to *Liberty Lately*," I say. "See how he likes it."

She snorts. "No you're not. Don't do that. You're going to get yourself in trouble."

"Don't worry. I won't send it from my work email," I say.

"Don't send it from any email, Darcy. Sending naked pictures of people is, like, revenge porn. And we're making a lot of assumptions. It might not even be the guy from *Liberty Lately*, let alone Douglas. Who knows?"

"Who else would it be?" I ask.

TRY NOT TO POST THIS ON THE INTERNET Joy texts me with a naked photo of her. It's her reflection in a bathroom mirror. Her hair and skin are wet, and the mirror is foggy.

I heart the picture, then take one under my shirt and send it to her.

FEEL FREE TO POST THIS ONE. EVERYONE'S ALREADY SEEN IT.

I save Joy's photo in a folder on my phone titled JOY NAKED. She is aware of the folder and finds it hysterical. I'm a librarian; someone concerned with preserving informational assets and memories. I've explained to her, "I save these pictures as an archive."

She laughs. "Mhm. I'm sure that's why you save them."

I scroll through the photos. In one, she's lying in our bed. Her hair is fanned out behind her. Her face is pink and sleep flushed. Some of the photos are of us together. In one, we're topless at a hotel, kissing in the mirror. In another, she's in the bath, with beads of water on her chest. There's a close-up of her back; there's a sunburn on her shoulders. Our legs are tangled together in another, both half-dressed, our skin pressed together. There's a blurry photo she took of herself naked and laughing—with her chin jutted into her neck.

Despite my better judgment, I attempted to introduce Kyle to Lou and Toulouse again. I followed the same protocol I did last time. I placed cat food on either side of the living room. I scattered boxes for them to hide in. I also purchased and sprayed a synthetic pheromone that was supposed to make the cats feel calm.

The pheromone did not make the cats feel calm. In fact, I think it might have made them angrier. This attempt was worse than the first. Lou charged at Kyle. Kyle stood his ground and fought back. Toulouse stood in the wings, howling, as if cheering Lou on. I was screaming. I had to pull the cats apart. I got scratched and severely bitten on my arm. The bite left two puncture marks near my wrist. It looks like I was bitten by a fanged vampire bat.

I've locked Kyle back in the workshop like a criminal in solitary confinement. I'm angry at Lou for biting him. I'm angry at Toulouse for egging her on. I've locked both cats out of my bedroom due to my disappointment in their behavior. I can hear them yodeling on the other side of the door, pawing, desperate to come in—but they're not welcome.

Instead, I'm staring into the blue glow of my laptop, nursing my wrist, scowling at Doug's Facebook page. I'm brooding about how despicable it is for this guy to screenshot my accidental nude and share it with anti-library, bigoted extremists. I've been nothing but kind to this guy. Despite some serious imperfections, I saw the good in him. I associated him with buffoonish fairy godmothers and loving his sister.

HI DOUG, I write on Facebook Messenger.

HEY, he replies quickly.

LONG TIME NO CHAT, I write.

YEAH, FOR REAL. WHAT'S UP?

CAN I SPEAK TO YOU ON THE PHONE?

WHY?

I HAVE A SERIOUS TOPIC TO DISCUSS.

OKAY, SURE. HERE'S MY NUMBER: 555-555-0156.

"Hello. Dougie speaking."

"Hi, this is Darcy," I say.

"Hey girl, what's up? How're you doing?"

He has a raspy voice.

I inhale, preparing to confront him. "I'm all right, thank you. How are you?"

"I'm okay. I think I know why you're calling."

"Oh yeah?" I narrow my eyes.

"Mhm. It's because you heard about Benny, right?"

My stomach drops.

He goes on, "I didn't see you at the funeral. I looked for you. I thought maybe you'd show. Were you there? I'm sorry if I missed you."

"O-oh, no," I say. "I-I didn't hear about it until after, unfortunately."

"Ah damn," he says. "I'm sorry. Maybe I should have messaged you or something. My bad. I didn't think of it."

I say, "Oh, that's okay. You had other things on your mind, I'm sure. I don't live in the area anymore, anyway. I probably couldn't have made it regardless."

"Right, right. So, are you calling to find out what happened, then?"

My throat is spasming. "Yes."

"Okay. So, it was a brain aneurysm. Apparently, it was really quick and it didn't hurt. He came home from work one day, and I guess there was this weak spot in his brain. The doctors told us it was instant. He may have had a headache before, but he didn't even know it was happening, and he wouldn't have felt any pain. That's what they told his family, and I don't think they were lying. I really think it was quick and it didn't hurt."

My eyes are closed. I have a hand cupped over them. I feel relieved he didn't kill himself, but I'm shaken by the details.

"Had you talked to him much recently?" he asks.

"No." My voice breaks. "We hadn't spoken in years."

"Ah, man. Well, you know, he always loved you," he says.

I'm crying. "Thanks, Dougie."

"No problem, honey. Take care, all right?"

"Thanks. You too. Bye."

CHAPTER
TEN

I'm sifting through the Rubbermaid bins filled with books, questioning if I should really get rid of them. It's three a.m. I can't sleep.

What if I regret getting rid of these books? What if I want to read them again someday? I change a lot. I have no idea who I'll be in a year, or five, and what I'll want to read in a few years. I could be a totally different person. I could love these books. I could hate everything I've kept.

I sit down and look around the cluttered room. I don't feel well. I put my hand to my forehead.

I wonder what it feels like to have an aneurism.

Maybe I should get rid of every single book in this house and start fresh. Maybe we have too many books. Maybe that's the problem.

No. What am I thinking? What about Joy? Maybe my mom is right. Maybe my problem is that I think about myself too much. I obsess about what I want. What I feel. What works for me. A lot of these books don't even belong to me. This isn't just my library. We collected most of what we have here together.

I keep seeing Ben's face on the inside of my eyelids. I hope he didn't know it was happening. I don't think he'd want to know it was happening.

Why am I organizing these books anyway? I won't read all these books again. I haven't even read many of them. What am I amassing these for? What am I going to do with them? What's the point?

"Someone just emailed me photos of myself," Mordecai says.

"That's nice," I reply mindlessly. We're both working in the back. I just returned from the bathroom, where I spent the last twenty minutes crying. I didn't sleep last night.

I keep picturing Ben collapsing without warning. His dad finding out. The funeral. Ben's body in a casket. In the ground.

I was able to compose myself and return to the desk, but I feel drained. Not just because I'm tired, I'm also dehydrated. I think I've cried all the liquid out of my body. I'm a prune of a person, just clacking at a keyboard, devoid of moisture, a dry husk, incapable of forming tears.

Is This a Cry for Help?

I want to distract myself. I try to focus on planning our human library program. It will be open to the public, but I'm also working with a teacher from a college in Pert City to invite her class of sociology students. The professor assigned a project dependant upon their participation in the program. I'm advertising that we'll have food, which I find also helps ensure attendance.

I need to coordinate more with the "books." Each human book comes prepared with a story to share. The "borrower" will ask the "book" questions, and they'll chat for fifteen minutes. The program is meant to bridge divides and combat prejudice by facilitating conversation between people from different backgrounds. So far, we have a firefighter, a person living with HIV, a person living without stable housing, a Muslim woman, a veteran, a cancer survivor, an ex-convict, a man who is blind, an Indigenous person from the Anishinaabe people, and a palliative care nurse.

"No," Mordecai says. "It's *not* nice. They sent me pre-transition photos of myself."

"What?" I look up from my computer.

He turns his monitor toward me.

The email is titled I KNOW YOUR SECRET, and old photos of Mordecai are attached. The photos depict him as a child, wearing dresses. One is of him as a teenager. He's at the beach building a sandcastle in a green tankini.

It's not a secret that Mordecai is trans. He worked here before he started transitioning, and he often mentions that he's trans. In fact, I've seen most of these photos before because Mordecai has shared them himself on social media. He often posts his old childhood pictures.

I get up and stand behind his chair. "Can you show me who sent it?"

He closes the photos so I can see the metadata in the email.

My mouth opens involuntarily. It's from EaglesNest88@gmail.com.

He says, "Who the hell is EaglesNest88? This is unnerving. And as if they 'know my secret.' Give me a break. This one is my profile picture on all my social media!"

It's of him at about seven, wearing comically large glasses. His hair is in pigtails and he's sticking out his tongue.

"This is supposed to be threatening, isn't it?" he says. "You know who I bet it's from, one of those protestors. They were hollering at me on my way to work the other day. The man who threatened to spit on me, screaming "groomer." I bet it's him. What should we do? Should we call Brenda?"

"Make sure he keeps the email," Brenda says. "Please don't delete it. We need to keep a record of everything. I'll talk to the police right away. Is he upset? How's he doing?"

He's standing beside me listening. He mouths, *I'm fine.*

"He's fine," I say.

"Okay. Please remind him we offer counseling services as part of the employee assistance program," she says.

"I'll let him know."

"Thank you, Darcy. While I have you, I want to mention that we've scheduled that community forum to review our policies next Monday. It's posted on our website."

"Good to know. I didn't see. Thank you."

"No problem. I'll see you there. Thanks for letting me know about this."

"Yeah, no problem. Sounds good. Bye."

When I hang up, Mordecai snorts. "As if I need counseling services because of an asinine email. How fragile does Brenda think I am?"

I frown. "It wouldn't make you fragile—"

"I'm fine," he assures me. "I'm outraged by the gall of whoever this is. If anything, it's ridiculous. I do think this email is intended to be harassment, but is it criminal? And would the cops care? I bet nothing's going to come of Brenda calling them. They did zilch after the protestors threatened us and blocked the library from patrons. The cops aren't going to care about someone sending me pictures of myself if they don't even care about that."

I rub my eyes. "You're probably right."

He lowers his voice and leans closer to me. "And you know what? Between you and me, I'd rather take it into my own hands anyway."

I furrow my brow. "What do you mean?"

"I mean *I'm* going to find out who emailed me this, and I'll deal with them myself."

I squint at him. Is he secretly involved in some back-alley, vigilante justice?

I glance around us to check if anyone is eavesdropping. Ahmad and Doris, who are both pages, are working nearby. They're sorting returned books, chatting to each other. I don't think they're listening.

"How?" I whisper. "What do you mean?"

He says, "I mean I'll find out who sent this myself."

"And then what? What will you do once you find out?"

He shrugs. "I'll decide what to do next once I know. Maybe I'll confront them. Maybe I'll publicly expose them."

We look at each other for a moment.

I like to follow rules. I appreciate protocol, established steps, clear guidelines, and order. I'm starting to recognize, however, that sometimes our established processes don't work, and deviation is necessary.

I say, "That's not a terrible approach."

He smirks. "Will you help me?"

I glance at Ahmad and Doris. They're inspecting a large book that appears to be damaged.

I say, "Yeah, I'll help you, but I need to confess something first."

"What?"

Very quietly I say, "EaglesNest88 emailed me too."

"*What?*" he says, way too loudly.

Ahmad and Doris both look at us. Mordecai says, "Sorry! I just got excited about something!"

I smile at them awkwardly.

They both turn back to the damaged book.

I whisper, "It happened last week. It was similarly vague and threatening. I'd accidentally posted a naked photo of myself on Instagram not long ago, and they somehow got their hands on it."

He gasps. "Did you tell Brenda?"

"No."

"Why not?"

"I didn't want her to see or know about the photo. Plus, I don't think she can do anything. I'm of the same mind as you.

I don't think Brenda or the cops are any more positioned to deal with it than I am."

"Than *we* are," he corrects me. "We're going to get to the bottom of this together."

Mordecai and I are now sitting at a desk, scrolling through Declan Turner's Facebook profile.

"He's the prime suspect," Mordecai says.

"But how would he get our photos?" I ask.

Mordecai is manning the mouse. He says, "And why does he post so many pictures of grass? Oh wow, and all the photos he's posted of himself are hazy selfies taken from an extremely low angle. I feel like I'm in his lap. Gross. Did he rub Vaseline on his lens before taking these? And he's not smiling in a single picture. What's his problem?"

He scrolls down. Declan has posted to his own wall several times, seemingly attempting to enter queries in the search bar.

LIBERTY LATELY

SHERYL ESTEVEZ

SHERYL ESTEVEZ

He's also posted a review for an HVAC company to his own wall. It says: "LET ME START BY SAYING THESE GUYS ARE TOTAL SCAMMERS. I'D SOONER HIRE A DONKEY TO SERVICE MY A/C. STRONGLY RECOMMEND IF YOU WANT TO WASTE YOUR TIME AND MONEY."

I snort. "He really doesn't seem like he's capable of breaking into our social media. I know it doesn't take a genius, but—"

"Yeah, this is a man who should really join us for Tech Literacy Tuesdays. There's no way he's breaking into our private accounts. But maybe it's one of his buddies?"

He opens up Declan's friend list and begins to scroll.

"Some of these people do look familiar. I think they were at the protest," Mordecai says.

I hear a ding from my computer. I get up to check it. It's an email from the bird patron. It says, CAN I ASK QUESTIONS THAT AREN'T ABOUT BIRDS?

I squint, wondering what's prompted this turn in their interests. It's hard to tell over email, but I sense a subtle, ominous shift in their tone.

I hit reply and type, YES, OF COURSE, YOU CAN ASK ANYTHING.

"How do you feel now that you know what happened?" Dr. Jeong says. I told her about the conversation I had with Doug last night. I didn't mention why I called him, and I didn't get into the nude photo issue. I just shared that I spoke to Ben's friend and learned how he died.

"I'm relieved it wasn't suicide," I say. "I'm glad he didn't die because he felt hopeless or depressed. But still, it's awful to think of him dying this way too. The way he died still feels—I mean. I guess there's no way he could die that would feel okay. It's horrible no matter what, but this feels senseless."

She says, "It does feel senseless when someone dies unexpectedly from something like an aneurysm."

"Yeah. It just seems, like, disturbingly casual. His life wasn't finished. It's—I don't know. It feels gross and absurd.

Though, to be honest, I'm struggling with talking to you so much about how *I feel*. Do you know what I mean? Like, when I come here and we talk about my feelings, it seems sort of insensitive. Like, Ben is dead. He can't feel anything, and I'm just obsessively talking about my own thoughts and feelings. It's sort of sickening. It makes me hate myself."

She nods. "People often feel self-absorbed in therapy. I appreciate your opening up about that. The purpose is to explore your thoughts and feelings, though. That's what we're doing here. It's important. It's not self-absorbed to talk about yourself in therapy."

I close my eyes and exhale. Maybe I'm just trying to avoid talking about how I feel. It would be nice if I could choose my own feelings. I wish that's how it worked.

I grimace. "I feel very guilty about Ben."

"I know you do."

My eyes are still closed. "I think I ruined his life."

"You aren't responsible for the trajectory of Ben's life."

I'm imagining what Ben's life would be like if we stayed together. He'd live in a nicer house. He'd take his kid fishing. Maybe I would have told him to go to the doctor for his headache, and they'd catch the problem. Or maybe he wouldn't have had the problem at all. How do aneurysms form? Is it stress? Did it grow because of me?

"I feel like I'm responsible," I say. My eyes are still closed, but my tears have slithered out of my eyelids and are slipping down my cheeks. "I feel responsible."

"Why do you feel you're responsible?" she asks.

I sniff. "If we hadn't gotten together at all, maybe Ben would have met someone else. He'd spend those five years we were together with another girl, or a few other girls. Or maybe he'd never date anyone. He'd take a different route in life, live free of any heartbreak, get a dog. Be happy."

"Do you feel Ben might also be responsible for those five years you lost when you were with him? Perhaps you would have met someone else. Perhaps you would have taken a different route in life."

I'm imagining what my life would be like if we stayed together. I would have been so unhappy.

I open my eyes. My vision is blurry. "No, I don't think he's responsible, but I'm happy where I am now. I don't really feel like I *lost* those five years. It's not like they were meaningless. I just wish it were different."

"You can wish things were different without being responsible for how they are."

"The way he died makes me feel like life is meaningless.

Maybe I shouldn't have said that. Telling psychiatrists you feel like life is meaningless is perhaps ill-advised. I want her to think I'm getting better. I don't want her to put me back into in-patient care. I didn't love the experience. I had to sleep in a room with my door open. The bed was small and uncomfortable. I was fed hospital food I found very off-putting. There was a lot of frozen cubed carrots and peas. Joy could only visit at designated times, and she was anxious when she did. I missed the cats, and our bed. I was eager to get better and go home.

"I know what you mean," Dr. Jeong says. "Questioning the meaning of life when someone dies, especially the way Ben died, is natural. I think most of us question that when we're facing death, especially death that feels random. It's okay to feel like life is meaningless."

"Really?" I ask.

"Yes. I think so." She nods. "I'm not sure it matters whether life feels meaningful. I think it matters whether you find it worthwhile. And am I right in saying that you do find it worthwhile? From our sessions, I get the sense that you care a lot about your relationships with people, even with Ben, and you value life."

I rub my eyes.

"Yeah," I say. "I do."

"I haven't been sleeping well," I tell Joy.

Toulouse is sitting on my chest, purring like a revving engine.

"Me either," she says.

"Because of the crying baby?"

"Partly, but I'm also just used to sleeping with you, in our bed. Have you been taking your sleeping pill?"

"Sometimes," I say. "But it's still hard to fall asleep when I'm alone here."

"Are you kept awake worrying about burglars breaking in, and me not being there to protect you?"

I snort. "If a burglar broke in, you'd be no help. I'm the one who'd be defending us."

She laughs. "Yeah right. You're dreaming."

I say, "The reason it's hard for me to sleep, actually, is because I'm so accustomed to hearing the dulcet hum of you babbling and snoring next to me. I can't sleep without it."

"I don't snore," she says.

I laugh. Toulouse jumps off my chest.

CHAPTER ELEVEN

HOW OLD DO YOU HAVE TO BE TO GET AN ABORTION? CAN YOUR PARENTS FIND OUT WHEN YOU'VE HAD ONE? AND WHERE DO YOU GO TO GET ONE?

This is the email I received this morning from Sammy, the bird patron. My heart sinks when I read it. *Is Sammy a pregnant minor?*

I begin to research the answer. I pause after a moment of typing. Why would there be an age restriction? There's no way the rule is, "You have to be at least twelve years old to have an abortion," right? That would be atrocious. It's not like riding a roller coaster or buying tobacco.

I rub my eyes, and the pressure triggers a visual response on the back of my eyelids. I see flashes of color and light. I'm not thinking straight. I really hope Sammy isn't a pregnant child. What a hideous thought. This poor little bird-obsessed kid.

I hope these questions are for a school project. Or maybe Sammy is just curious. I read it over again.

Can your parents find out when you've had one . . . where do you go . . .

My heart sinks again.

Juice drips from the tangerine I'm peeling. I'm sitting outside on the picnic table. It's well past six, but it's still light out.

I had an abortion when I was twenty-three. I got pregnant near the end of my relationship with Ben. It was a shock. I was on birth control. I missed some days, though. It was exam season. I was busy and stressed. I forgot to take a pill one night, then took it the next day. There were other days when I took the pills at irregular times. I wasn't the best at staying on top of it, to say the least.

I put a tangerine slice in my mouth.

After feeling sick for several days, I decided to take a pregnancy test. I was in a Walmart bathroom. The test was positive, so I took two more. They all said I was pregnant.

There's a seed in the tangerine. I spit it across the grass.

The next day I went to a clinic where I was given two forms of medicine. Mifepristone and misoprostol. Mifepristone blocks progesterone, a hormone needed to maintain a pregnancy. The next day, I took the misoprostol. I had to put four little pills between my cheek and gums. That gave me contractions. It was painful. I took the painkillers they'd prescribed. For the most part, it felt like having an intense period. I told Ben I was sick and sat in the bathtub for a day. I continued to bleed for about three days. I pretended my period came early, and then I thought about all the things I'd been pretending.

I thought I wanted what Ben wanted, but I didn't. I dreaded the idea of him touching me, let alone the prospect of us getting married. I was on one side of a wall—aching, bleeding into our bathtub—and he was on the other side, playing video games, oblivious.

The woman I cheated on him with came to mind. I remembered her breath in my ear. The amber scent of her skin. I thought of the conversation we had that night; her voice, her opinions, and how she saw the world. I remembered looking into her face, and the recognition I saw in her eyes. I thought of all women and all men. I tried to picture myself as an elderly woman taking care of my elderly husband, and I felt sick. I then imagined myself as an old woman, holding another old woman's hand.

While I sat in that gross, murky bathwater, I felt myself split in two. I was no longer the person I knew myself to be. I understood the world differently. I felt both older and new. I just knew. I was gay.

I've shared Sammy's email with Mordecai to ask for his opinion about how best to handle it.

"Is there anything I should do besides answer?" I ask. "I need to help this kid."

He's furrowing his brow, reading the email for a third time.

"So, this person's sent us several emails in the past, right?" he asks.

"Yes, but the previous emails were completely unrelated to this one. All their other questions were about birds."

He tilts his head. "When did they start sending us those bird requests?"

I think for a moment. "I got the first one when I returned to work. I think it was on my first day back, actually. Why? What are you thinking?"

He hums. "I think it's strange for this person to email us this question. They could google the answer."

I squint at him. "Okay. Yes, but that's the case with a lot of reference questions, though, isn't it?"

"This is more urgent. This is a time-sensitive problem, and there are so many resources for someone in this situation. Something about it just isn't making sense."

I frown. "I guess. But what's your point? They did send it to us, so—"

"I have an inkling that this is from one of the protestors," he says. "I think they're fishing to see how we respond to questions like this. They want to make us out to be abortion-loving, porn-obsessed perverts. They're probably trying to concoct some story for *Liberty Lately*."

"What?" I say, shocked. "That can't be it. Could it? This person has been sending us bird requests for weeks. Why would they ask us all those questions? What would be the point of that?"

"I don't know." He rubs his jaw. "Maybe they thought we'd let our guard down."

I look at the email and wonder if he's right. Would they really go to these lengths for a weird long-con? I frown at the words on my screen. *How old do you have to be . . .* Part of me hopes he's right. I hope weirdos are just harassing me, and there's no actual pregnant kid.

I ask, "What should we do?"

He says, "I have no idea."

I stare at my monitor. I already know what I have to do. I exhale.

DEAR SAMMY,

THERE ARE NO AGE RESTRICTIONS IN OUR AREA TO GET AN ABORTION. THERE IS NO REQUIREMENT FOR PARENTAL CONSENT, AND HEALTH CARE PROVIDERS AIM TO MAKE SURE PATIENTS RECEIVE CONFIDENTIAL TREATMENT.

NOTE: IN CASES WHERE A DOCTOR DEEMS A PATIENT UNDER THE AGE OF SIXTEEN INCAPABLE OF UNDERSTANDING THE NATURE OF THEIR MEDICAL TREATMENT, THEY MIGHT DISCUSS PARENTAL INVOLVEMENT; HOWEVER, MINORS HAVE THE RIGHT TO PRIVACY REGARDING THEIR HEALTH CARE.

I HAVE ATTACHED A LIST OF LOCAL CLINICS IN THE AREA THAT PROVIDE ABORTION SERVICES. MANY HOSPITALS ALSO PROVIDE ABORTIONS SERVICES.

PLANNED PARENTHOOD, WHOSE WEBSITE AND CONTACT INFORMATION I'VE ALSO ATTACHED, IS AN EXCELLENT RESOURCE FOR ADDITIONAL INFORMATION.

IF YOU NEED ANY MORE ASSISTANCE, PLEASE LET US KNOW.

"I didn't tell anyone I had an abortion, including Ben," I tell Dr. Jeong.

I brought this up because I couldn't stop thinking about Sammy. I also thought maybe discussing it might help me come to terms with the choices I've made.

"Why did you keep that to yourself?" she asks.

"I knew Ben wouldn't want me to get an abortion," I say. "He'd be upset, maybe even angry, if I suggested it. I knew it wouldn't feel like an option anymore if I told him, so I didn't."

"Have you told others about it since?"

"Yes. I've told Joy," I say. "I've told friends also. I mention it to people. It's not a secret."

"And how do you feel about the abortion now?"

"I feel good about it. I've always felt good about it, though. Immediately after taking the medicine, I felt intense relief. I thought I'd feel sad, maybe I'd cry and wonder how I could have gone through with it. But I didn't feel any regret at all."

I remember sitting in the Walmart bathroom, looking at the positive tests. I knew if I told Ben, he would want to marry me. It wouldn't be ideal to be pregnant before the wedding, but we would have figured it out. I'd be done with my master's degree by the time the baby was born. My mom would be upset at first, but then happy, maybe even relieved. I looked at the test and realized I could become the person I always thought I wanted to be. Everything I thought I wanted would come true.

I say, "I think that pregnancy is what helped me realize that Ben and I needed to break up, actually."

"Why is that?" she asks.

"I remember feeling something inside me resist. I looked at the positive pregnancy tests like they were cursed. The idea of going through with it felt wrong. I had this deep sense that it wasn't right."

It was around this time that I felt extreme clarity, like my brain abruptly finished developing, the smoke dissipated, and I was lucid for the first time in my life. I felt like someone who'd been in a trance, waking up.

I say, "I realized the prospect of *really* having a baby, *really* getting married to Ben, *really* committing myself to the life I'd been working toward felt grim. It helped me realize I wanted to take a different route in life."

Rather than attempt to introduce Kyle to Lou and Toulouse face-to-face again, I've taken a step back. I've carefully carried him inside the house and shut him behind the door to our bedroom. I've directed Lou and Toulouse to the other side of the door, so they can sniff at each other with a barrier between them. I've placed treats and cans of salmon pâté on both sides of the door in an attempt to make the interaction more pleasant.

I'm now standing with my arms crossed outside the room, observing Lou and Toulouse. I am a cat bouncer. I watch them sniff at the crack beneath the door. After several hearty whiffs, they both leave their mouths open slightly. They look comically shocked, but I know this is called the flehmen response. Cats do this to draw scents deeper into this organ they have in their mouths that helps them process and analyze pheromones.

I hear a low, guttural moan from Kyle on the other side.

Toulouse starts hissing. Lou is swatting at the door.

"You're okay," I say serenely, in a vain attempt to calm them down.

There's a loud bang on the door. Kyle is thrashing himself against it, like an angry man in a cage.

I'm in bed looking at the ceiling. It's smooth. Secure.

The ceiling above the mattress I slept on with Ben collapsed on us one night. There was a loud buckling sound before it fell. It was dark. We couldn't tell where the sound was coming from. The ceiling crashed down on us while we were sleeping.

We held our heads where the plaster hit us. Ben flipped on the lights. We found the room clouded with dust. Chunks of plaster debris lay in our blankets, and all over the room. There was powder in our hair. I remember hacking, looking up into the exposed structure of the ceiling. We could see the wooden lath, the joists, and insulation.

In retrospect, it's strange how startled we were. There had been this huge, visible crack for a long time, and all these little hairline cracks, and they kept getting bigger, and bigger. My heart was racing. I couldn't believe it finally fell.

"Do you have a minute? I have an idea," Mordecai says.

I'm sitting at the reference desk like an undead person. I still haven't slept through the night. I feel slow and devoid of energy.

I nod, and he leads me to a computer. He sits down at the chair, and I stand behind him, rubbing my eyes. He's opened the email he received from EaglesNest88. He clicks the ellipsis next to the reply arrow in the email header, then clicks *Show Original*.

As he clicks, he explains, "I'm looking for a line that starts with "Received: from" in the message headers. It'll show the IP address."

He finds it. He then opens the *Liberty Lately* website. He opens the Command prompt by searching CMD in the Windows search bar. He types: "ping LibertyNews.com," then clicks enter. The IP address of the website is in the command output.

While he compares the two numbers, he says, "IP addresses can be rerouted, so it's not perfect, but—" He gasps. "It's the same."

"What?" I squint.

He looks at me. "It's the same IP address. It *was* Declan."

"Wow," I say. "Are you serious? How the hell did he get that picture of me?"

"I have no clue," he says.

"Wait." I frown. "Can you open one of those bird emails now?"

"Sure," he says. He clicks through the reference email inbox until he opens the abortion email that we got from Sammy. He goes to the email header and clicks until we see the IP address enclosed in square brackets.

He copies the number and pastes beside the other two. We're both silent.

They're all the same.

***

"It was Declan," I tell Joy. I'm sitting outside on the picnic table.

I explain how Mordecai tracked the IP addresses.

"Holy shit," she says. "That's unnerving. Is this man a psychopath? He's gone to those lengths to, what? Intimidate you? What's his end goal? What the fu— *Wait*. How did he get that picture of you?"

"I don't know," I say. "That's what's disturbing me too. I guess maybe someone who follows me took a screenshot and sent it to him?"

"Wow. But who would do that?"

"I don't know," I say. "I was thinking, maybe my cousin Tucker?"

He's the only person remaining on my list of suspects.

I've had several uncomfortable conversations with Tucker at family events. We don't see eye to eye. He's mentioned that he doesn't support gay marriage, immigration, pronouns, vaccines, and he loathes the liberal government to a degree that I consider fanatical. He has bumper stickers about it. He wears branded, anti-liberal clothes. I'm often tempted to delete him off social media, but I've resisted because it would upset my mother.

She says, "How would Tucker be associated with Declan, though? Tucker lives where you grew up—that's like three hours away."

"I don't know," I say.

"God. I don't like this. Do you feel unsafe?"

I say, "No, I feel safe. Don't worry."

"Well, I *am* worried, but I have some good news," she says.

"What?"

"I'm coming home tomorrow, so I can protect you from the creeps."

I sit up. "Are you really coming home?"

"Yes. I was already planning to before I heard about this, but I'm glad I'll be home soon."

I grin.

"They all seem to know each other," Mordecai says. He and I are in the lunchroom. A local bakery brought us doughnuts. I'm eating a honey cruller.

I told him about Tucker. I say, "I don't think there's anyone else who follows me who would send my picture to an alt-right news source. Maybe I'm overlooking someone or something. I don't know. My cousin does run in a crowd that's similar to Declan's."

Mordecai puts his apple fritter down. "You know, I realized something when I was digging into this. Everything that's happened—the protests, the article—it's all the same group of people. They go to libraries all over. You can see the same faces in the photos. Most of them aren't from this area. If your cousin is involved in similar online communities, I think *it is* possible he's involved. It's a relatively small group. They're the ones trying to get books banned too. Did you know that? There was this analysis that found only eleven adults file sixty percent of book challenges. Isn't that wild? It's a very small number of vocal, determined people, and they all know each other."

I'm combing through Tucker's social media. He doesn't follow *Liberty Lately*, or Declan Turner, but he does follow quite a few similar accounts. Alternative and conservative news outlets. Alt-right political leaders and celebrities. Anti-feminist, men's-rights influencers.

I think of Tucker as a direct and blunt person. He's unable to interact with me without mentioning that he doesn't condone my "lifestyle." I know a lot of my extended family are uncomfortable with my politics, and with me being gay, but most of them don't say anything. They awkwardly avoid discussing it. Tucker, on the other hand, struggles to keep his thoughts to himself. There have been several instances when he and I have gone head-to-head.

In some ways, I appreciate that he's honest and up front. I know where he stands. There's no ambiguity. I don't have to waste mental energy interpreting him. He demonstrates emotional honesty, and I admire that. I also think that being exposed to people like Tucker has helped me better understand who I am. I've never felt more affirmed, or certain of myself or my beliefs, than the times I've sat across from Tucker at a family dinner and listened to him express his opinions.

I only see him once every couple of years. Despite that, I do think I could ask him if he knows Declan, and he'd tell me.

"Tucker speaking."

I texted my aunt, his mom, asking for Tucker's phone number. I've never called him before.

"Hi, Tucker, it's your cousin Darcy. This is going to be a strange conversation," I warn him immediately. I'm cutting right to the chase.

"Hey Darcy. Okay. Uh, it's already strange that you're calling me, to be honest. I don't think we've ever spoken on the phone before, have we?"

"Do you know Declan Turner?"

"Hm. That name does sort of ring a bell. Why? Who is he?"

I inhale. "He runs *Liberty Lately*. Have you heard of them?"

"*Liberty Lately*? What's that? Like, news?"

"Sort of. Can I ask you another question? It's a little bit of a weird one."

"Sure. Hit me."

"Have you ever taken a screenshot of something I've posted on social media? Like an Instagram story?"

He takes a beat to reply. "No, I don't think so. Why do you ask?"

"Maybe you wanted to share it with someone else?"

"What?" he says. "Why would I do that? Oh, actually—you know who does screenshot your shit?"

"Who?" I ask.

"Your mom."

I frown. "My mom?"

"Yeah. She's constantly posting everything you share on her Facebook."

I make a face. "What?"

"My mom says it's because you moved far away and you barely talk to her. Is that true? Your mom is constantly posting things like *Darcy went to the mall today*. Then she attaches a picture you already shared on Instagram. I had to mute her account. It's been relentless."

"Are you serious?" I put a hand on my chest.

"Yeah, don't you have your mom on Facebook?"

"No."

What the hell is wrong with my mom?

He tuts. "Well, you should really check out her profile. It's a shrine to you."

"Jesus Christ."

He snorts. "Why would you think I'd do that? You've got only-child syndrome, Darcy. You always have. We're not all out here obsessed with you, you know."

I scowl. Tucker is an only child too.

Rather than argue with him, I say, "Thank you. I'm going to let you go now."

"Yeah, no problem. Are you visiting this year for Christmas? You didn't come last year, did you? I don't think we've seen you in a while."

"I was with my wife's family last year. We'll probably try to come this year."

There's an awkward silence. He says, "I didn't realize you got married. Man, I still don't get why you chose to live this way. I remember that guy you were dating before. What was his name?"

I close my eyes. "Ben."

"Oh yeah. Whatever happened to Ben? I liked him. You guys made a nice couple, I thought."

I inhale. "I have to go, Tucker. See you at Christmas."

"All right, all right. See you."

"Bye."

I search my mom's name on Facebook and click her profile.

She has no privacy settings whatsoever. Her entire profile is open to the public. I scroll down and see that it is as Tucker said. She's screenshotted almost everything I've ever posted on Instagram, including the photo I took in the tub, and reshared it to her own wall.

I look at the naked photo of me. I don't think she's noticed I'm naked in the reflection of the tap. She has poor eyesight and has to wear her readers when she uses her phone. She captioned her post: DARCY IS RELAXING TONIGHT!!!

I sigh deeply. It's not hard to find out my mom's name. All you have to do is search my name, find my grandma's obituary, and boom. Declan must have found the photo from her profile.

I brought Joy home to meet my parents after we'd been dating for two years. It was awkward, but overall, it went fine. After dinner I found myself sitting in the living room with my dad. We watched baseball while my mom sat in the kitchen with

Joy. She was showing her our family photo albums. I overheard my mom say what a beautiful little girl I was.

I have no memories of her ever saying anything like that to me. I was taken aback when I heard it.

My dad noticed the change in my expression. He asked, "What's with the face?"

I said, "I've just never heard Mom say anything like that about me before."

He cheered for the game, then said, "Well, your mother loves you, slugger."

Sophie posted the first photo of January on social media. In it, January is wearing a furry white onesie, and a hat with little bear ears. She has big dark eyes, long eyelashes, and little red blotches on the bridge of her tiny, button nose.

Beneath the photo, Sophie's written:

WE'RE SO EXCITED TO WELCOME OUR LITTLE BABY GIRL INTO THE WORLD. SHE IS PERFECT. I'M OBSESSED WITH HER EVERY BLINK, AND ALL HER NOISES. BECOMING A MOM IS A MIX OF AWE, WONDER, AND THIS HORRIBLE, CRUSHING WORRY. I'M SO TERRIFIED I'M GOING TO MAKE MISTAKES. I WANT EVERYTHING GOOD FOR YOU, JANUARY. I'M SO LUCKY TO BE YOUR MOM.

My parents met at church when my mom was sixteen and my dad was twenty. They got married two years later. Whenever I hear the story, I am reminded that, "Things were different back then."

My mom cooked dinner every night. She hung the laundry on the line. Did the dishes by hand. My dad worked, mowed the lawn, and took care of the cars. Mom greeted him at the door when he came home at six p.m. and fixed him a drink.

And I was their baby. A little girl watching her mom, trying to understand how to be a person.

And at one point my mom was a baby too. A little girl watching her mom.

I remember her teaching me how to cross-stitch. We were sitting in the living room with hoops and aida cloth on our laps. I kept making mistakes. Mom helped me rip my stitches out, rethread my needle, and said, "It's okay. I made mistakes when I learned how to do this too."

CHAPTER
TWELVE

"Hi, Mom," I say.

"Oh, wow. To what do I owe the pleasure? I feel like we just spoke. Normally we have to wait at least a month to hear from you again. Actually, it's usually more like three or four months—"

I interrupt her. "You've posted a naked photo of me on the internet."

"What?" she says. "No I didn't. What a ridiculous accusation. I would *never*—"

"You did. It was an accident. It's okay. Please delete the photo you posted of my bathtub. It was about two weeks ago. There's a purple bath bomb in it."

She's flustered. "I-I don't know what you're talking about. I didn't do anything wrong. I just—"

"Are you logged on to your Facebook right now?"

"Yes. I'm at the laptop. How do I delete a post?"

"You just click the three little dots in the upper right-hand corner of the post. Do you see that? Then there's an option that says move to trash. It has a little garbage icon. Do you see it?"

"Yes," she says. "Got it."

"Perfect." I exhale. "Thank you."

She huffs. "Why did you share that picture of yourself to begin with if it was going to be an issue? It's not like I—"

I close my eyes. "It was an accident. But yes, you're right, Mom. It was my fault. Don't worry about it. I'm not upset. It's fine. How are you? How's Dad doing?"

She exhales. "Oh, Dad's all right. We just had a pot roast for dinner. I made an apple cake. Now he's in his chair, watching the game."

"Is our team winning?"

She shouts at my dad. "Are we winning, Larry? Are we? Okay, he says yes. We are."

"That's good." I inhale. "So anyway, I was thinking of visiting you in a couple weeks. On a Saturday, maybe? Would that work for you? Do you guys have any plans I should work around?"

"In a couple weeks? Oh. No, not really. Um. There's a community yard sale on the sixteenth we were planning to go to, but you could join us if you come that day. It's for the whole neighborhood. There's a bake sale, and a book sale too. Do you like yard sales still?"

"I love yard sales, yeah. That sounds fun. Okay. I'll come up on the sixteenth, then. And while I'm there, I'm going to adjust your privacy settings on Facebook, okay? Right now, your profile is way too open. Strangers can see what you post."

She gasps. "They can?"

"Yeah, don't worry about it, though. I'll fix it. I have to let you go now, though, okay? I have to pick Joy up at the train station."

"Okay. Tell Joy she should come visit too," she says.

"I will," I say.

She says, "Bye, honey."

"Bye, Mom."

I watch the automatic doors open and close for strangers exiting the train station. I crane my neck, anxious to spot Joy. I feel weirdly nervous. When I haven't seen her in a while, I feel the residue of the nerves I felt when we first started dating. I look at myself in the mirror. I check if there's anything in my teeth.

Her train arrived ten minutes ago. The tracks are several minutes away from the pickup spot, so she has to walk a bit. A lot of people are leaving the station. She should be here any minute—

I spot her. She's rushing through the doors. I smile and wave her down.

She sprints toward the car, rolling her luggage behind her. I have the trunk already open for her bag.

"Hi, stranger." She grins at me.

"Hi." I extend my arms open. She rushes to hug me. Her hair smells like roses and a newborn baby. After we let each other go, I pick her bag up and put it in the car for her.

While we drive home, I put my hand on her leg. I'm smiling. It's after dusk. The sun has set, and we've rolled our windows down. Cool night air is blowing into the car. Our hair is whipping in the wind. I'm playing a song I know she likes, and she's belting along to the words.

One of the lyrics says, "Will you still love me if it turns out I'm insane?" She sings that part turned to me, touching my chin, like she's asking me the question.

I nod while she sings the next line, which is, "I know what you'll say."

I carry her bag inside for her, and we kiss after shutting the door.

"I'm so happy to be home." She smiles while our mouths are still touching. "And the house smells so nice."

"Mhm," I say. "I told the cats you were coming, so they got to work. They were mopping. Doing laundry. Lighting incense."

She snorts. "Oh, did they do all that? I should thank them. Where are they?"

They've both entered the room. Lou is meow-screaming. Toulouse is rushing toward us. She's also meowing, but because she's running, she sounds like a vibrating duck.

"I have to warn you, the living room is a mess," I say, ashamed. "I'm sorry. I decided to organize the books, and it totally got away from me. It's a disaster."

"Oh, I don't mind a disaster." Joy sits down on the floor. Both cats slink into her lap. They strain their necks to butt their heads against hers. Both are purring loudly.

She pets them and says, "I missed you, ladies. You look so beautiful. Have you done something different with your fur— Oh my god!" She looks up at me. "Where's Kyle? Show me Kyle!"

"Oh no. He's so cute." She pouts at me.

She's crouched beside him, petting him.

"I know," I say.

He's closed his eyes. She's petting him under his chin.

"I wish he got along with the girls." She frowns. "Should we try introducing them again?"

I look at Kyle. He's a fluffy cat. He has big round eyes and a pink nose. Little tufts of fur grow around his cat-toes. He looks so tame and innocent. Unfortunately, he turns vicious at the sight of Lou and Toulouse. Though so do they. It's not all Kyle's fault.

"I don't know," I say. "I probably don't have it in me tonight, honey. The last time I tried I got bit. My arm is still healing. I think we need to wear, like, falconry gloves when we try it again."

Joy takes a quick shower to wash the train off, while I turn down the house. I close the windows and switch off all the lights downstairs. I wipe down the counters, start the dishwasher, fill the cats' water dishes, check the thermostat, and make sure all the doors are locked.

I climb upstairs and enter the steamy washroom to brush my teeth while Joy showers. She's singing behind the curtain. I put some toothpaste on her toothbrush for her for when she comes out.

I go into our bedroom and open the window above our bed. I can hear the frogs croaking by the lake. Owls are hooting. The air is still cold at night, but Joy and I both like to sleep in the cold.

She comes out of the bathroom while I toss an extra blanket on the bed. We crawl under the covers together with no clothes on, and curl into each other. We fall asleep almost immediately. I wake up briefly, around two a.m., to Joy babbling "I love you" in her sleep. Shortly after, she says gibberish. It sounds like she says, "Toads eating biscuits."

I wake up before her in the morning. Both cats are lying on her chest. I climb out of bed quietly and amble down the stairs. I put on a pot of coffee and take two mugs out of the cupboard.

While the coffee maker percolates, I open all the curtains and windows on the main floor. I look outside at the lake. There are loons on the water. It's six a.m., and the sky is orange.

I return to the kitchen and spoon brown sugar into Joy's mug and take the cream out of the fridge. I hear the stairs creek while I pour coffee into our cups. When Joy reaches the kitchen, she takes her cup from me with both hands and smiles.

We walk barefoot outside together, down the stone path that leads to the lake. We sit on our dock and sip our coffee in silence.

If I were asked to picture my dream house when I was in my teens or early twenties, I would have envisioned a modern, ostentatious, new build in a sprawling suburban development. It would have a two-car garage, floor-to-ceiling windows, a manicured lawn, and a chandelier in the foyer. The house would look like the set of a family sitcom, or something you'd see in the background of a rich family on social media. People like my parents would be impressed by it. At that time, I dreamed about living somewhere that showed I'd arrived at what I thought to be success.

Joy and I don't have a lawn. We have moss, creeping thyme, and wild strawberries. There are spiders in our kitchen, the floor creaks, and the house is difficult to heat, but I wouldn't move even if we won the lottery. I like hearing the lake; it cracks and pops in the winter when it's frozen, and laps against the shoreline when it's not. All our rooms are small and cramped, there's problems with the foundation, and the mortgage eats most of our money, but the sun hits the front windows in the morning, and I hear frogs croaking every day. I'm happy here. I know I'm lucky to have a house at all—let alone one I feel relieved to pull up to at the end of the day. I would hate to live in the house I thought I wanted when I was younger. I hope I die here.

"I'd like to call this meeting to order," the chairperson says into the microphone.

Joy offers me a piece of gum while the board members do roll call and approve the agenda. Joy and I are sitting near the back of the room. I'm off the clock. We're both here as community members. We're in a municipal building in a sizable hall. There's a platform at the front of the room where the board members are sitting on wooden chairs. At the center of the hall, there's a large screen that projects the word's COMMUNITY CONSULTATION.

The room is packed. It's a good turnout. I've spotted a few regular patrons as well as some of my coworkers in the audience. Patty. Ahmad. Brenda. I also notice the back of Declan's blond head and some of the familiar faces from the protests. Mostly, though, the room is full of people I don't know.

"Which one is Declan?" Joy whispers.

Before I can point him out, the chairperson says, "Welcome everyone! I hope you're enjoying the lovely weather. It's so nice that spring has finally sprung. Thank you for joining us here today."

While she introduces the members of the board, I discreetly point Declan out to Joy. We look at the back of his head. His hair is thinning at the crown.

"This consultation was arranged in response to an influx of community concerns relating to our collection development and program planning policies. Rhonda Wheeler, library CEO, is here to briefly present those policies to us. Following that, we'll open the floor for public comments."

The projector in the room flashes and is now displaying a slide titled COLLECTION DEVELOPMENT & PROGRAM PLANNING.

Rhonda stands up. She has her glasses on the end of a long gold chain. She's wearing orthopedic Mary Janes, a long dark skirt, and a gray knit cardigan. She has her hair in a low, tight gray bun. She looks like the archetype of a librarian, a spitting image of the picture next to the word "librarian" in an encyclopedia.

She addresses the room. "Hello everyone. Thank you for your presence today."

Rhonda is not a quiet, stereotypical librarian, however. She has a deep, loud, booming voice. Before she spoke, people in the audience were chitchatting. The room is now silent and sitting at attention.

I glance at Declan. Before Rhonda spoke, he was leaning over, talking to the man sitting beside him. He's now leaning forward, looking smug.

Rhonda scans the crowd. "I'm going to share some context with you. First, our policy suite was renewed sixteen months ago. For your awareness, we review our policies on a four-year schedule. This review is an extensive process; it involves consulting legal, the public, and our various governance bodies."

The slide changes. It now says SELECTION CRITERIA.

"We have criteria we use to evaluate the material in our collection. We consider community demand and relevance to our community's needs. We also consider quality, including literary merit, accuracy, authority, and currency. In addition, we consider availability, and of course, budget. More detail about our criteria can be found on the library website."

The slide changes. It now says PROCEDURES. Rhonda's voice booms, "We have a number of procedures that support our policies. Today we're following the one established to address challenges and complaints. The first step in this procedure is to reaffirm our principles."

Next slide. It says PRINCIPLES.

I notice Declan tilt his head while he reads the slide.

Rhonda speaks, as if she's pledging allegiance, "We believe in equitable access to information. We believe in providing inclusive, welcoming, and accessible services that embrace diversity. We defend intellectual freedom. We are committed to community development, lifelong learning, and literacy." She pauses, then says, "Thank you."

As she turns around to sit back down, Robert, a member of the board, stands up. "Thanks a bunch, Rhonda. All right, so the content that's been challenged recently have been brought to the board and documented. The list of the challenged material is now displayed on the screen."

It's a long list. Among the contested books, I see:

>*The Bluest Eye*
>*Gender Queer*
>*The Hate U Give*
>*All Boys Aren't Blue*
>*This Book Is Gay*
>*And Tango Makes Three*
>*The Family Book*
>*The Perks of Being a Wallflower*

Robert looks back down at his paper. "A reconsideration committee was formed. We assessed the material using our selection criteria, which Rhonda just shared. We've now reached this stage of the process, public participation. We're here to solicit input from you, the public. I'd like to welcome you to come up to the podium." He gestures to his right. "Please come up and share your thoughts and opinions. They'll be put on record and used to support our final decision. We have the next forty minutes. Try to share your thoughts as succinctly as possible to save time for others. Thanks all."

He sits down, and Declan immediately stands up. I watch him walk over with assured determination. As he marches toward the microphone, I try to picture him as a little boy. I wonder what he was like when he was a kid. I wonder how his parents treated him.

"Hello, everyone. My name is Declan Turner. I'm a local reporter, as well as a concerned father and citizen."

Declan is not a good-looking man. He has a gaunt face and deep-set eyes. He's very thin, and his clothes don't fit well. He has poor posture; always slouched. I wonder if he was picked on as a kid. I wonder if he had many friends. The people who came here today with him seem to respect him. I think he's made friends through organizing this group.

He continues, "I hope I speak for the majority of the people here today when I say we need to protect our kids from sexual deviants. At this time, I firmly believe opportunists and predators are drawn to our library because of the books and events we promote."

I tilt my head while I watch him speak. I wonder why he believes that. Does he really think that's true? I have no doubt that there are predators in every community and know they're drawn to public spaces where there are vulnerable people. Parks. Schools. Churches. Libraries. I don't believe, however, that predators are drawn especially to the library because of our books or events. I don't buy that picture books about gender, racism, or lesbian moms are luring in pedophiles.

He says, "Recently, I reported on an incident in our library that involved a man watching pornography on the public computers. I was told this was allowed by the librarian on duty. I've also been made aware of concerning events hosted by our library that promote sexual deviancy and gender ideology."

I wonder if he realizes that the people who watch porn in the library tend to be people experiencing homelessness and mental health problems. They generally don't have access to their own devices or the internet. They don't have housing. They often struggle with addiction, lack social awareness, and struggle with compulsive behaviors. I wouldn't classify them all as opportunists or predators; they're mostly marginalized people who lack access to resources and support.

"There are books on our shelves dealing in topics that are absolutely inappropriate for kids, including sexually explicit content, offensive language, critical race theory, and many other disturbed and immoral ideologies."

I squint. Why does he consider critical race theory disturbed and immoral? It's a framework that examines systemic racism, and studies how racism is woven into the fabric of society. What's his issue with that? Maybe he doesn't know what it means. Did someone tell him it means something else?

Or maybe he does know what it means, but I don't understand why he would oppose it. Is he threatened as a white person by the idea that our social institutions favor us? He doesn't seem to be excessively wealthy, and I know he didn't go to college. I'm sure he's struggled in his life. Maybe he doesn't like the idea that the world is easier for him in some ways, because it still feels hard.

I try to picture him as a six-year-old boy. I imagine he was smaller than most boys his age. I don't know, of course, but he's not tall, and he's very thin. I imagine he was a little, sickly-looking kid. Maybe he got bullied.

"What is the educational purpose of these books?" he asks. "And how do drag queen story times help our kids graduate high school? I know the answers. This isn't educational. This is indoctrination. There are deep-rooted issues in our libraries that require our immediate attention for the well-being of our children. I strongly believe we need to reassess the books we keep on our shelves, the behavior we allow in our tax-funded buildings, and the events that we host. Libraries should be child-friendly, educational spaces. Period. Thank you."

He steps away from the podium to a smattering of applause.

Joy whispers, "What a piece of work."

I watch him walk back to his chair. I find it strange when people say libraries should center children. We have children's sections. Does he think the entire library should be for kids? What about seniors? Parents? Mature students? New immigrants? People looking for jobs? Genealogists? Adults with disabilities? Artists? Entrepreneurs? Reading groups? People experiencing homelessness? People looking for legal aid? Victims of domestic abuse? What about everyone else?

A line formed behind Declan while he was speaking. A woman in a blazer takes the mic. "Hi. I'm Paula West. I share the concerns raised by Mr. Turner. Also, I'd like to point out that a lot of what Ms. Wheeler said earlier was peppered with buzz words like 'diversity' and 'inclusion.' I want to ask, does diversity and inclusion also embrace incestuous relationships? Or books that promote pedophilia? Where's the line? This is virtue signaling. Who are we being inclusive of exactly? I'm a taxpayer and a member of this community. I don't feel the library is being inclusive of me, my family, or of anyone in our community who has traditional values. I believe we need to have better moral standards for our library, and that one of our objectives should be to protect the innocence of our children. I urge the board to reconsider the books and programs our library offers, and to uphold the traditional, moral principles of our community."

I look at the books projected on the screen. Almost all of them are about LGBTQIA+ people or people of color.

She steps aside and the man behind her takes the microphone. "Hi there. I'm Duncan Hughes. I just want to say this is a Christian community. Our library should reflect the values of the people who live here. I don't support promoting sexual content to kids, or porn in our public spaces. Frankly, it's disturbing that this is controversial. Kids don't need to read about sex, whether it's gay or not. That's for adults."

Joy stands up.

I look at her. "What are you doing?"

"I'm going up."

"*Are you sure—*" I say while she walks toward the line.

A woman in purple overalls is at the microphone now. She has a baby strapped to her chest. "Hi. My name is Anita Maple. I'm a parent. I don't understand why a small group of people think they should be who determines what my children, or any kids in our community, can and cannot read.

I want my kids, and our whole community, to have access to books that depict a diverse array of people. Furthermore, Ms. Wheeler mentioned these policies are current and were updated last calendar year. Why would we spend money on updating policies that are current? I don't support appeasing a small group of people whose interests don't reflect our communities. And by the way, this isn't a Christian community. This is a public library. My next-door neighbors are Sikh. I'm Jewish. The library is full of Christian books. I'm not asking us to ban books about Easter regardless of having no interest in sharing those with my kids. This is a community space. No one should be banning books. Thank you."

A man takes the microphone. "Hello. I'm Isaac Jackson. I agree with the woman before me and want to state that I'm who is responsible for my child's education. Me and my wife. It's not the business of anyone here to decide what my kid can read. That is a parental choice. I want my child to have access to books with kids who look like her—which a lot of the books listed on the screen up here do. Why would we take these away? Please don't take these books out of circulation."

An elderly woman takes the mic. "Hello. I'm Judy-Lue Kline, and I'd just like the record to note, I firmly believe this hysteria is politically manufactured to rile up support for specific ideologies. I'm upset to see it's reached our community, but I don't believe it reflects us as a whole. Our community wants these books to stay. My family and I don't support banning any books."

An old man in a wheelchair is at the front of the line now. Judy-Lue helps him reach the microphone. "Hiya. I'm John Karnes. I'm a conservative man, who has conservative values; however, these sorts of complaints go well beyond conservativism. I don't support banning or burning books. It's tyrannical. I agree that what a kid reads is up to his parents. Thank you."

Joy is standing at the mic now. "Hi. My name's Joy Carpenter. I've lived in the area for about six years. I moved here with my wife. We actually picked this area partly because we saw its inclusivity. There are rainbow flags on the shops on Main Street. We looked at statistics and saw the community here is made up of people from various cultures and backgrounds. Unfortunately, I've experienced harassment and violence in relation to my sexual orientation, and my partner and I chose to move here partly because we felt safe. I didn't read a book with a lesbian in it until I was twenty-five years old. Not seeing myself in books impacted how I understood myself and how I connected with others. I think I might have realized I was gay sooner if I'd been exposed to more stories with people like me in them. I'm grateful that there are books for kids today that feature the people and families they see mirrored in their own lives. We need to see ourselves in stories. We need to see people who aren't like us too. Diverse books that feature characters of different races, cultures, gender, sexual orientation, ability, religion, and family structures help us develop understanding and empathy. What is the point of reading? What is the point of the library? We want to learn and connect with other people. Our library needs to be a community space that welcomes and values everyone. Please don't remove any of these books from our shelves. Thank you."

She steps away from the microphone. I watch her walk by Declan. His head follows her as she walks.

"How'd I do?" she whispers as she sits back down beside me.

"Good," I put my hand on her leg while others take the microphone. A large line of people has formed.

"I'll be quick. I don't support removing these books."

"Banning books infringes on free speech. I don't support it."

"The government shouldn't be involved in deciding what books people can read."

"Book banning is censorship. It's a slippery slope. I don't support it."

"We should support our teachers and parents in educating kids rather than blocking books from kids. Don't remove these books."

"Our community has the right to read whatever we want."

"I support protecting kids, but banning books isn't the way to do that."

Several more people make statements until Robert speaks into the microphone by his chair.

"Thank you all," he says. "I'm sorry, we're at time. We really appreciate your involvement today. We've captured all this helpful feedback. The decision regarding these complaints will be communicated through the library website, where you will also find the appeals process. There's more coffee on the table over here. Please help yourselves. We're adjourned. Have a great evening."

CHAPTER
THIRTEEN

"Rise and shine," Joy says.

It smells like coffee. I open my eyes. She's standing at the end of our bed with a tray in her hands and a tea towel flung over her shoulder. "Happy birthday!" She grins.

I sit up while she puts the tray over my lap. I say, "Wow. Thank you so much."

I rub my eyes. I slept through any noise she made in the kitchen.

"I tried to be quiet. I almost set the fire alarm off, but I opened the windows just in time. And don't worry, I cleaned the kitchen as I cooked. I've got a whole day planned for us. I'm going to have a quick shower, okay? I got pancake batter in my hair. I need to wash it off so we can start celebrating."

I'm not fully awake yet. I sip coffee from the mug on the tray.

"Did I say thank you?" I ask as she walks into the bathroom.

She pops her head out of the doorframe. "Yes, you did. You're welcome, babe."

I hear the rumble of our water heater turning on, and the patter of the shower running. A breeze wafts through our window and moves my hair off my neck. I look around our room. The clothes Joy and I wore yesterday are folded on a sitting chair in the corner. It's a bright, sunny morning. The light from the window creates a block of sun on the foot of our bed, where the cats are basking in its glow. The shadow of my head and shoulders is obstructing the light, and Lou is lying slightly in the shade of me.

I close my eyes. I'm a year older. It's strange, getting older. Sometimes I feel like an old lady remembering moments I had when I was younger. I'm conscious of how lucky I am to be alive, healthy, in a safe place where I live with someone I love and who loves me.

I wish I always felt this way, and that everyone could live comfortably in a safe place too. I wish there were no threats to anyone's safety or happiness.

I open my eyes and look down at the breakfast Joy made. There are dried yellow roses in a little glass vase. A cup of cranberry juice. Sliced oranges. She's placed blueberries in the pancakes to write out thirty-three, which is how old I'm turning today.

I puncture a berry with my fork. Purple juice saturates the surrounding pancake like a bruise.

Ben was thirty-three when we broke up. That was over ten years ago. I find that staggering. The difference between me now, and me ten years ago is stark. The disparity feels as dramatic as the difference between me at eight and me at eighteen. I was a different person. I didn't hear the same assured voice in my head I have now telling me what do. I wasn't a kid, but I had *just* been a kid. I didn't understand what I wanted in my life the way I do now.

I wish I didn't think of Ben on my birthday. I wish I could exist in this moment without carrying the baggage I've collected throughout my life. I like being older. I'd rather be me now, than me any age prior. But there is this heaviness to aging. Who I am was built on the shoulders of the person I was last year, and the year before, and before, and before. I'm not just thirty-three; I'm twenty-seven. I'm eighteen. I'm nine. I was just born. And I have to carry all of those versions of myself, the feelings they have, and the mistakes they've made, everywhere I go.

I close my eyes. If I'm an old lady remembering her life, I wonder if I'll understand things differently than I did when I was thirty-three. I wonder what mistakes I will have made that are weighing on me. I hope I'm making fewer mistakes.

Ben died when he was forty-three. He was born in July. On one of his birthdays, when we were together, we went to the batting cages. He loved going there. He played baseball as a kid. I remember cheering for him from behind a chain-link fence. I can see his face grinning at me over his shoulder. He had a bright, friendly face. Kind hazel eyes.

Ben called me "dove" because I tripped over one on our first date. He and I were strolling in a park, eating soft-serve ice cream. A pack of pigeons were scattered across the path ahead of us. I wasn't looking down, and a slow bird didn't scuttle out of my way in time. The bird was fine, but I fully tripped to the ground. My waffle cone went flying.

Ben rushed to help me up, concerned, but found me laughing.

I cackled. "Did I just trip over a fucking bird?"

He laughed too. We were both laughing so much that he struggled to help me up. He stood over me, holding both my hands, while we both wheezed, mouths open.

Later that afternoon, he changed my name in his phone to "Dove."

I told him it wasn't a dove I tripped over. It was a pigeon.

He said, "Aren't doves just pretty pigeons?"

I didn't know the answer and I've never looked it up.

"Do you want your present before we go out, or later tonight?" Joy asks. She's out of the shower, drying her hair with a towel.

"Whatever you want," I say. She smells good. She uses this bodywash with patchouli, black pepper, and vanilla in it.

"I'm excited to give it to you," she says while pulling it out of the closet. "Sophie and I got it while I was with her. I saw it and thought, *Darcy'd love that.*"

She puts the gift down on the bed. It's big and rectangular. I tear the paper and see that it's a framed print. It's Auguste Toulmouche's 1866 oil painting, *The Hesitant Fiancée*. It features a disgruntled-looking bride-to-be sitting in an opulent room. She's being attended to by her bridesmaids while she sports a strikingly petulant expression.

I love art that features hostile, angry-looking women.

"Do you like it?" she asks.

I smile. "Yes. I love it."

She grins, and I stand up to kiss her. I hold her arm above her head, and she spins like we're dancing. We often pretend to dance. Though I guess it isn't really pretending. We're actually dancing, I guess.

I say, "Thank you for my present."

Joy took me out for more coffee at a shop I like, then to a bookstore, and now a petting zoo. We just held yellow chicks and fed the goats. She packed us a picnic to take on a hike after this, and later, we're meeting up with some of our friends for dinner.

I'm holding a baby lamb. Her fleece is soft and she's radiating this gentle heat. She feels lighter and more delicate than I expected her to. I've never held a baby lamb before. I'm overwhelmed by how vulnerable I sense she is, a trusting, fragile creature.

Joy is taking my photo. I smile, but I have tears in my eyes.

She tilts her head after taking the picture. "Are you touched by how sweet this little lamb is?"

I nod. "Yes."

The lamb is sniffing my face.

We meet up with Hodan, Ada, Matthew, and Marco for dinner. We're at a restaurant that serves small plates. We've just been served our drinks.

"So, have there been any more porn watchers in your library?" Hodan asks.

I put my mint julep down. "There's actually been less lately than usual, despite the press."

"There's porn in the library?" Marco asks.

"Don't get me started," I warn him.

Hodan laughs.

"You're the same age Jesus was when he died, did you know that?" Matthew says.

"Am I really?" I ask.

"Yes. Do you have any wisdom to share with us now that you're Christ's age?"

Everyone looks at me.

"Uh," I say. "Don't drink." I sip my drink.

They roll their eyes. Ada says, "Come on, give us some advice. What's something you learned this year?"

I clear my throat. "All right. Um. What happened this year? Oh, Joy and I got married." I smile at Joy. She's sitting beside me. She bats her eyes melodramatically at me. "That was the highlight, for sure. What else happened? Um—"

I feel a pang in my chest. I picture Ben's face and feel my smile fade. My mouth is open but I'm not saying anything.

They're all waiting for me to speak. "Uh," I say. I picture Ben looking over his shoulder, smiling at me.

"I had a mental breakdown," I say quietly.

Joy puts her hand on my leg under the table.

"You what?" Hodan leans forward.

"You had a mental breakdown?" Matthew asks.

Our waitress has come back to our table. She's placing plates down. We're all silent except for repeatedly saying, "Thank you" to her with pained smiles.

After she leaves, I put a Brussel sprout in my mouth.

"What happened?" Marco asks.

My mouth is full. I cover it with my hand. "Maybe we should pretend I didn't say that. Sorry. I'm a vibe killer."

"Who among us hasn't had a mental breakdown this year?" Hodan says generously.

"We don't have to talk about it if you don't want to," Joy says.

They all nod. Ada says, "Yeah. You don't have to. If you *want* to talk about it, though—"

"Oh, I've been talking about it a lot already. I'm in therapy," I say.

"We love therapy." Hodan holds her glass up.

"I'm in therapy too," Ada says.

"Aren't we all in therapy?" Matthew says.

Everyone except Joy nods.

"I'm thinking of going, though," she says. "As I'm sure everyone is aware, I have health anxiety. I've got an inkling, based on that anxiety, that I have many other very troubling issues too."

We laugh.

"All right, so have you gotten any wisdom from therapy, then, Darcy?" Ada asks.

I consider the question. "Yeah, I guess. My therapist said something about it being okay to feel like life is meaningless."

Matthew laughs. "Wow, where'd you find this therapist? A booth behind a Wendy's?"

I laugh. "Yeah, exactly, we shared a Baconator and she said it matters that I feel like life is worthwhile, not necessarily that it means something."

"Oh, I don't mind that," Ada says.

Joy holds her glass up. "Cheers to another meaningless, worthwhile year, then."

We clink our glasses.

Ada touches Joy's arm. "You didn't tell us about your visit with your sister, Joy. How's she doing? And how's your niece?"

"They're good," Joy says. "January was born with some minor limb differences. She's missing fingers."

"Oh no, is she okay?" Marco asks.

"Yes, she's fine. I went with Sophie to a pediatric geneticist appointment while I was with them. They did some testing. The doctor said she's perfectly healthy. Some of her fingers just didn't grow. I guess it was just a random case."

"Is Sophie doing okay with all that?" Hodan asks.

Joy nods. "Yes. At first, she was rattled, but we talked about it a lot. Having a baby with missing fingers is hard because we have all our fingers, so we don't know what it would be like not to. It's scary to have a baby who is going to have hardships you haven't. But the doctor told us similar kids with limb differences do very well, and it shouldn't impact the quality of her life. The actual function she has is good. There's nothing wrong with her, really. The only real issue is how other people might treat her. That's what Sophie is worried about. We just don't want January to be treated badly."

"How was your weekend?" Mordecai asks.

I'm pouring coffee into my thermos in the break room.

"It was good, thanks. How was yours?" I twist the lid on my cup.

"It was too short." He yawns. "I did a bunch of yard work. Planted a mulberry bush. I also went to visit my friend Lucy. She just moved to Oldewood Street. Oh, and I went to my brother's for dinner. Brought a homemade lemon meringue pie. I'm exhausted. And we've got the human library program at the end of the day, right?"

I nod. "Yes we do."

He pours coffee into his mug and says, "You know what, I wanted to say, I've been thinking about this whole Declan thing, and I'm so sorry that you're dealing with this. Especially right after being so sick. It's like you came back to work just in time to be harassed. I'm sure after dealing with whatever your health issue was, this has been especially insufferable. I hope it isn't impacting your recovery—"

"It was a mental health crisis," I tell him.

He raises his eyebrows. "Oh. You didn't have to tell me that. I'm sorry if I made you feel like you had to tell me—"

"No, it's okay," I say. "Someone I used to be close with died unexpectedly and it really shook me up. I had a series of panic attacks. I'm doing a lot better, though. I still feel a little off, but I'm all right."

"Oh, I'm so sorry."

I sip my coffee. "That's okay. You didn't kill him."

He doesn't laugh.

"I was joking," I say.

"Good one," he says without laughing. He adds, after a beat, "Who was he?"

He's prying.

I say, "An ex-boyfriend. His name was Ben. We dated for five years before I realized I was gay. We were together from when I was eighteen to twenty-three. He was twenty-eight to thirty-three."

He raises his eyebrows. "A ten-year age gap? That's quite the May-December romance. You know, I had a similar experience, actually. I dated a man who was twenty when I was a teenager. He hasn't died, though." He looks at me. He adds cautiously, "Sadly."

I snort into my coffee.

"Was that an insensitive joke?" he says quickly. "You said that thing about me not killing your ex, so I thought maybe the tone made it acceptable—"

I laugh. "You're a terrible person, Mordecai."

He snorts. "Fuck off."

The human library event has begun. We placed chairs around the room for patrons to sit and chat with their human "book." I set up a table with coffee, cookies, and other refreshments. We have a good turnout. The participants have all been paired up already. We've given everyone a moment to get settled.

I'm standing in the middle of the room to open up the

program. I project my voice. "Thank you all for coming to our Human Library! We aren't the first to host this kind of event. These events were inspired by the Danish concept of "Menneskebiblioteket," which I'm sorry, I probably just pronounced poorly. The event aims to bridge divides and combat prejudice by facilitating meaningful conversations between people from different backgrounds. We're so excited you're here to participate."

Mordecai is helping with the event. He adds, "You've all been given a pamphlet with some sample questions to get the conversation going. There's also a quick survey. We'd love your feedback."

I say, "Thank you all again for joining us today. I hope you have wonderful conversations. Please feel free to get started!"

The participants eyes move from us to the person they're paired with. The library starts to become loud with conversation.

I watch people begin to talk to each other. While I scan the room, I'm startled to spot Declan. He's standing by a large sign I placed by the entrance to the library. The sign says:

WELCOME TO THE HUMAN LIBRARY!
CHECK OUT A LIVING BOOK, SPARK MEANINGFUL CONVERSATION, BRIDGE DIVIDES, AND CONNECT!

Mordecai notices Declan's presence too. He nudges my arm. "Why is he here?"

Declan looks up from the sign toward us. My eyes connect with his, and he starts walking in our direction.

"Hi," he addresses us as he gets closer.

"Hello," Mordecai and I reply in unison.

"I'd like to participate in this program," he says.

I wonder why he wants to do that. Is he trying to monitor the conversations? Perhaps the words "diversity" in the promotional material felt like a red flag to him.

"Why?" Mordecai squints at him.

I grit my teeth. He probably shouldn't have asked him that. It sounds unwelcoming. I wonder why too but—

"Am I not allowed?" Declan raises his voice. "I want to see what you're doing here. I'm a member of the public. I have a right—"

"Did you sign up?" Mordecai asks. "All our human books are already claimed."

Declan shakes his head. "That's disappointing. I came all the way here."

I wonder how he would have behaved if we had paired him with someone. I'm not sure I would want to subject one of the participants to his slander.

Mordecai says, "We're sorry for the inconvenience, but the event started fifteen minutes ago and—"

I interrupt them. I have an idea. "You know what, I'm available. We could pair you with me if you like?"

Mordecai frowns. "What? You're not signed up as a book."

"We put a lot of effort into encouraging people to come to our programs," I say. "I would hate for Mr. Turner to come all the way here just to be turned away. Would you like to borrow me as a book and have a conversation?"

Declan's eyes scan my face.

"Sure," he says. "Let's talk."

Is This a Cry for Help?

Declan and I are sitting in two chairs facing each other in a corner of the library. We're in the 900s section where history and geography books are shelved.

"Would you like to grab a coffee or a snack before we get started?" I offer.

"Maybe in a bit, thank you," he says. He's leaning forward. His elbows are resting on his knees, and his hands are clasped together.

We look at each other.

I inhale. "Should we get started, then? What would you like to know about being a librarian?"

He looks at me. "I think it's obvious what your political and ideological beliefs are, and I'd like to know what measures you take to ensure the books and services you offer here don't promote a particular agenda."

I brush my hair behind my ears. "We have collection development policies that we have to follow. We have rules when it comes to what books we acquire and what programs we offer. It's not up to me as an individual."

He squints. "There are a huge number of books in this library, especially books for children, that push gender ideology, critical race theory, radical feminism, and other ideas that I strongly oppose, but sense you likely support. Can't you admit it's suspicious that this building is full of books aligned with the political beliefs that you as an individual have? Can you understand how that looks to someone from my point of view?"

He is speaking calmly, but I sense he's preparing for us to argue. His neck is red. I don't want to argue with him. It would be nice if we could actually communicate.

I say, "We get complaints about material that is more politically right-wing too. We have books and content I personally think is awful, to be frank with you. We have a large range of resources that cover a variety of viewpoints, including ones that are aligned with right-wing ideologies, even extremist ones. We've also had speakers visit, like authors, who are definitely very conservative. This is meant to be a space for all members of our community, including people I don't personally agree with."

He tilts his head. "So, you admit your personal beliefs oppose mine, right? You support things like critical race theory and changing your gender?"

I look at him. He has eyebrows when you're up close to him. They're just blond and hard to see.

I say, "On a personal level, it's important to me that the library is a space for everyone, regardless of their ideological beliefs. My job is to uphold the principles of intellectual freedom and inclusivity."

"And my job is to protect our community from moral bankruptcy." He leans forward more in his chair. "I find it hard to believe that you actually want this to be a space for everyone. I feel like this space is not welcoming to me, my family, or anyone who has traditional values. Can you acknowledge there are biases here? Don't you think most of your coworkers are politically left-wing too?"

I consider the question. "I honestly don't know what my coworkers' political beliefs are. I know that higher levels of education are associated with greater support for progressive policies. So yeah, anyone who has a job like a librarian, or a lawyer, or a teacher, or any career that requires that sort of education is probably more likely to be left leaning, but not always. There are lots of people I work with who seem to have conservative beliefs. And most people who work here aren't librarians. We've got library techs, pages, and volunteers."

"It's condescending to say that more educated people are more likely to be left-wing," he says.

"I wasn't trying to be condescending," I say.

He's projecting his voice. "I have valid concerns about this place. I think it's reasonable to want libraries to demonstrate ethics and moral values. I don't want my tax dollars promoting lifestyles or behaviors that aren't good for our country. I think we're accommodating a loud vocal faction, which you're a part of, rather than accommodating most of our citizens, who I believe agree with me."

I look at him. "I want you to know that most of the work we do here doesn't have anything to do with political belief. We host programs about how to do your taxes, or write a résumé, and we lend out Wi-Fi hotspots. We do puppet shows. We read *Clifford the Big Red Dog* to children. I understand you have reservations about some of our materials and events, but I—"

"I have more than reservations. I'm appalled."

His face is red. He has hazel eyes.

I ask, "What specifically troubles you?"

"I think you're promoting an agenda. You're pushing ideologies that go against traditional values that endanger children. How would you feel if government institutions that you pay taxes for weren't aligned to your beliefs, and were actually boldly opposed to them?"

I look at him. "I already feel that way."

He squints.

I add, "And our goal really isn't to push an agenda. It's to offer a safe and welcoming environment for everyone."

"Well, I don't feel safe or welcomed," he says.

"I'm sorry to hear that," I say.

He crosses his arms. "I don't think you really are sorry, because to make me feel safe and welcome you could start by removing the books we've requested."

I exhale. "But that would make other people feel unsafe and unwelcome. Do you understand that?"

He leans back in his chair. "I don't think we're ever going to agree, are we?"

"I agree," I say.

"How do you think your conversation went?" Mordecai asks. We're cleaning up now that the program has ended.

I'm tossing empty paper cups into a recycling bag. "I guess it went as well as I could have anticipated. He didn't really budge. I didn't exactly expect him to change his—" I pause.

"What?" he asks.

I frown. "Damnit. I didn't say anything about the emails. God. I'm so sorry. I should have. I wanted to confront him about sending us those pictures. And I forgot to talk to him about the bird and abortion emails too. I was too focused on talking about *Clifford the Big Red Dog*, and what libraries do. I wanted to get our mission across—"

"Oh man," he says. "That's okay. It might not have been safe to anyway. What if he got angry? I was surprised he didn't. Though I have a feeling we're going to have to suffer through a *Liberty Lately* article about that soon."

I close my eyes and shake my head, pained.

***

"Do you need me to bring home anything?" I ask Joy. I'm sitting in the car, about to drive home from work.

She says, "Yes. We need Band-Aids."

I frown. "Band-Aids? Why? Did you hurt yourself?"

"Um. I got a little scratched. I, uh, tried to introduce Kyle to the girls again, and it went poorly."

I make a face. "Jesus Christ. Are you okay? I don't think those cats are going to get along, honey."

She says, "I know. They really don't like each other, do they? I don't know what to do. I was thinking, maybe Kyle could just live in the workshop permanently? He could be our workshop cat. He could—"

I sigh. "No, honey, he can't always live in the workshop. He won't be happy in there."

Her voice is quiet and subdued. "But I want to keep him. I love him."

I say, "I know you love him, but we can't keep him."

CHAPTER
FOURTEEN

"Hey you." Someone clasps my arm.

Joy and I are at a farmers' market. We're buying produce and pie.

I turn around and see the woman I cheated on Ben with.

"Oh. Hi," I say, startled to see her.

My heart starts racing. I didn't mention her to Joy.

Joy is looking between the woman and me. She has a confused expression on her face.

"Wow, we must be magnets to each other." The woman winks at me.

I feel my face heat up.

"Good to see you again." She smiles as she pushes toward a booth selling local honey.

"Who was that?" Joy asks as we walk out of the crowd toward our car. We're carrying a peach pie, and a library-branded tote bag full of fruit and vegetables.

I stammer while I unlock the car. "S-she's, uh. I don't actually remember her name."

"Why are you being weird right now?" she asks.

"I'm not."

"Yes, you are. If I didn't know better, I might think there was, like, something going on with you and that woman."

"What? Don't say that. Of course there isn't," I say.

We put the pie and tote bag in the trunk, then sit down in the car. I turn the air-conditioning up.

As we pull out of the parking lot, Joy says, "Okay. It weirdly kind of seemed like—"

"She's someone I hooked up with," I explain while trying to get out of the parking lot.

Joy puts a hand to her chest. "What?"

"No, not recently obviously, like when I was twenty-one," I stammer. "It was a really long time ago."

I glance at her. Her face looks sort of pale now. She says, "But the way she just interacted with you seems like you've spoken recently."

"Yeah, I randomly ran into her at the library last week," I say.

We're finally out of the parking lot now. We're on the road headed toward home.

"Why didn't you mention that to me?"

Her voice is eerily calm. I can tell she's mad.

"I don't know, honey. You were away. I'm sorry. I—"

I glance at her. She's furrowed her brow. "That is really weird of you, Darcy."

"I'm sorry. You're right. It is weird. I've felt off lately, like I'm wading through this brain fog. I—"

"Why didn't you tell me about running into her?" Her voice is louder than usual.

"I should have told you," I say.

"I know. Why didn't you?"

I glance at her. Her face is red. "Because I was twenty-one when I hooked up with her. I didn't think it mattered."

"I don't care how long ago it was, Darcy. If you interact with someone you've had sex with, you should tell me. I would tell you. We're married. It's weird."

"No, no, I mean—like, I was twenty-one. I was dating Ben at the time. That's why I didn't tell you. I-I didn't want to talk about it."

"*What?* You were dating Ben when you hooked up with that woman?"

My throat feels tight. "Yeah."

"Oh." I can feel her eyes scanning my face as if she hasn't seen me for a long time.

"You were at Sophie's when I ran into her," I babble. "I planned to text you about it, or mention it on the phone, but things got busy, and I'm all over the place. I—"

"Don't make excuses. You could have told me. You didn't want to tell me."

"No, I—"

"Don't lie," she says. Now she's looking out her window with her arms crossed. "You didn't tell me because you didn't want to tell me. I'm always honest with you."

I don't know what to say, so I don't say anything. We drive silently the rest of the way home.

When we pull up to the house, Joy unbuckles her seat belt and asks, "Can you bring in the bags? I want to go upstairs to think about this for a bit. I need some time alone, okay?"

She always wants to be alone after we have an argument.

I frown. "Okay."

There was this infomercial that used to play on TV when I was a kid, warning people not to smoke weed. It featured a woman sitting on a couch, deflated. She was a balloon-ish mannequin with no air in her body. The advertisement warned DO NOT SMOKE POT.

I can't remember the last time I smoked weed, yet I feel like that deflated balloon woman. I'm sitting on the couch, limp. I wish I'd handled that conversation differently. I feel stupid.

I close my eyes. Once, when Ben and I got into a fight, he punched a hole in the wall. I can't remember what he was mad about, but I think he'd been drinking. It was unlike him to get angry like that, though it happened a couple times.

It's been almost three hours since Joy went upstairs. I can't tell if she wants me to go talk to her or give her space, but it's nine p.m. and we usually go to bed around nine thirty. Maybe she wants me to sleep on the couch.

I climb up the stairs and stand in the doorframe of our bedroom. Joy's lying in our bed facing away from the door. She's either asleep or ignoring me.

"Hey, I'm sorry," I say quietly from the door. "Do you, uh, want me to sleep on the couch?"

She doesn't say anything, but I can tell by how she's rustling that she's awake.

I inhale. "I'm really sorry, Joy. I didn't want you to think of me as someone who's cheated on someone before. You've said that you think people who cheat will always be cheaters, and I didn't want you to put me in that category. I know that's unreasonable of me, and you have the right to know the truth, to decide how you think for yourself. I'm sorry. This was obviously a stupid way to handle this. It makes me seem even more dishonest. I'm sorry. I have this constant worry that you might realize I'm a bad partner. I was an awful girlfriend to Ben. And I don't think that's just because I'm gay. I think I'm selfish. And I know it's complicated because he was way too old for me and he had issues too, but I think if we put all that aside, I'd still come out as someone who was in the wrong a lot. I think I made a mess of that relationship, and I've always tried to be a better partner to you, but I'm worried it's, like, something that can't be fixed. Especially now. I'm worried I might just be a shitty partner."

She doesn't say anything.

"Am I?" I ask.

She rolls over and looks at me. "Sometimes."

I frown.

She exhales. "But not always."

"That means I am shitty," I say. "You can't *sometimes* be a good partner. You're either a good one or a bad one—"

"No," she says. "Not everything is so clear-cut. You aren't a good partner or a bad one. You aren't a good or bad person either. You're a person. There's this gray area."

We look at each other.

She sighs. "I don't care that you cheated on Ben. I'm upset that you kept something from me."

I frown. "You really don't care?"

"Well, I mean. I don't think that's very nice, but *he* wasn't very nice."

"Don't say that." I wince. I don't want her to talk badly about him.

"I know you have complicated feelings about him, and I'm sorry you're still dealing with that. I think maybe you're still a little brainwashed when it comes to him, though."

"No, you don't understand. It wasn't like he was this awful person—"

"I know," she says. "I get it. You have a lot of sympathy for him. But I have more sympathy for you. I'm going to forgive you for lying to me because I know you're sorry, and I understand that people make mistakes, but I'm upset, and I want you to be more considerate and thoughtful in the future."

Both cats stroll past me into the bedroom. They rub their bodies against my legs as they pass. They jump on the bed and lie down on my side.

Joy breathes air out of her nose. "But I guess you're sleeping on the couch regardless. The girls have claimed your spot."

I walk into the room and lie at the end of the bed the way a dog might. "Can I sleep here, Lou and Toulouse?"

"Hm. They don't look impressed," Joy says. "I think they want you to sleep on the floor."

I snort. "Jesus, girls. Be reasonable."

I lie there pathetically for a moment, then say, "I get why this upset you. I really am sorry. I'll be more considerate and thoughtful from here on out. Thanks for telling me how you feel."

"No problem," she says while she puts her feet on me like I'm a footrest.

I wake up, reach my arm out to the spot where Joy should be, and find it's empty. The bed feels cool. I open my eyes and sit up. Where is she?

Is she still mad at me?

I climb out of bed and amble down the stairs.

Did she leave?

I walk into the living room, panicked. I spot her in a robe. She's putting our books back on the shelves.

"There you are," I say. My heart is racing. "What are you doing?"

"Oh, good morning. I'm just helping," she says. She has

her arms full of books. "I've made these sections. What do you think? This area here is poetry, and I've organized by period. So, this shelf is contemporary. Renaissance is over here. Neoclassical. And over here we have children's lit. Lit fic is over here. Nonfiction books are on these shelves. This row here is gender studies. This is feminist literature. I've organized everything into these groupings, but I didn't order alphabetically by author. So things are where they should be generally, but in no specific order. I thought maybe it would be a good compromise. Everything has a place, but there's still a little chaos. What do you think?"

I look at her.

"Do you like it?" she asks.

Her hair is gathered in a claw clip on top of her head.

"Yes," I say.

"I know you prefer things to be perfectly organized, but—"

"A little disorder is okay," I say.

She smiles at me. "Exactly."

I told Dr. Jeong about Joy, the woman at the farmer's market, and the fight we had.

She says, "We've talked a lot about your relationship with Ben, but you haven't shared much about your relationship with your wife. Would you be open to telling me a bit more about her?"

"Sure," I say. "What would you like to know?"

"How did you two meet?"

"We were at a library conference," I say. "Joy's a bookbinder. She had a booth. She had a copy of *The Velveteen Rabbit* on her table. I told her that was my favorite book when I was a kid. She said it was hers too. She'd restored this old edition she found in a secondhand shop. She used velvet and foil stamping for the cover. She gave me her business card and wrote her cell phone number on the back. I still have it in my wallet, actually. The conference was out of town, but we chatted a bit at her booth and learned we both lived in the same city. She asked me if I wanted to have dinner with her, so we went to a Mexican restaurant."

"And how long have you two been together?" she asks.

"About seven years," I say. "She gave me that Velveteen Rabbit book, actually, on our first anniversary."

Dr. Jeong says, "That's a thoughtful gift."

I nod.

Before I broke up with Ben, I felt like a lab monkey living in a cage who spent her days being tested on. When we broke up, it was like I'd been released back into my natural tropical forest habitat, and when I found Joy, it felt like I finally met another chimpanzee.

"Have you found your relationship with Joy has been impacted by the challenges and grief you've recently faced about Ben?"

The longer we were together, the less time we spent drumming, laughing, and swinging from branches. We spent more time quietly picking through each other's fur and nesting. The static excitement of being with someone I liked was replaced by this sort of calm, contented, easy feeling.

Lately I've felt less calm, though. I feel sort of shaken,

vulnerable, and nervous. I've been reminded of the lab, and the mistakes I made there.

I nod. "Yes. I think it has."

"Can you expand on that for me?"

I wish I were a chimpanzee who was born in the forest. I wish I never spent any time in a lab. I wish I never had a handler who was kind to me, or mean to me, or who I bit. I wish I was born where I was supposed to be.

"I don't feel totally like myself lately. I feel anxious, and sort of faraway. I find myself thinking about Ben a lot. I space out. I'm distracted by it. I've spent a lot of time ruminating about our relationship. I feel this strange sort of guilty grief."

She says, "I understand."

I don't know if this therapy is helping. I'm worried I'm going to feel like this forever.

"Am I a bad patient?" I ask.

She looks at me. "No. Why do you ask that?"

"I just feel like I'm bad at this. I want you to think I'm getting better."

"You want *me* to think you're getting better?"

I look down at my nail beds. "Yes."

"You know I'd rather you didn't center my thoughts in relation to your treatment here. Why do you think you might be doing that?"

I stare at a hangnail. "I don't know. Because I have people-pleasing tendencies?"

She hums. "You do, yes. But you also demonstrate a desire to pursue honesty over performance. You set boundaries. You express your feelings. You prioritize yourself, and your own approval over others. You stand up for yourself. I care much more about your own thoughts, about your progress, but for your awareness, I do think you're getting better. Don't you?"

I look over at her hands. Her nails are painted mauve, and she's wearing a wedding ring. I wonder who she's married to.

I say, "I don't know. I still feel terrible about Ben. Is there something more I can do to get over this?"

She writes something down. "It's natural to want to get better, and I understand why you feel that way. This doesn't have a quick fix, though, and it might not be something you get over. What we're doing here is finding ways for you to cope and move forward."

I would like a better answer than that. I want to be given something I can do.

"What do you think about writing a letter to Ben?" she says, as if she were reading my mind. "I think that could help you. It could give you an outlet for some of your complicated feelings. It might offer an opportunity to honor your memories and say goodbye."

I say, "Okay. I'll try anything."

Joy is talking to her mom on speakerphone. I have my head in her lap. I'm reading poetry. She has her free hand in my hair.

Tammy is going to visit Sophie in a few days now that Joy has come home. She lives a few hours away from Sophie, so she hasn't met January in person yet. She and Joy decided to space out their visits so Sophie has the most support at all times.

"I was just on the phone with Sophie," Tammy says. "She seems like she's doing so much better since your visit."

Joy says, "I think she is doing better, yeah, but I do worry she might have postpartum. Especially considering her genes, and how badly you were affected by it."

Tammy is quiet for a moment.

"You know," she says, "postpartum is strange. It's hard to say what parts of it are hereditary, or even chemical. For me, I don't know how to differentiate between what was postpartum, and what was my own personal crisis. I was definitely affected by how my hormones shifted through pregnancy and childbirth, but there was more to it. I was only twenty-three years old when I had Sophie, and I was even younger when I had you. After Sophie was born, I had this strange feeling. It was like I'd just been transported into my body. I felt suddenly aware of the fact that I was married, and a mom. I'm not sure that's hereditary or something we need to worry about when it comes to Sophie's genes."

I look up at Joy. She and I have talked about how I felt that way when I left Ben. Tammy had a similar experience too. She dropped out of college and took a year off when it happened to her. I think there's this moment for a lot of people as we age when we sort of, wake up. It might especially happen to those of us raised as girls. So much of our lives are mapped out for us. It's assumed by everyone around us, even by ourselves, that we'll take a socially prescribed path.

"I was reading *The Bell Jar* when I was pregnant with Sophie," Tammy says. "And I got to the part about the fig tree. You know, where Esther is sitting in the crotch of a fig tree, trying to decide which fig to pick. Each fig represents a different path she could take in her life. Be a wife. Travel the world. Be a mother. Be a poet. She can't pick them all, and they start falling. I felt really affected by that. I was too young when I got married, and I didn't have the time to consider what life I'd pick for myself. I just took the life served to me. I really think Sophie is suited to be a mother. She might look back at the life she didn't pick, but I don't think she'll truly regret having January. I don't regret having you girls, either. I hope you know that. I'd always pick to have you. But I do think it's important for everyone to reflect on their life and the path they choose. To make choices for themselves—rather than forge ahead however the world pushes them to go. I think I left that year because I realized I hadn't chosen my own life. Though I really would choose to have you girls again, honey. I promise I don't regret—"

"Don't worry. I understand, Mom," Joy says.

Tammy often laments about the year she left, and how regretful she is about it. She's assured Joy and Sophie numerous times that she regrets leaving, that she loves them and is grateful they've forgiven her.

"I wouldn't have married your father, though," she adds.

Joy laughs.

Lou is purring in my lap. I'm sitting on the floor of our home library, struggling to write my letter to Ben. So far, I've only managed to write, "Dear Ben."

The windows are open, our curtains are swaying, and the room is tidy. After Joy organized our books, I vacuumed,

Windexed, and wiped down all the surfaces. All our throw blankets are folded. The plants are watered. It smells crisp and citrusy.

I shift to stretch my legs. As I do, my eyes catch something under our couch. A dusty ball of cat hair. Gross. I must have missed it while I was vacuuming. I squint at it, wondering how long it's been there. I must have missed it a few times.

I tilt my head back and look at the shelves. I wonder if any of our books outline how to write a letter to a dead ex-boyfriend. I doubt it. Unfortunately, there aren't guidebooks for everything, and even if there were, who's to say how to do this properly?

My eyes continue to wander through our shelves until I spot a book placed in the wrong section. I stand up to put it where it belongs, but as I pull it off the shelf, I hesitate. I decide to flip through it instead.

I read a poem about letting go of judgment, stepping outside rigid categories, and the limits of language.

I sit with the book on the floor. I feel a sort of cosmic magic finding me in this poem. I read it again. While I run my hand over it, I think about how we organize things to make them easier to find—but I found this book because it was in the wrong place.

I think sometimes I get lost following steps. I think too rigidly and lose sight of the objective. It doesn't matter if our library is organized perfectly. What's the point of organizing it? It's to find things, to make this room neat.

I look at the words, "Dear Ben" in my notebook.

The point of writing this letter is to help me get closure. It doesn't have to be perfect.

I look up and see Declan Turner exiting the grocery store with a woman, a teenaged girl, and a little boy. They must be his family. I watch him push their cart through the parking lot. His son is riding on it. His wife is reviewing their receipt, and his daughter is straggling behind.

I unbuckle my seat belt. I want to ask him about the emails. It's probably not the best time, since he's with his family, but why should I care about that? He wouldn't care to consider that for me.

I step out of my car and walk toward them.

"Declan!" I shout as I get closer.

He and his wife turn to look at me. It takes him a moment to register who I am. His face drops when he does. He says, "I'm with my family right now—"

"This will only take a minute," I say. "I just want to understand something. Humor me, please."

His wife looks concerned. His children are looking from his face to mine.

Rather than wait for him to reply, I say, "I wanted to ask you about those emails you sent.

I think I understand what motivated you to send me those emails from that EaglesNest account. You wanted to blackmail me because you see me as a dangerous person in our community. Fine. But I don't understand what you were doing with the bird questions. Were you trying to get the inside scoop about how we handle reference questions, or something? What's your angle? What are you planning?"

He makes a face. "I don't know what you're talking about."

"Please. I'm not trying to pick a fight. I really just want to know the answer. I'm a librarian. I like to get to the bottom of things. I don't understand why you wrote to the library with two different email addresses."

"I didn't write to the library with two email addresses. I did . . . " he trails off.

"What?" I ask.

He turns to his wife and children. "Go to the car, guys. I'll meet you there in a minute."

His wife squints at me over her shoulder while she directs their children to the car.

After they've walked out of earshot, Declan says, "I did send the emails from the EaglesNest account. And I, uh, believe I owe you an apology. I shouldn't have sent those photos. I'm sorry."

I look into his eyes. I'm surprised at his apology.

He adds quickly, "I'm not sorry for standing up for my beliefs, but I think I may have crossed a line with the photos. So, I'm sorry."

I narrow my eyes with trepidation. "Thank you. I appreciate the apology, and the honesty. But you also sent the bird questions, right? I know you did. We tracked your IP address."

He squints. "What are you talking about? What bird questions?"

"Come on, let's stay honest. I really want to know. I just want to understand why—"

"I am being honest. I don't know what you're talking about." He's looking right into my eyes.

"Really?" I ask.

"My hand to God," he says, before turning toward his family. They are paused at a distance from us, watching.

I stay where I am as he rejoins them, and they all walk the rest of the way to their car. I exhale. I guess confronting him with his wife and kids was a poor choice. I just wanted to understand. I hate not understanding something, wondering why, with no route to an answer.

I watch them trek forward, and just as I begin to accept that I don't get to know why he sent those emails, his daughter looks back at me.

"Hurry up, Sammy," he says to her.

CHAPTER FIFTEEN

DEAR SAMMY,

I'M WRITING TO SHARE A QUICK NOTE AND A BIRD FACT WITH YOU.

DID YOU KNOW DOVES AND PIGEONS ARE SCIENTIFICALLY THE SAME? THEY'RE BOTH COLUMBIDAE. THE SMALLER BIRDS ARE OFTEN CALLED "DOVES," AND THE LARGER ONES ARE OFTEN CALLED "PIGEONS," BUT THERE'S NO REAL SEPARATION BETWEEN THEM. I LOOKED THIS UP TODAY, AND THOUGHT PERHAPS IT MIGHT INTEREST YOU.

I ALSO WANTED TO TAKE A MOMENT TO REASSURE YOU, IN CASE YOU HAVE ANY CONCERNS, THAT THE QUESTIONS YOU SEND THIS LIBRARY ARE COMPLETELY CONFIDENTIAL. THE TRUST BETWEEN OUR PATRONS AND THE LIBRARY IS SOMETHING WE TAKE VERY SERIOUSLY.

PLEASE DO NOT HESITATE TO REACH OUT TO US AGAIN. WHATEVER YOU'RE INTERESTED IN—BE IT BIRDS, BOOKS, OR BIGGER QUESTIONS—WE'RE ALWAYS HERE TO HELP.

A psychologist is leading a story time for children going through divorce. She's read two picture books to the room. One is about having two homes, and another is about how their family is still a family even if they don't live together. I should be at the reference desk right now, but I stood up for a moment to peek in.

"My dad made me a new room," a little boy tells the storyteller.

"Did you get to help decorate?" she asks.

He nods. "Yes. It's green."

"Mine is purple," the little girl beside him says.

I look back at the reference desk. A man is hovering by it. From my peripheral vision, I can see that he keeps glancing at me. He's pretending to inspect a stand with booklets about local events. I walk back to the desk and sit down.

While trying to put a brochure about the hot-air balloon festival back, he accidentally knocks over the entire display. He swears, then kneels down to pick up the fallen brochures. His pants don't fit him well, so he's yanking them up while

Is This a Cry for Help?

he leans, to avoid exposing his butt crack; however, he's unsuccessful. I avert my eyes.

After putting everything back, he says, "I'm sorry about that."

I look at him. His face is bright red. I smile. "Oh, don't worry about it. Thanks for cleaning it up. Can I help you with anything?"

He inches closer to my desk and mumbles something.

I say, "I'm sorry, I didn't hear you."

He glances around, then says, "Yes. Um. I-I'm actually the man who was watching porn here a few weeks ago."

I blink. I didn't recognize him at first, but I see now it is him. What am I supposed to say to this guy—

"I'm writing something," he says.

I open my mouth. I don't know the script for this one. I spit out, "That's, uh, nice. Is it, like, erotica—"

"No. It's psychology. I'm doing an analysis of vulva appearance in pornography. I'm researching the impact that imagery has on people's psychological well-being. There are certain beauty standards in relation to genitals. My internet was down, so I came here. I could have gone to the college library, but it's a forty-minute drive. I live right around the corner. I had a deadline. I'm sorry for the trouble I caused. I wanted to offer to speak to the news."

His face is flushed.

I say, "The news?"

"Yes, I've been seeing all the hullabaloo it caused. I feel bad. I-I thought perhaps I could explain how this all started."

He's fidgeting, sweating, and stammering. I have an inkling, based on the way he carries himself, that appearing on the news might be his worst nightmare.

I say, "No, sir, you don't need to do that—"

"I want you to know I'm not a pervert," he says. "I'm not a very sexual person at all, actually. I've never really had any interest—"

I stop him. "I don't need to know that."

"Sorry, sorry." He bats his hands. "I just want to explain myself. I was just absentmindedly working. I'm sort of desensitized to it. I'm constantly scouring porn for vulvas, and I just wasn't thinking—"

"It's okay, sir. Really. It's fine."

He sighs. "I'm sorry."

"There's nothing to be sorry about. Please let me know if I can find any resources to help you with your work."

"Hi, Darcy."

I look up from my desk and see Brenda has entered the back room.

I smile at her. "Hello. What are you doing here?"

It must be raining out. She's wearing a damp Gore-Tex jacket.

She approaches my desk. "I was going to call you but I happened to be driving through the area, so I thought I'd pop in and share the good news in person."

"What is it?" I ask. *Did Declan take back all his complaints and promise to stop disturbing us?*

"You got it." She smiles.

"Got it?" I repeat, confused.

She says, "The job. You got the branch manager job. HR will send a formal email and the letter of offer, but we're officially offering you the job. I was so excited, I had to come tell you myself."

"I got it?" I frown. *How could I possibly have gotten the job? I only did the one interview.*

"Assuming you still want it," she adds.

I stare at her blankly, my mouth slightly ajar. "But I-I only did one interview . . . and it was months ago. I thought. I-I didn't realize—"

"We just put it on hold while you were off sick, and then other priorities came up, but we all agreed you were the best candidate. The second interview was just a formality, really. We would have just taken that time to tell you the job was yours, frankly. If you need time to think about it—"

"No, no, I do want it," I say, "I'm sorry. I'm just surprised. I-I—"

Mordecai is standing behind Brenda in the doorway, eavesdropping. He's beaming at me and holding both his thumbs up.

Brenda says, "I know you'll do a fabulous job. Congratulations."

I smile. "Thank you."

"I'm so proud of you." Joy beams.

We're in the kitchen. I just told her the news.

She says, "You should have called to tell me. I would have made us something nicer to celebrate. Should we toss this soup in the fridge and order something? Do you want sushi? Do we have any wine? Or should we go out?"

There's a large cast-iron pot of mushroom soup simmering on our stove top.

"No, I love your mushroom soup," I say. The kitchen smells earthy, like mushrooms, garlic, and butter. I have my arms around Joy's waist. Her hair is up. I pull her in closer. "And I don't want to go anywhere."

She exhales. "If you say so. Well, this is so exciting! I'm over the moon— Oh, I forgot! I have a little news too. I found a home for Kyle."

"Did you really?" I ask.

"Yes. Hodan and Ada said they want him."

I frown. "They do? But I thought they wanted a dog."

"Yes, well, they realized a cat would suit their lifestyle better."

That's such good news. I know he'll be safe with them.

I smile. "I'm so happy."

I jump into the shower. Hot water is hitting my back. While I lather my hair with shampoo, I spot strands of Joy's hair stuck to the tile. She's arranged the hairs into an outline of a woman's body. One strand forming the slope of her shoulder, another the dip of her waist. Rather than rinse the hair off, like I usually do, I leave it there.

"Did you write your letter to Ben?" Dr. Jeong asks.

I have it in my hands. I hand it to her. "Are you going to read it?"

"That's up to you," she says. "I don't have to read it if you'd prefer to keep it private, but if you'd like a witness, I'm also happy to read it."

I think about that for a moment.

"Maybe you could read it when I leave," I suggest.

"Okay," she says. "That sounds good to me. Shall we do some breathing exercises to get started?"

I feel the weight in my chest become lighter.

I nod. "Okay. Sure."

Dear Ben,

I used to picture running into you in a store somewhere in the future. You'd be with your wife and kids. We'd both have a little gray in our hair. Fine lines in our foreheads. Our eyes would connect across the store. I'd smile at you. you'd smile back and nod.

It's hard for me to write this. I'm having a hard time finding the words. I feel a lot of guilt, regret, remorse, anger, but also, sympathy for you. For several years after we broke up, I considered you someone I'd hurt, and I thought of myself as this grisly lesbian monster. I tried not to think about you. I blocked your number. But you turned into this intrusive thought. I saw flashes of your face the way I imagine conscionable murderers see their victims. In quiet moments, when no one was talking and my mind wandered, my heart sank to the dark pit in my stomach where I kept you.

We broke up because I was gay. I didn't tell you that because I thought that would wound you too severely. Instead, I told you I needed to be alone for a while. I'm sorry. I should have been honest with you. For what it's worth, I think I did need to be alone for a while. And I think that even if I weren't gay, we needed to break up.

I felt comfortable with you. You were a bighearted person. I saw the good in you because there was a lot of good in you. There were also times when I felt trapped and mistreated by you, though. It's hard for me to reconcile the complicated feelings I have about you. You and I started dating when I was only eighteen, and you were a full decade older. During our relationship, I was a staunch defender of our age gap. I felt older than the people my age. I felt like you and I were peers, but we weren't.

I'm the age now that you were when we broke up. It's hard to believe that was a decade ago. I really buy into the idea that our frontal lobes don't fully develop until we're in our mid-twenties. My brain wasn't totally formed when I met you, but yours was. You were your fully fledged self when we first met. I was green to the world. I thought I wasn't, but I was. Easy to manipulate, and eager to be liked. I didn't know who I was yet.

I'm around eighteen-year-olds at my job sometimes. It would offend them if I infantilized them by calling them kids, so I won't, but they are inherently different than who I am. I think of them as people I should protect. I can't imagine dating an eighteen-year-old when I was twenty-eight. The thought of that not only turns my stomach, but it feels sinister and sad.

I feel guilty about the mistakes I made in our relationship, and I have a lot of compassion for you. You were, and will always be, an important person to me. I'm devastated that you died, and am haunted by the idea that I contributed in any way to the *suffering you experienced in your life. I really hope that you're in a peaceful state now.*

I learned a lot from our relationship and I'm grateful for that. If I controlled how things work, you'd be alive right now, living with a woman who really loved you, you'd get a dog, and you'd be happy.

You were a flawed person, like I was. I wish you were here so I could forgive you and ask you to forgive me.

Instead, I'll share this poem by Rumi that makes me think of you:

> **Out beyond ideas of wrongdoing and rightdoing,
> there is a field. I'll meet you there.**

Darcy

Joy holds the door open for me while I carry our drinks outside. Our wisteria is blooming; there are bunches of pink flowers cascading over the awning on our deck. We walk barefoot along our stone path toward the lake. The ice cubes in our cups clink against our glasses.

We sit down at the end of the dock, Joy kicks her Birkenstocks off and puts her dirty feet in my lap. We sip our drinks and listen to the grebes make weird bird sex noises.

WAYS YOU CAN SUPPORT YOUR PUBLIC LIBRARY

GET A LIBRARY CARD.

BORROW BOOKS AND CHECK OUT MATERIAL.

VISIT A BRANCH IN PERSON.

PARTICIPATE IN LIBRARY PROGRAMS AND EVENTS.

ENCOURAGE YOUR FRIENDS AND FAMILY
TO USE THE LIBRARY.

VOTE FOR POLITICIANS WHO SUPPORT FUNDING LIBRARIES.

ATTEND CITY COUNCIL AND LIBRARY BOARD MEETINGS.

WRITE YOUR ELECTED OFFICIALS EXPRESSING YOUR
SUPPORT FOR LIBRARIES.

ASK THE STAFF AT YOUR LOCAL LIBRARY
HOW ELSE YOU CAN SUPPORT THEM.

ACKNOWLEDGMENTS

Thank you, person reading this. Somehow this is my fourth novel, but it remains strange that anyone reads stories I write. You're even reading the acknowledgments! I'm grateful for your support and time. There are so many books to read. It means a lot to me you chose to read mine.

This book came to be with the help of my literary agent Heather Carr, who I always feel so supported and encouraged by, and whose knowledge, judgement, and taste I really value. These stories and I are lucky to have you, Heather.

Acknowledgments

This book was edited by Jade Hui, Brittany Lavery, and Sean Delone. Jade, you are such a supportive and kind person who brings so much a sincerity to your work, and my books and I are fortunate to have benefitted from your effort and talent. Brittany, it's meaningful to have the support of someone who I know connects with me and this story, and your notes, as well as your championing of my writing overall, really mean the world to me. Sean, thank you so much for everything you put into sharing this book. I'm so grateful to you for the time and effort you poured into this.

This book was surrounded by a team of people who do such a great job of packaging, publicizing, and marketing stories. Thank you so much for your work, Gena Lanzi, Jolena Podolsky, Cayley Brightside, Kelli McAdams, Liz Byer, Stacey Sakal, and everyone at the Friedrich agency, Atria, and Simon and Schuster Canada.

Thanks to Bridget for confirming the spelling of almost every word in this. Thanks also to Corrina, Brock, Mal, Mitch, Ainsley, Chad, Aaron, Joel, Tunny, Huckle, Rivvy, Aileen, Matthew, Christina, Lou, and the rest of my friends and family.

I wrote this book while listening to "Motion Sickness" by Pheobe Bridgers, "We're in Love" by boygenius, "Fast Car" by Tracy Chapman, and "Your Ex-Lover Is Dead" by Stars.

Lastly, thank you to all librarians, but especially my school librarians at St. Gabriel's, St. Raphael's, and St. Joe's, the public librarians at the St. Thomas Public Library, and the academic librarians at King's College and Western

Acknowledgments

University. Thanks also to my teachers and classmates in Western's Library and Information Science program, and to my librarian coworkers, including the folks at Ottawa Public Library. I only worked at OPL briefly, but I left with so much admiration for the work done there, and at all public libraries.

ABOUT THE AUTHOR

Emily Austin is the author of *We Could Be Rats*, *Everyone in This Room Will Someday Be Dead*, *Interesting Facts About Space*, and the poetry collection *Gay Girl Prayers*. She was born in Ontario, Canada, and received two writing grants from the Canadian Council for the Arts. She studied English literature and library science at Western University. She currently lives in Ottawa, in the territory of the Anishinaabe Algonquin Nation.